Lucky Charm

Reverse Fairytales

book 2

J.A.Armitage

Contents

The Coronation

I felt the weight of the royal crown bearing down as the bishop placed it firmly on my head to rapturous applause and the bright lights of the media. Six months since my father had died and I was now the official Queen of Silverwood.

The national anthem played as cameras flashed, blinding me with their brightness. My only job was to stay still and look regal as the massive congregation lifted their voices in song around me. Long live the queen!

When the music had stopped and the cheering had died down, Luca came bounding over and gave me a kiss on the cheek. He held my hand as I stood, trying not to fall over with the weight of the bejeweled monstrosity on my head. He looked resplendent in his immaculate royal attire decked in golden trim and epaulets. I, on the other hand, looked like a royal golden meringue with the biggest dress Xavi had ever dared to dress me in. Colored white with a golden lace overlay that nipped in at the waist; it billowed out at the skirts. Over the top, I wore a golden velvet cape edged in ermine that trailed along the floor behind me. Needless to say, I hated it and couldn't wait to get home and into a pair of comfortable pants.

I walked down the aisle of the huge cathedral, marveling at the vaulted ceiling so far above me, which was the reason for the amazing acoustics of the singing people. I walked arm in arm with Luca who was doing his best to keep me upright and not trip over my voluminous dress himself. I tried not to think about the next time we'd be making this particular journey. In five months time, we'd be taking the same walk, only then, it would be on our wedding day as husband and wife.

Despite the all-time low ratings of popularity for the monarchy, a surprisingly large number of people had turned out for the coronation. The enormous gothic cathedral was packed with the kingdom's elite filling all the pews, not to mention various celebrities and royals from other lands, and the roads outside of the cathedral were crowded with people. I gave Elise a quick smile as I passed, and she smiled back. She looked more radiant than ever, probably due to her honeymoon glow. Leo had proposed to her at Christmas, and with mother's blessing, they'd had a discrete family wedding in the palace on New Year's Day. The only people they'd invited were family and Daniel and Dean. I envied them for the intimacy of it. My wedding plans were shaping up to be a complete nightmare of epic proportions, thanks to my mother, Jenny, and Xavi collaborating. In my mother's mind, I needed a wedding even more spectacular than the last one to make people forget what had happened at it. As many people had died including the groom and the king, I thought having a bigger wedding cake and better-dressed bridesmaids probably wasn't going to cut it, but I kept my mouth shut and let her plan it her way. It was easier than arguing.

I tried to get my wedding out of my mind and concentrate on the matter at hand, putting one foot in front of the other without losing my crown or tripping over the long skirt I was wearing. As everything was being televised and shown to tens of thousands of people throughout the kingdom, I knew any misstep would result in more damaging press for our family, and that was the last thing I needed on my first day as the monarch.

Security was at an all-time high to prevent the same disaster as the one at the palace six months ago, and as I left the cathedral, I was flanked by ten guards specially brought in from the Silverwood Army. They led me through the snow to the awaiting golden carriage, but it was Luca that helped me through the door with my large skirt.

Thousands of people screamed and cheered as we were taken through the crowd-lined streets back to the palace. I waved and smiled as I was expected to do and tried not to look as uncomfortable as I felt. I'd been preparing for this ever since the moment my mother uttered the words, "Your father is dead" but I still wasn't ready for the enormity of it. I'd planned how I wanted to rule the country and spent night after night unable to sleep, fretting about how I could turn Silverwood around, especially with the Magi situation. What I hadn't practiced was holding a crown on my head and keeping a smile on my face. Jenny had warned me that I needed to, but for some stupid reason, I'd put the health of the country over the importance of wearing the correct outfit and shoes for the coronation. As it was, my feet and my head were warring for most painful part, with my stomach coming up third, nipped in as it was by a corset that was so tight, I doubt I'd be able to eat anything for fear of it snapping open.

I'd protested, of course, when Xavi had asked me to wear it, but as it was the only way I could fit into the tiny waisted dress, I had no choice. I made a mental note to go to wedding dress fittings instead of eschewing them in favor of meetings with Silverwood's leaders as I had with my coronation dress fittings.

"How are you feeling your majesty?" whispered Luca in my ear.

I turned away from the crowds for a second to look into his handsome face. "Exhausted," I replied honestly. "You?"

"I'm feeling like the luckiest man in the world right now. I cannot believe I'm going to be marrying you in a few months. You look every inch the queen, and if it wasn't for the eyes of every person of Silverwood currently watching us, I'd be kissing you right now."

I smiled. I wanted to kiss him too, but I couldn't be seen kissing him in public before our wedding day. It just wasn't the done thing for a lady of society, let alone the new queen. At least that's what Jenny had told me. I looked up to Jenny for help at every turn as she knew every law and rule of Silverwood as long as it pertained to etiquette. Instead of sharing a kiss, I reached out for his hand and squeezed it.

We lapsed into an easy silence. I felt comfortable in his presence and couldn't think of anyone I'd prefer to be with on the day of my coronation.

There is one other

The voice in my head piped up. I couldn't think of Cynder. Not now. I'd not seen him in over six months, and as much as I hated to admit it, he was a part of my past that had no place in my future. I ignored the little voice and, instead, concentrated on my new role as monarch.

It was a role for which I'd had so little training, and I felt wholly unprepared. I'd only found out I was going to rule Silverwood when my elder sister, Grace, died, and my father's death unexpectedly followed soon after. I'd spent the five months prior to my father's death learning how to eat soup without spilling and picking out a man to marry. It all seemed so frivolous now. I should have been learning more about my kingdom. In the months that had passed since I learned of my father's death, I'd spent as much time away from the spotlight as possible, trying to figure out how to rule a land. But it felt like too little, too late. Luca had been as helpful as possible, and so had Leo, who had just the head for business I needed. I'd not hesitated at hiring him as my chief advisor, a role into which he'd thrown himself wholeheartedly. And still, even with the help of Luca and Leo and all the other people I'd surrounded myself with, the thought of unifying a separated land was a task that seemed so daunting that wearing painfully high shoes paled in comparison.

"My father made it look so easy," I said, sighing.

"Your father was a tyrant and a murderer," Luca reminded me.

"Yes, but the people loved him. They hate me."

"They hate all royalty because of what happened. You've told the people the full story. You can't make them believe it."

It was the truth. As soon as I found out that my father had died, I'd gone to the press to tell them the truth about the riots. I'd also gotten Cynder cleared of all charges. What I hadn't expected was for the people not to believe me. No one wanted to hear the truth that it was the fault of my father and Xavier when it was convenient to go on blaming the Magi.

"Why does no one believe it?" I asked Luca for the thousandth time.

Luca took my other hand in his. "Because for a long time, people treated the Magi like dirt, fueled by the belief that they were to blame for all of Silverwood's problems. No one wants to be the bad guy, and so it's easier to believe a lie than to face up to what they have done."

I knew he was right, but it was of little consolation. I'd naively thought that I could tell the truth about my father and invite the Magi back and everyone in Silverwood would be happy. I soon found out that anti-magi feelings ran much deeper than I had expected. My father's legacy of hate had lived on even if he hadn't.

I turned back to the window and plastered on my fake smile again. There were so many people out there, and yet, nothing about it seemed real.

I looked at the crowds as the six white horses pulled the carriage through the heavily guarded gates of the palace. Even now, six months after the riot, I could still see a number of people demonstrating against the Magi. Today was not a special occasion for them. It was just another excuse to bring their placards and spew their vitriolic bile. They had been there all winter. Not even the harsh weather conditions we'd experienced had put them off. When the Magi themselves had demonstrated last year about their appalling treatment, the police had used brute force to move them. These guys were left alone. The police didn't do a thing. It was something I was going to change as soon as I got the chance.

The carriage came to a halt at the palace doors, and two footmen opened the door and helped me out. The palace itself looked better than ever after all the restorations that had been done on it, and the only reminder of the disaster that had happened all those months back was the lingering smell of wet paint. Paint that had been used to cover up the blood stains and new plaster filling the bullet holes in the walls.

"I'm going to get changed," I said as Luca and I entered the main hall. The dress was weighing me down, and I couldn't wait to get out of it.

"Do you need any help?" Luca replied, eyeing up the multitude of buttons.

"They are just for decoration," I smiled. "I think I'll be ok. Why don't you get changed too?"

Luca nodded, but I could see he was put out. Royal protocol demanded that we not be too intimate until our wedding night, so apart from the occasional stolen kiss, we'd not had much in the way of romance. The long wait until we were married was difficult for him, but apart from kissing him when no one was looking, there wasn't much I could do about it. He was living full-time in one of the guest houses on the grounds. Of the four, his was the only one occupied now that Leo had moved into the main palace.

I watched him leave before running upstairs to my room. Xavi had laid out a simple, but elegant, dress for me to wear for the rest of the day. I heaved a sigh of relief as I took the heavy crown from my head and eased myself out of the hefty gown and crushing corset. I lay down on the bed in my underwear, reluctant to get changed and go out to face the next part of the day—meetings with the press followed by a huge banquet of celebration.

I stood up and made my way over to the window as I had many times. Peeking through a crack in the curtains, I looked out over the snowy white grounds to the apartment that had once been occupied by Cynder. I'd spent so many fruitless hours gazing at the window, hoping that I'd see the light on or any other sign of life in there.

Not that I needed any reminders of Cynder. He pervaded my every thought, and at night, he filled my dreams. I'd been naive when I thought agreeing to marry Luca would help me forget. Nothing helped me forget, but in truth, I wasn't sure I wanted to. He was still out there somewhere. Still on the run, despite no longer being a wanted criminal. I'd not seen him in over six months. I told myself for the umpteenth time that it was for the best, and yet, it was harder to believe than it was to crush myself into a corset.

The protesters were at the back gate too. I could just about see them through the iron bars. It wasn't enough that they stood at the front gates of the palace every day; they had to completely surround the outer walls to drive their point home. I pulled out the telescope that had been sitting in my room for the past few months and angled it towards the gates. The signs they held were getting worse. As I watched, one managed to scale the wall. The guards were on him before I had a chance to worry, but the banner he was carrying gave me a jolt of fear. On it were three letters and a death threat.

MDS Forever

Death to the Monarchy

It looked like it wasn't just the Magi they were after; they wanted to kill me too!

I shook my head and tried to collect my thoughts. I'd never heard of the MDS before today, but it looked like whoever they were, they weren't my biggest fan.

Taking a deep breath, I turned and stepped out of my room, ready to take up my duty as the new queen of Silverwood.

Blackmail

My eyes felt blinded after the myriad of pictures the press wanted of us in every combination. My mother; my mother and Elise; Elise and Leo; Luca; Luca's parents, etc. And in every one, me at the front smiling graciously as though I'd been born to the role. Some might say that I was born to it, but there wasn't a day that went by when I didn't think of my elder sister Grace. It should have been Grace standing here, taking center stage with a handsome beau on her arm. I often wondered what would have happened if she were still alive. Would she have been forced to marry Xavier or would she have stood up for herself and waited for true love? Knowing Grace, she'd have done what was best for the country, but I'd seen her diary. I knew that she didn't want to marry Xavier any more than I did.

I looked over to Luca. He was smiling at the camera. A reporter was interviewing him with his parents. He'd become quite a star since being chosen to be my husband, and he'd taken to his new role like a duck to water. His parents, the rotund King Theron and the willowy Queen Sarina were both beaming with pride. It made me feel pleased that they were all so happy. It was one thing I felt I'd done right. If only everything else about being queen would fall into place now, then I could be truly happy.

Or at least, as happy as possible without the boy who makes my heart flutter.

I ignored the little voice once again as a photographer grabbed me and lined me up with Luca, Leo, and Daniel for a throwback shot. Luca held my hand while Leo and Daniel stood on either side of us. All three of them looked so handsome in their smart clothes. I really felt lucky to have them with me. Of the three men from the ball, one had become my fiancé, one, my great friend and one, my brother-in-law. I couldn't have asked for a better outcome. After the photo, I kissed Daniel on the cheek and gave Leo a hug. It made me feel so happy that because of the ball, all three of us had found love.

Is it really love?

The voice again. I did love Luca. He was a wonderful man, but I had to admit, I didn't feel the goosebumps when he walked through the door. My heart didn't race in his presence the way it did when I thought of Cynder. And yet, he was so perfect for the role in a way that Cynder could never hope to be. Cynder had grown up as a second-class citizen. I hated to admit that. To me, there was nothing second-class about him, but he'd not grown up learning how to rule a country as Luca had. No, things had turned out for the best, I just had to keep telling myself that.

My family and friends were led away to the great banquet hall to join all the guests who had been invited for the coronation, while I stayed behind to give a full interview. I'd written my speech carefully with the help of the royal advisors. This was no wishy-washy speech like all the others I'd had to give about choosing a husband. I'd filled it with my wishes and plans for Silverwood and the political ideals I held. It had taken me weeks to write and polish, and now I felt confident that the people of Silverwood would see me as a political force and not some flouncy-dress-wearing princess.

I sat down in the sitting room-cum-media room opposite a tall wispy man with the thickest, most luxurious hair I'd ever seen in the most garish, yellow blond. On his lapel, he wore a small golden pin in the shape of a rose. His name was Frederick, and he had taken over Sadie's role as Royal Media Correspondent when she died. This was the first time I'd met him. I got the impression that the interviews with him weren't going to be as frivolous and light-hearted as they had been with Sadie which I was glad about. I needed a serious interviewer for the topics I wanted to talk about, not just someone who would ask me who designed the dress I was wearing.

"Your Majesty," he began, "how are you enjoying your first day as Queen?"

I'd expected this question and had a prepared answer.

"The ceremony was beautiful. Thank you." I turned straight to the camera now. I wanted to address Silverwood, not Frederick.

"I want to thank each and every one of you that came out today to wish me well. It has brought happiness to my heart to think that we can now be a kingdom as one, not divided by race, color, gender or magical ability." I emphasized the last one as it really was the only thing that did divide our kingdom. "The past year has been a difficult one for many of us, but I'm confident that if we all pull together, we can make Silverwood a stronger, happier place to live for all of us."

"I noticed there were some anti-magi protestors outside the palace," interjected Frederick.

"Yes, there were. There is still a lot of anti-Magi feeling in the kingdom, and it is my wish that we can all learn to live together in peace. Silverwood will be a place where we can all feel safe."

Frederick stared at me, putting me on edge. "And how do you propose making Silverwood safe for the Magi? There aren't many left."

"I've talked a lot about Magi rights in the past. As you know, Frederick, it is a topic very dear to my heart. Silverwood has become a divided nation, something which the monarchy of the past has had a lot to do with. I've gone on record and told the truth about the palace's involvement. I can only ask forgiveness from those who have been hurt, but I plan on making changes. No more will the Magi be treated differently than anyone else. We are all people of Silverwood and, therefore, will all have the same choices and chances. University admission will be opened up to all, and no employer will be allowed to discriminate on the grounds of magical ability. There will always be jobs here at the palace for those magi that left. My home and my kingdom are open to them."

"That's a very different approach than that of your father," Frederick reminded me.

I really didn't want to bring my father up again. I'd spent the last six months trying to change people's opinions. They still loved him.

"My father had his own reasons for not wanting the Magi in Silverwood. I, personally, would like to look to the future and put the past where it belongs."

I hoped that would be the end of it, but he carried on, wanting to know what exactly were my father's reasons. I'd told the truth about my father to the press, but there were a lot of things I'd kept from them. They didn't know that Xavier was my cousin, and they didn't know that my sister died at their hands.

"A lot of people think that your father had the right attitude and that you are tearing down the monarchy." Frederick smiled in such a way I wanted to punch him. Being queen, that was high on my list of no-no's. I was appalled by his words, but I could hardly show it on live television. Instead, I smiled sweetly.

"People are always afraid of change, Mr. Pittser, but I assure you that I will do my best for this kingdom. I am committed to being a ruler that the people of Silverwood deserve. I..."

Frederick cut me off, "Well I expect that they'd all like to see another reality TV show about it. The last one certainly won hundreds of thousands of viewers. I, for one, was taking bets on what color dress you'd wear next."

Sadie would have probably said something similar, but with her, it would have been genuine. Frederick Pittser had said it to put me down, to show the world I was nothing more than an airhead princess. I wanted to fight him, to tell him and the world that I wasn't that person, but the truth was, that's all they had ever seen of me. It didn't matter what I said to him now. What would matter was what I did in the coming months and years. His views weren't unusual, unfortunately, but that didn't mean I liked them. I'd hoped for an interview where things would be resolved, but Frederick Pittser seemed determined to make me look bad, as if I needed the help. I made a mental note to call the network to speak to them about Magi rights and, hopefully, find someone more appropriate to be the royal correspondent. For now, this interview was over.

"I'm afraid I must go and join my guests," I said, standing. "They can't eat until I'm there, and I'm sure I heard Prince Luca's stomach rumbling during photographs."

Frederick gave a forced laugh and turned to the camera to wrap up. I had left the sitting room and was halfway down the corridor when he caught up with me. He grabbed me roughly by the arm, spinning me towards him and taking me by surprise. His pleasant but boring TV manner had left him, and instead, he had a fierce look on his face that startled me.

"What are you doing?" I asked, alarmed. A quick glance up the corridor told me that we were alone. "Get off, you are hurting me."

"I know, Your Majesty," he hissed.

"What?"

"I know more than you think." He pulled back his lips to reveal a ghastly grin that put me completely on edge.

After a second or two, he let go of my arm and smiled a sickly smile as though he'd not just assaulted me. I rubbed my arm where he'd grabbed it. A year ago, I'd have gone to my bedroom and cried, but I'd seen too much to put up with this kind of behavior.

"I don't know what you think you know, Mr. Pittser,"—I raised my voice.—"but I cannot and will not have you touching me without my permission. I'll be calling your network and telling them what you just did."

I tried to sound as intimidating as possible. It obviously didn't work.

"No, you won't. I know about your affair with the kitchen hand. If I lose my job, I'll tell the world. I don't think Prince Luca would be too happy to find out what his fiancé was up to behind his back would he?"

I felt sick, hearing what he was saying to me, but there was no way he could possibly know how I felt about Cynder.

I crossed my arms and stood as tall as I could, still barely coming up to Pittser's chest. "What do you want, Mr. Pittser, because I don't take kindly to being blackmailed for something that didn't happen."

"I want you to stop the Magi scum from re-entering. Silverwood was doing fine before you decided to stick your oar in."

"There were bombings and riots!" I reminded him. "People died!"

"Keep them out, and we won't have to find out if the people believe that your affair didn't happen, will we? The MDS will rule."

There it was again. The MDS. He turned on his heel and left me standing alone in the corridor in a state of bewilderment.

Frederick Pittser was wrong. There'd been no affair. I'd not seen Cynder in over six months, but it was true that I'd never told Luca about him. What was the point? Cynder was in my past. Luca was my future. I didn't want anyone else to know either. I'd had enough questioning from the press about why I was so interested in Magi rights. If they found out I was in love with one of them, it would make a mockery of everything I'd achieved. Ok, I'd not achieved much, but if the world knew about Cynder and me, it would only push the cause backwards.

I was still walking down the corridor when I realized that in trying to think everything through, I'd automatically thought of myself as being in love with Cynder.

I rubbed my arm and sighed. It was going to be a long day.

My arm still throbbed as I walked into the banqueting hall. I tried to put Frederick Pittser and his threats out of my mind as I took in the scene before me. My mother had outdone herself with the decorations. Everything was golden from the cutlery to the floral arrangements. The whole place sparkled. I plastered on a smile as hundreds of guests, the elite of the elite, rose from their places to greet me. A cheer went up, and the applause thundered through my ears as I made my way to the head table. I was popular in here, at least.

The last time the banquet hall had been this full was the night of the ball. This time there was to be no dancing and, hopefully, no drama or explosions.

As I was served the most ludicrous fancy meal, I thought back to when Cynder had brought me a plain chicken dish.

"Is it ok?"

I looked to my left to see Luca gazing at me. "You've been looking at your plate for the last five minutes, and you are yet to pick up a fork. Everyone is waiting."

"Hmm?" I looked around. He was right. I'd forgotten that no one was allowed to eat until the monarch started their meal. Everyone had been waiting patiently for me to start. I picked up my cutlery, feeling embarrassed and nodded my head at everyone. As soon as I took my first bite, the sound of hundreds of pieces of cutlery being picked up filled the hall. I could almost hear the collective sighs of relief as they were all finally allowed to eat.

"Oops," I whispered under my breath.

"Don't sweat it. It's your first day on the job. It will get easier." Luca speared a potato and popped it into his mouth.

"What would I do without you?" I smiled back at him.

The meal went without a hitch, and the champagne party afterward went late into the night without any problems or interruptions. Part of me was on edge, waiting for a bomb to go off or a riot to break out, but apart from a couple of tipsy guests, everything went smoothly.

That night, Luca escorted me my bedroom.

"You did gloriously today, My Queen." He did a small bow, and I swiped him playfully on the sleeve.

"Thank you. I wouldn't have been able to do it without you."

"My parents want us to do an official visit to Thalia next month. I was hoping you'd say yes. I'd like you to meet my brother, sister-in–law, and my nephews."

"I'd love to!" I exclaimed. I'd invited the whole family to the coronation, but as Luca's sister-in-law was a Mage, they felt it would be safer to stay at home, and only his mother and father attended. I hated how, even now, some of his family didn't feel comfortable in visiting Silverwood. "I'll speak to Jenny and my mother to arrange it. Can you let your parents know that we'll definitely come?"

Luca grinned. I don't think I'd ever seen him so happy.

"I love you. I'm so grateful you picked me."

I wanted to say his words back to him, but as usual, something stopped me. He was so free with his language and had expressed his love for me on so many occasions, but I was yet to say those three words to him. Instead, I leaned forward and kissed him.

Kissing Luca was always a pleasure. He was as beautiful on the outside as he was on the inside and as for kissing—he was an expert. As soon as our lips touched, he moved towards me so our bodies were slammed together. He took the back of my head in his hands and kissed me with an urgency and a passion that one day I hoped to match. I fell into his embrace savoring every moment.

He peppered my neck with kisses until he got to the neckline of my dress. I thought that's where he would stop, but he pulled down slightly on the material, causing me to step back.

"We can't," I whispered. "Not until the wedding night."

"Why not?" asked Luca, looking put out.

"You know why not. It's not protocol."

"Who will know?"

I nodded my head to the far end of the corridor where a guard stood on duty. He wasn't watching us, but he had to be aware what we were doing.

"He's not allowed to tell anyone. It's part of his contract."

Luca moved back to my neck, but I pulled back again.

"We have to wait until our wedding night," I repeated, feeling foolish.

He scrunched his eyes up. "Do you want me, Charmaine?"

"Yes," I replied a little too quickly. "I just want our wedding night to be special."

His features softened. "It will be. I'll make sure of it." He kissed me on the nose and reluctantly left me alone with my thoughts.

I threw myself on my bed, exhausted after the full day. I'd lied to Luca. Well, partially. I did want our wedding night to be special, but that wasn't the reason for holding back. I wasn't ready. I enjoyed his kisses, the feel of him against me, but there was something stopping me from taking it further that had nothing to do with my wedding night.

You know exactly who's stopping you!

I pulled the covers over my head to try to drown out the voice.

The Chief of Police

I'd specifically cleared the week after my coronation from my calendar so I could spend time with advisors planning what path to take for my kingdom. Jenny, who had somehow morphed from being my nanny into my personal assistant, planned what meeting I was supposed to be in and where, but more often than not, I would find her colluding with Xavi and my mother on wedding matters.

On the third day after I became queen, I called her into my office. It was the same office my father had used, and as I'd not had a chance to decorate, the whole place reeked of him, both figuratively and literally. I could still smell the faint scent of his tobacco, and it was his choice of pictures that decorated the dark room. Everything in there was wood or leather and without any windows, it made me feel claustrophobic. The only part of the room I liked was the large desk. Made by Daniel and his father, it was exquisite in its craftsmanship. I made a mental note to get some decorators in to brighten up the room. The desk was staying, but everything else could go.

"Yes?" asked Jenny as she bustled through the door. She was wearing a mixture of flowers in her hair and had drapes of fabric swathed over her shoulders.

"Fancy dress ball?" I enquired, struggling to figure out just exactly she was trying to be.

"We were in the dressing room going over samples for the tablecloths and centerpieces."

More wedding talk. I should have guessed.

"Have you made an appointment for me to speak with the chief of police? I need to speak to him about the demonstrations. They were out there on my coronation day, and they are still out there now."

Jenny pulled out a notebook from a pocket hidden somewhere in her voluminous skirts and began to flick through it, licking her finger with each page turn.

"Two o'clock this afternoon." She looked at her watch. "You'd better get something for lunch quickly, it's one already, and I made the appointment for you to go to the station."

I glanced up at the clock. It would take me at least half an hour to get to the police headquarters. Sighing, I stood and walked past her. "Please, can you get my coat and tell the stable hands I'll need a horse."

"Don't you want a carriage? It's freezing out there."

I shook my head. I was going to see him alone, and the royal carriage would stand out a mile. I didn't want the protesters to know where I was going.

Half an hour later I was trotting down the back driveway on one of the royal horses. The guards seemed surprised to see me, but they let me past without question. It felt so different to six months previously when I had to sneak out. Now I was in charge, and no one could stop me. The protesters were thankfully in small numbers around the back, the majority taking up a more prominent place at the palace's front gates. Going through the gates reminded me of the letters I'd seen on one of the banners three days previously. Some of the nastier banners had the same three letters today. The same letters Frederick Pittser had uttered at me. I'd completely forgotten about them until now, but I made a mental note to ask the chief of police about them. The protesters jeered, but, at least, no one tried to attack.

I'd never been to the large police headquarters before, but I knew the building. As imposing as it was bland, its stark architecture and sleek lines, always gave me the chills as though it was built only to house criminals. It did just that on the lower floors, but it was also the central hub for the whole of Silverwood's police force. The top four floors housed hundreds of the kingdom's finest men and women police officers from the constables that roamed the streets, to the chief on the top floor. Any crime committed anywhere in any city in Silverwood was processed at this place. To me, it looked like a very large square box.

The security guard on the door was ready for me as I walked in. He led me past the long line of people demanding to speak to an officer, and to a stairwell.

As I walked up the seemingly never-ending stairs, I realized that I'd never actually met the chief of police before. I'd seen him speaking to my father on a number of occasions, but I'd never had the opportunity to discuss matters with him. I remembered him as being a rather pugnacious man with wispy hair and a thick mustache that covered up his rodent-like face.

He was sitting ready for me as I was shown into his office. It was as bland as the outside of the police headquarters, and no effort had been made to decorate it. There were no plants or pictures of family. Perhaps he didn't have one. The nameplate on his desk read Monty Grenfall.

"Would you take a seat, Your Majesty?" He gestured to the grey chair at the opposite side of his desk. I noticed he didn't stand as I walked in—his way of asserting dominance.

I held out my hand for him to shake it, making sure it was slightly out of his reach. He either had to stand or leave me there with my arm outstretched—my way of asserting dominance.

His mustache twitched for a second before he rose to shake my hand, his handshake weak for a man of such power.

"I'd like to talk to you about the Magi," I began, finally sitting in the seat.

"I suspected that's why you wanted to speak to me."

"On the contrary. I wanted to meet with you to introduce myself formally. We will be working together to promote a healthy, happy, and safe kingdom, and I thought it would be proper to establish those ties now while it is still early in my reign. The Magi, however, are my prime concern."

"As well they should be," he replied.

"Anti-Magi protesters have been demonstrating outside the palace for six months now. I've sent numerous requests to you to do something about it, but even as I left this morning, they were still there."

"There is no law in Silverwood banning demonstrating. They are well within their rights unless they have caused damage or physically threatened you. Have they done either of those things?" I thought back to the man who'd scaled the wall. He'd not gotten anywhere close to me. There was also Pittser, but his threats had been more of the blackmailing kind rather than one of force.

"No," I conceded, "but that's hardly the point. Last year when the Magi were demonstrating, you used tear gas on them."

"Do you wish me to use tear gas on the demonstrators now?"

"No, of course not. I just want you to ask them to stop. I'm trying to build a tolerant kingdom. A kingdom where everyone is equal, and it can't be done if the Magi don't feel safe enough to even live here."

"They aren't safe to live here. I've spent almost my whole career getting rid of that scum. I'm not about to have my life's work ruined because someone killed the king."

He slammed his hand down on his desk, causing his nameplate to fall over. I picked it back up for him and placed it back on the desk.

"You know as well as I do," I said, "that the king died because of the decisions he made. May I remind you that it was the fault of the police that started the riots in the first place?"

His mustache twitched again, and I could see he was getting irked. Well good. He deserved to be.

"There's simply nothing I can do about the demonstrators. If you want to change the law, you are well within your rights as the monarch. But I caution you, if you change it for the anti-Magi protestors, you'll have to change it for the Magi protestors too. That is if they ever decide to come back, which I certainly hope that they don't."

While I hated his views, I couldn't fault his logic. The demonstrators disgusted me, but they hadn't actually broken any law. If I had them arrested for peaceful protests, I'd have to do the same in the future for other protesters. I collected my thoughts.

"Have you ever heard of the MDS, Mr. Grenfall?"

"No, I can't say I have," he replied, but the way he spoke, his eyes shifting to the side, told me he was lying. It looked like I'd have to find out from elsewhere what MDS stood for.

I decided to call him out on his views. "You must have seen on television that I've made it law that people cannot discriminate against the Magi, and that has to include you. You are one of the most senior ranking people in our whole kingdom and people look up to you..."

"They look up to me to keep them safe. I can't do that with the Magi here. Since they've been driven out, crime has gone down by nearly forty percent, and I'm not just talking about here in the capital; that statistic is for the whole of Silverwood." He folded his arms and gave me another smug look as if what he'd said overruled my feelings on anything.

"The crime was high because they weren't allowed to work," I pointed out. "They had no money and very little food. I wonder about your crime statistic. How many of those crimes were for stealing food?"

"Well, I'd have to look that up," he blustered.

"Don't bother. I can already guess the answer. The problem was never with the Magi, but with how we as a society treated them."

"We will have to agree to disagree then."

"Actually," I began "No we don't. It's your duty to follow and implement the laws of the land. Laws set out by the reigning monarch. As I am the reigning monarch, those laws are made by me and my advisors. Over the past few months, I've made sure that every university in this kingdom is open to all, no matter their magical ability. No employer can discriminate, and that means within the police force too. If you can't stick to the laws of the land, I'll be forced to find someone who can. Good day, Mr. Grenfall."

I stood and turned without letting him say anything else. I was in no mood to argue the point; I just wanted the law followed. My threat about replacing him was said in the moment, but as I left his room, I realized I might just have to follow through. I allowed myself a small smile. I'd stood up for myself and, more importantly, for the people of my kingdom. Maybe being a queen wouldn't be as difficult as I had thought after all.

The Trip to Thalia

The six white horses that pulled our carriage over the rugged mountain roads between Thalia and Silverwood looked like anything but the beauties they had been when we set off. Cold, wet, March weather combined with mud had turned them into woeful bedraggled creatures. The horses of the guards in front and the ones that followed hadn't fared much better. On a good day, the journey would take two full days to get to Luca's parents' palace, but we were already on our fourth day and no closer to getting there. We probably would have been there much sooner if I hadn't insisted on stopping for plenty of rest breaks and long nights in cozy inns. No one complained. The guards were glad to be out of the rain, and the horses were happy for the chance to rest their feet. Luca, on the other hand, was getting anxious. The path between the two kingdoms was usually safe, but with the mess my father had made in Silverwood, he was worried that the Magi might try to stop us in some way.

"The guards will keep us safe," I said for the hundredth time. This was the part of the journey he was most worried about. The path through the mountains provided a haven of hiding places for anyone who wanted to accost the royal carriage and was notorious for hiding thieves and highwaymen. We'd kept the visit as low key as possible, but it had somehow gotten out via the media which is why Luca was biting his nails and staring out of the window. "How far do we have left to go?" I asked. Anything to take him out of his thoughts.

"Another half day if we get through these mountains alive."

I looked out. It was so dreary and damp that anyone wanting to hurt us wouldn't need to hide in a cave. The fog was so thick that they could be standing ten feet away, and we wouldn't see them.

I sighed. I'd been looking forward to this trip ever since Luca had first mentioned it, but we weren't even there yet, and I was wishing it was all over. I knew that once we got out of the miserable weather and to the palace, we'd both feel better, but I was beginning to think that would never happen.

Despite my constant reassurance to Luca that we would be alright, I felt nervous myself. His nerves had put me on edge, and with every minute that passed, I expected someone to jump out at us. An hour of silently peering out the window later, the fog lifted. The sun finally peeked through, showing the most wonderful vista ahead of us. As we were so high up in the mountains, I could see for miles. Thalia was spread out before me in glorious Technicolor.

"Wow!" I breathed as the carriage crested the mountain and began the long descent.

"I told you Thalia was gorgeous in the spring. The flowers really make it something don't they?"

And they did. It was like a multicolor patchwork quilt was laid out below us as fields and fields of flowers bloomed.

Luca had moved over to my side and was visibly more relaxed than he had been for the previous part of the journey. He put his arm around me as we followed the steep road to his home.

"See over there?" He pointed to a huge building in the distance. Made of pale grey stone with hundreds of turrets topped with red slates, it rose majestically from the beautiful landscape surrounding it. "That's my home."

I gasped at the enormity of it. I'd thought my own palace was huge, but it was nothing compared to this magnificent building. Just the sight of it took my breath away.

"It's certainly something. It looks like the jewel in Thalia's crown."

Luca kissed my cheek playfully. Now that we had gotten through the mountains without incident, his demeanor had returned to normal.

"I've never heard it described like that, but you are right. I missed this place."

I'd forgotten how hard it must be for him. He'd not been home once since the ball. When I'd picked him out of the hundred men, he'd had someone bring more clothes and his belongings and had stayed at the palace in Silverwood ever since.

"I'm sorry we didn't visit sooner," I said, meaning every word of it.

"We've been busy," replied Luca. "Don't worry. We're here now."

He was as giddy as a schoolboy for the rest of the journey, and even though I was cold and tired, his enthusiasm was infectious.

After a couple of more hours, we finally pulled through the massive wrought iron gates of the Thalian Castle. The carriage was directed under a portcullis, through an archway to a massive courtyard where four uniformed guards were waiting for us.

I'd barely stepped out of the carriage when Queen Sarina ran up to me. She threw her arms around me and squashed me against her bosom.

"Darlings!" She let go and hugged her second son. "I'm so glad to see you both. Was the journey dreadful? This awful rain has lasted for weeks. I'll be glad when it's summer again.

"The rain helps the flowers!" King Theron clapped his wife on the back and then did the same to Luca. "The Thalian flowers are our biggest export you know!" He gave me a wink making me blush.

I'd met them both on two occasions. Once when they came to visit Luca and the second time when they'd come to the coronation. On the first occasion, I'd found Sarina to be sweet but quiet and Theron to be loud and boorish. Now, in their own castle, they seemed transformed. Sarina practically dragged me into the palace, chattering away about how worried she'd been about us all.

I was directed to a beautiful apartment within the castle. It opened into a large sitting room with a beautiful bright pink floral sofa and matching chair. To one side, a door led to the most luxurious bedroom I'd ever seen with a bed that was, at least, twice the width of my bed at home. I was sure it could comfortably fit five people in it. There was also a bathroom with a round tub, and there was even a small kitchen.

"We don't expect you to cook," said Sarina, pointing it out, "but it's there if you want to. The fridge is stocked with cold drinks and chocolate."

It put our palace to shame. My whole bedroom at home wasn't much bigger than the bed here.

"I'll leave you be," she continued. "I know you must be exhausted from your journey. I'll have someone bring up your bags and then you can have a nap until dinnertime. I've organized a small family dinner tonight. I didn't think you'd want such a fuss after traveling so far. Tomorrow, we'll do the big visit thing and invite the press. I've also invited some people for a ball. It's going to be wonderful. Is there anything else I can get you?"

"No, thank you. This is superb. I think I'm just going to have a bath in that wonderful bathtub."

"Press the button on the side," she whispered, "bubbles!"

After she left, I ran the bath. It was so large that I had to wait twenty minutes for it to fill to the top and when it had, I jumped in. Water splashed all over the sides into drains in the tiled floor. I pressed the button and jets of bubbles percolated around me.

Small, matching bottles of bath creams and lotions and bubble bath stood on a tiled shelf to the side of me. I added some of the bubble bath which immediately turned into a mountain of foam. By the time I'd found the switch to turn the jets off, there was at least a foot of foam on the surface.

"That looks like fun!"

I squealed and looked up. Luca was standing there with a big grin on his face.

"You should have knocked! I'm in the bath."

"I see that you're in the bath. I brought your bags up."

"Ok, thanks. Can you leave them in the bedroom."

"Are you ok? You seem on edge."

How could I tell him that I was on edge? When we'd first started dating, I'd looked forward to his kisses, his touch; but recently, everything had become much more urgent. His kisses were no longer just kisses to him, but a prelude to something else. Something else that I couldn't give him. At least, not yet. He'd never seen me naked, and even though I was completely covered in foam, I still felt extremely exposed.

"I'm fine," I covered, trying to sound nonchalant. "I was just wondering if we should dress up for tonight. Your mother said it was an informal dinner."

"I'm sure that whatever you choose to wear, you'll look as stunning as always."He moved closer, and as he stepped, I involuntarily moved back. He noticed my hesitation, and I saw his spine straighten. "Wear the navy blue dress. You look great in that." He took another look over the foam and left. I heard the outer door click as he left the apartment.

What was wrong with me? He was my fiancé, my chosen life partner. I'd craved his intimacy once, but now that it was real, I was scared, and I didn't know why.

When Elise had told me all about how good it was to be with Leo, I'd been jealous that I had to wait for so long. She'd waited for her wedding night, but her wedding night had come so much sooner than mine. Maybe she'd been scared before just like I was and just hadn't told me?

I felt so mixed up. I wanted Luca. He was beautiful and attentive and everything a girl could dream off; and yet, when it came to reality, I shied away from him.

"I need to reach out to him!" I said to myself, jumping out of the tub. "I need to show him that he's wanted."

I needed to go to his room tonight. No one would have to know and who cared if they found out? We were going to be married soon enough.

Once I'd made up my mind, I felt better about my decision. It was as if deciding it had taken some of the pressure off.

I pulled on my navy blue dress and tried to coax my hair into something resembling hair rather than a rat's nest. I applied a little lipstick and mascara, all the time wishing Xavi and her team were here to help me. When I was, at least, halfway presentable, I made my way down to the main part of the palace. I had to ask a guard for directions, and he took me to the royal dining room. It was much smaller than the banqueting suite at my palace, but I guessed this room was reserved for family meals. I had no doubt that there was a massive hall for parties somewhere in the palace.

Luca was already there as where his parents. There was also a handsome man that could only be Luca's older brother. Next to him sat the most exotically beautiful woman I'd ever met, with long dark brown hair and beguiling brown eyes. Next to her were two young boys who looked just like her. Luca's sister-in-law and nephews I presumed. Luca stood and guided me to the only empty seat with a place setting at the table. Luca sat next to me, and I had one of his nephews sitting opposite. I gave the little boy a smile, and he stuck his tongue out at me. As he was only about four, I quickly did the same, and he grinned back.

I was just about to do the same to his elder brother when one of the waiters behind him caught my eye. My heart jumped into my throat, and I gasped. Behind the little boy stood the one person I'd not ever expected to see again. It was Cynder.

Cynder

His eyes flicked up, and he noticed me at the same time that I noticed him. I saw his eyes go wide and light up, before the spark went out and he looked away, staring straight forward in front of him like the other waiters, waiting for their orders.

No one else noticed that my heart had nearly leapt out of my chest. The whole room seemed to go silent around me. He looked exactly how I remembered him except he was more careworn. Even from across the room I could see scars on his face, and even though he was fully covered from the neck down, I knew there would be more scars underneath. I wanted to jump up and run to him, but how could I? No one knew about us. He wasn't even looking at me now.

Someone brought in a huge tureen of soup, and the waiters took it in turns to serve. First the king, then the queen. I watched where Cynder went, hoping that he would head straight to me.

"Charmaine!" I jumped at the sound of my name. Luca, sitting next to me, squeezed my hand. "You were daydreaming. Are you ok?"

I looked at Luca. "I'm fine...sorry," I replied, feeling flustered.

"You were miles away."

"I'm just tired after the journey," I replied, yawning for good measure. "I'll be fine."

"I was just introducing you to Tomas and Seraphia."

Tomas, Luca's brother, nodded his head curtly, but Seraphia gave me a huge grin.

"And these two little monsters are Jacob and Michael."

The two boys stuck their tongues out at me again, but I was too confused to care. Instead, I smiled at all of them at once and said hi.

A dish of soup was laid down next to me. I jerked my head to the side to see who had served it and found myself looking at a kindly old waiter who smiled at me. Looking back around the room, I saw that many of the waiters had already left, probably back to the kitchen to let us eat in peace. Cynder was one of them.

Why had he not served me? Was he mad at me? I could only assume he was. Why wouldn't he be? I'd told him I loved him and then promptly gotten engaged to someone else. Even though I'd hired a private investigator to find him, he'd come up with nothing. Six months ago, Cynder had completely vanished into thin air. I wondered how many of those months he'd been here.

"It's so lovely to meet you," Seraphia leaned across the table and spoke directly to me. "We should meet up after dinner. I've been really looking forward to meeting the one that finally got Luca to settle down."

"I'd like that," I replied, absent-mindedly and went back to eating my soup. When the main courses came, I sat up straight, waiting for Cynder, but he never reappeared.

After we had finished eating, we were all invited into a small wood-paneled room for drinks. A fire roared at one end with a couple of leather sofas and two matching leather chairs all pointing towards it in a kind of semi-circle. The smell of the burning logs filled my nostrils as a glass of whiskey was thrust into my hand by Theron.

I saw Seraphia winging her way towards me, but it was Luca that got my attention by pulling me back outside to the hallway.

"What's the matter?" he barked.

"Nothing. Why?"

"You've been acting strange all during dinner. You barely said a word to anyone. It's not like you."

I immediately felt bad. He was right. I'd been so caught up in Cynder that I'd not paid attention to anything going on around me.

"I'm sorry. I'm always nervous around people I don't know. I guess I felt overwhelmed." It was partly the truth. "I'll go back in there and talk to everyone."

"Thank you." His voice softened. "My parents love you. You know that. I want Tomas and Seraphia to love you too."

"I'll try," I promised, turning towards the door. Luca pulled me back around and tugged me into an embrace. His tongue teased my lips apart, "but I resisted.

"Not here," I said, pulling back. Your family is in there."

"So?"

"So, we should go and talk to them."

He looked so downhearted, and yet, I couldn't bring myself to pretend. I'd made a promise to myself to visit him in his room that night, but now that I'd seen Cynder, I knew I'd not be able to bring myself to do it.

When I went back into the parlor, I was the life and soul of the party. It was my way of making up for everything. I hated that Luca was disappointed in me. He deserved better. I sipped lightly on my whiskey, hoping the burning sensation it produced would drown out the pain I was feeling inside. King Theron grabbed my waist and pulled me into a sideways hug, almost crushing me in his bearlike arms. All the while, he jovially talked to the others about how proud he was that Luca had finally found the right girl.

I'd not really noticed it when we were sitting around the table earlier, but he'd used the same word that Seraphia had. "Finally." Both of them had used it when describing Luca. It was almost as if they thought that Luca would never settle down.

After quite a number of whiskeys on Theron's part, I was finally able to escape his clutches. He was being nothing but lovely to me, but after drinking so much, he was beginning to repeat himself. I think he was more excited about our wedding than my mother was, and that was saying something.

I walked across the room, glad to be away from the oppressive heat of the fire. Seraphia took the opportunity and came over to me.

"Don't you like whiskey either?" she asked, nodding at my still mostly full glass. "Theron never asks, he just gives you alcohol. I think if everyone else drinks it, it makes him feel better about drinking so much of it himself. Would you prefer some champagne because I know I would."

I nodded my head gratefully. The whiskey wasn't taking my pain away, it was just stripping the lining from my throat. I much preferred the freshness and bubbles of champagne. Seraphia left the room and came back a couple of minutes later with a young servant carrying two champagne flutes and a bottle of champagne in an ice bucket.

"I'm so glad you're here," she said, taking the bottle and pouring me a glass. I never thought I'd see the day when I'd get a new sister-in-law."

"Why do you say that?" I asked, although I knew full well the reason. Reputations don't happen for no reason, and Luca had quite a reputation for the ladies before I met him.

Her face fell as she realized what she'd said.

"Oh, it's just that I didn't take Luca as the marrying kind, that's all. I was surprised when he told us that he'd put his name into the drawing for the ball last year."

"He wants the chance to rule a country. He told me so."

"I think it's more than that. He's a different person since meeting you. Look at him." I looked over. He was chatting animatedly with his brother. He did seem to be happy.

"He would make a great leader, though," she continued "He's done so much to help me promote Magi rights recently. He told me that is something very close to your own heart."

I nodded enthusiastically; glad to be finally on the subject. "It is. I don't want a kingdom separated by hate. A lot of mistakes have been made in the past, and I want to rectify them. Everyone will be an equal in Silverwood."

"It's not that easy, though, is it? Luca tells me that you are having a hard time changing the views of the people."

"It's almost impossible," I admitted. "I thought it would be easy once I was queen, but the kingdom has become more segregated than ever. I've opened up the palace and the universities to the Magi, but no one is taking me up on my offer. They are either too scared after all the violence last year, or they have gone. I've not seen a single Magi since the panic at my wedding to Xavier. If there are any left, they are all in hiding."

"Keep at it! You are doing a wonderful job. People will come around eventually. Look at Luca."

"What do you mean?"

She leaned in towards me and lowered her voice. "He didn't like me when I first married his brother. I think he thought that Tomas marrying a mage would lower the monarchy somehow. It took a while, but he came around eventually, and now we are good friends. I have faith in you, and if you ever need any help, you know where I am."

I thanked her, but her words were futile. It wasn't even safe enough to invite her to my palace at the moment. I couldn't see a way to make things better.

My head was beginning to hurt with the whiskey and champagne, so I said a hurried goodnight and slipped out of the room before Luca could spot me leaving.

I wished I'd had a chance to speak to Cynder. To tell him that whatever we had had between us was over for good. I wanted to explain why things had turned out the way they had and to apologize for my part in everything.

And you want to see him again.

"No, I don't!" I whispered to myself, not entirely sure if it was the truth or not.

Walking the castle corridors was eerie compared to my own palace at home. I had become so accustomed to guards on every corner, that it felt weird to be roaming this huge house alone.

I managed to get to my bedroom without spotting a single other person. The beautifully made bed looked so inviting to me right now, but there was something I wanted to do before closing my eyes. I pulled out one of the cases I brought with me and searched through it. Xavi had packed most of my bags, filling them with gown after gown for every occasion except the occasion of just lolling around. The case I had on my bed was reserved exclusively for jewelry. When I opened it, I noticed that she'd put little notes on each piece telling which dress I should wear it with. I couldn't help but smile. She didn't trust me to be able to dress myself appropriately. Not that I could really blame her. I pulled out a small purse I'd thrown on top just before leaving Silverwood and opened the zipper. Inside was a little silver bracelet with a carriage charm and a silver slipper charm. No matter how much I wanted to pretend that Cynder wasn't taking up my thoughts, the truth was, he'd not left them since I saw him at dinner. The fact that I'd brought this bracelet with me in the first place proved I'd not really stopped thinking about him at all.

I slipped the chain on my wrist and closed my eyes. I could see him as clear as day. His curly hair and those caramel colored eyes of his were branded on my brain.

I played around with the bracelet as I lay down on the bed, not even bothering to get undressed.

I could have asked myself why I wasn't getting into my nightgown and slipping under the covers when I was so exhausted, but I knew it was because I was expecting a visitor. Cynder had seen me, I was sure of it, and he would know which room had been reserved for me. I didn't have to wait too long. Within fifteen minutes there was a light knocking at my door. I jumped up out of bed, knocking the case with all the jewelry over and scattering diamond-encrusted tiaras and necklaces all over the floor. I jumped over them and with a hammering heart opened the door.

"I wondered where you went."

Luca kissed me on the mouth. I could taste the whiskey on him. I wanted to enjoy it, but all I could think was "what if Cynder sees?" I pulled him into my room, which he took as an invitation. His kisses became more insistent, and his hands wandered lower and lower.

"I was hoping you'd be in your night clothes," he said when he came up for air.

"I'm not ready for this!" I said, pushing him back guiltily. I'd said no to him so many times that it was causing a rift between us. To my surprise, he didn't seem upset.

"I'm sorry, my love. I know you want to wait. I got carried away. I'd promised myself I'd leave you alone, but I fear I've drunk too much whiskey. The wait will make our wedding night all the sweeter."

He kissed me again, but this time much more softly. It was warm and nice. There was no pressure in it. It was what it was, and for the first time in quite a while, I enjoyed it. I found my body responding to his touch in a way it had long since forgotten. Without the pressure of things going too fast, I remembered how much I enjoyed these kisses. When he pulled back, I almost followed him.

"Will you walk me to my room?" he said, clearly too inebriated to get there himself. How he'd managed to find my room, goodness only knew. I put his arm over my shoulder and walked him to his suite further down the corridor. His room was similar to mine but slightly bigger. I could tell he'd had this room since childhood as it was filled with his things. Framed photographs lined the walls, and the shelves were filled with knickknacks and trophies and the clutter that accumulates over time. I helped him to his bed where he fell asleep immediately. His heavy breathing turned into the lightest of snores. I wanted to leave him there as he was, but he was still wearing his dress uniform which looked extremely uncomfortable to sleep in. I rooted through a set of drawers until I found his pajamas and then began the task of removing his clothing. It was strange. We'd been engaged for months, but I'd never seen him without a shirt on before. I pulled off his jacket and slowly unbuttoned his dress shirt. His chest was smooth, with just a smattering of dark hairs and as I looked down on him, naked from the waist up, I realized just how beautiful he was. I ran my hand lightly up his chest, marveling at the hard muscles covered in warm skin. Something stirred within me. This was the man I was betrothed to. I'd promised him my life. Why was I waiting for a kitchen hand to come to me? I pulled his trousers down, leaving him only in his underwear, before quickly sliding his legs into the pajama bottoms. Once he was fully in his pajamas, I pulled his bed covers over him.

He looked so happy and peaceful in sleep and now that I'd had a view of what to expect on my wedding night, I knew I should throw away my childish thoughts of Cynder once and for all.

I was just about to leave when a golden pin, lying on the bedside table caught my eye. It was in the shape of a rose. I'd seen the symbol before. Frederick Pittser had been wearing something similar.

I headed back to my room and closed the door. After a second's thought, I locked it. If Cynder came to see me, I couldn't open the door. I got changed and hopped into bed. In my mind I pictured my gorgeous husband to be, sleeping just down the corridor. Within minutes I was asleep, and the picture of Luca transformed into one of a kitchen boy doing dishes whilst dancing to the beat of his own music.

The Interview

I awoke with a start an hour or so later. Despite my promise to myself to only think of Luca, my dreams had been plagued by Cynder. I jumped out of bed, wondering if a knock on the door had awoken me, but when I opened it and looked along the corridor, I saw it was empty. I should have gone back to bed. I should have kept my promise, I should have done a lot of things. What I shouldn't have done was grab my dressing robe and head out into the dark corridor, but that's exactly what I did.

'I need to tell Cynder that I'm marrying Luca to help the Magi,' I said to myself. I wasn't sure if I was trying to persuade myself that that was the truth or not, but either way, I knew I'd not be able to leave this palace without seeing him again. If nothing else, I had to tell him I was sorry.

I stole down the corridors silently, scared that someone would see me. Except for my own quiet footsteps, there wasn't a sound. Everyone in the palace was asleep. I was a mere ghost within its walls. I didn't know where the kitchen was, but I had a strong feeling that if I carried on heading downwards, I'd eventually stumble upon it. In all houses as magnificent as this, the kitchen was usually on the ground floor or in the basement below.

I hurried down staircase after staircase, getting completely lost in the maze of corridors. Eventually, I came to a small wooden staircase. It wasn't nearly as grand as the others, so I took it to be the servant's stairwell. I hesitated before slowly heading down. Every step I took felt illicit and wrong, and yet some unseen force was guiding me onwards. At the bottom was a door. Upon it was a wooden plaque saying kitchen. I opened it slowly, my heart hammering in my chest. I'd waited so long to see him again, and yet I was scared to rush through the doors. The lights were on.

Someone was down there. I could hear the clinking and sploshing of cutlery being washed up. As I opened the door wider, I saw plates and cups flying through the air before dunking themselves in the sink. They were being washed up by magic. I burst through the door, unable to wait any longer and crashed straight into a young girl. She screamed loudly at my presence before realizing who I was and curtsying. The plates that had been held up by magic crashed to the floor where they shattered into hundreds of pieces.

The scream or the sound of the plates smashing brought down a big burly man wearing blue striped pajamas, who appeared in the kitchen just behind me. He looked like he'd just jumped out of bed, with his hair standing up in all directions and a decidedly sleepy look on his face.

"What's going on here?" he asked, taking in the strange scene.

"I'm sorry, sir," said the young girl, her face turning the color of a plum. "I had an accident."

"No," I replied quickly. "It was my fault. I scared her. I should have given her warning."

"Your majesty," began the man. "It's not customary, nor is it necessary, for a member of the royal family to be down in the kitchen. If you want something brought up to your room, you only need to pull the bell cord next to your bed, and someone will come to you."

"I'm sorry. I've not seen the bell cord," I answered truthfully. "I didn't know."

"No harm, no foul. What can I get for you? I'm assuming you are hungry."

"I just came for a drink of water," I improvised.

"Amanda, can you get her majesty a glass of water. I'll tidy up this mess."

He pulled out a wand and flicked it quickly. The broken shards rearranged themselves into full pieces of crockery and piled themselves up neatly on the counter. I was so in awe of the magic, I almost didn't notice when Amanda handed me the glass.

"Thank you," I said taking a sip. "I'll head off now."

"Be sure to use the bell cord," shouted the man as I left. "It's what we are here for."

"Will do," I shouted back as I made my way back up the stairs with the glass.

I'd never felt so foolish although I truly didn't know about the bell cord. It was not an excuse I could use again. Maybe it was for the best. I headed back to my room and placed the glass of water on the bedside cabinet, noting the bed pull hanging above it.

I got back into bed and closed my eyes.

The next morning, I had to be up early for a day of royal engagements. Xavi had left me strict instructions on what to wear for each occasion, but I was still unsure as I pulled a long blue velvet gown over my head. I topped it off with one of the tiaras I'd spilled on the floor the night before. The notes on each one also scattered, mixing them up, but the tiara I'd picked had a sapphire of the exact same shade of blue as the dress, so I figured it would be ok.

My hair and makeup was another matter entirely. Without Xavi's crew, I'd have to do it myself. She'd packed me a small case of makeup and hair equipment, but it looked like a rainbow of disaster. I knew if I picked the wrong eyeshadow, I could mess everything up. I settled for some nude lipstick and a hint of mascara. It wasn't on the same level of makeup expertise I had gotten used to, but, at least, I didn't look strange. I brushed my hair back into a tight ponytail and twirled it into a bun. Hopefully, the tiara would hide most of it. Looking into the mirror, I found that I didn't look quite as bad as I thought I might. Xavi would be proud of me. No doubt, she and Jenny were watching every move I made on the TV. Xavi would be critiquing my attire, and Jenny would be doing the same with my manners and the way I held myself. I found Luca in the breakfast room along with the rest of his family. When he saw me, he jumped up and bounded over, pulling me into a hug.

"I don't remember undressing myself last night," he whispered in my ear. When he pulled back, he gave his eyebrows a wiggle, which made me laugh.

"You look stunning, by the way. That blue really suits you." I kissed his cheek and took my place at the table. Even though I tried not to look up at the waiters dotted around the room, I couldn't help but glance up at them. Cynder wasn't there. I wasn't sure whether to be relieved or upset. I decided on the former after my decision last night. Seeing him again would only complicate things. Instead, I concentrated on getting to know Luca's family a bit more. I made small talk as we all ate. Breakfast was a rather hurried affair as we were all expected for photos and interviews.

I thought we would be taken to a room in the palace, so I was rather surprised when I followed the rest of the family down to the courtyard where a carriage awaited us.

"Where are we going?" I asked Luca as he helped me up into the beautiful black carriage with the royal crest on the side.

"The TV studios."

"You don't let the cameras into the house?" I asked, thinking back to last year when there seemed to be TV crews in my palace all the time.

"Not if we can help it. The studios have a special room just for royalty. Any time you've seen a professional photo of the Thalian Royal Family, it's been taken there."

As we headed out of the castle gates, a roar went up. Just as they had in Silverwood, the people came out to see the royals in Thalia. Thousands of people lined the streets, waving both the Thalian flag and the Silverwood flag. It was a pleasure to see and made me feel more confident about my presence here.

The journey itself only lasted about ten minutes. On arrival, there were hundreds of people behind barriers, most of whom held bunches of flowers. I walked down the barriers accepting bouquet after bouquet. Those that could not reach me, who were two or three people deep into the crowd, threw their bunches so the ground around me was littered with flowers. I smiled a genuine smile trying to speak to as many people as I could before I was finally ushered in. Once inside, we were all taken to a huge room filled with lights. A mock-up of a castle room had been made with a painted backdrop, and a long red velvet sofa sat in front of it.

"We've had our photos taken in front of that backdrop so many times, I'm sure that's where people think we live," whispered Luca into my ear. I grinned. I was feeling so happy, thanks to the warm welcome from the people of Thalia, that nothing could upset me today. The photographer came in and put us into the position he wanted us to shoot. The theme of the shoot was our upcoming wedding, so the rest of the family were only needed for a few shots, while Luca and I were put in pose after pose until the photographer was satisfied.

Then came the interview. I was prepped beforehand. It was to be a light-hearted interview about the wedding. I was assured that, even though I'd be the center of attention, there'd be no difficult questions. I felt calm and happy as I took my place in front of the cameras on a sofa. Luca's parents sat on one side, and Tomas and Seraphia sat on the other with myself and Luca in the middle. I smiled. For the first time ever, I was excited to be interviewed. My mother had talked about the upcoming wedding so much that if I was asked any questions about the dress or the flowers for the ceremony, I'd be able to answer almost without thinking.

I arranged my dress so it wouldn't crease and waited for the interviewer.

The door opened, and a tall wispy man walked in. My mouth dropped when I saw who it was. I'd almost forgotten about Frederick Pittser and the way he assaulted me in my own palace. What was he doing here? He introduced himself to the camera before welcoming me to Thalia.

"It's wonderful to have you here, Your Majesty. Thank you for coming, and welcome to the rest of our royal family. If I may start with you, Princess Charmaine, how did you feel when you found out you were going to become the queen?"

"I was initially upset," I replied, trying not to sneer at him. Where was he going with this? I felt like a deer caught in the headlights. "My father had just passed away. Eventually, I began to see it as a great honor, a way to make Silverwood better again."

"But Silverwood has descended into chaos since you took over."

"I wouldn't say it's chaos," I argued. "We have problems as does any kingdom, but I feel confident that Luca and I will be able to work together to help to solve them. Our wedding is coming up in a few months, and we are fully prepared to put our kingdom first."

"Forgive me Your Majesty, but were you putting your kingdom first this morning when the news of another riot in the capital of Silverwood came in because I've not seen you responding to it yet?"

I looked to Luca for help. No one had told me about a riot. I wanted to stop the cameras and find out what had happened, but we were broadcasting live.

"I wasn't aware of that," I said, trying to keep both the aggravation and the worry from my tone.

"It seems that the unrest has grown since you abandoned Silverwood. There are reports of numerous demonstrations from both sides, both Magi and non-Magi. What do you say to that?"

"As I already stated, Mr. Pittser. I've not been made aware, but I assure you, I'll look into it as soon as we are off air. The welfare of my people is my utmost concern."

"So what are you going to do about it once you make yourself aware?"

His hostile tone was unmistakable and making me nervous, and yet, I kept my composure.

"She's already said, she'll look into it," interjected Luca, saving me from having to answer. "Once we know what we are dealing with, we will do everything we can to sort out the situation. We were under the impression we would be talking about our wedding today."

"Yes, I apologize. I've noticed your lovely tiara, Princess Charmaine and the beautiful bracelet on your wrist. Can you tell us all where you got it?"

I looked down. There on my wrist was the simple silver charm bracelet that I'd put on last night. I'd forgotten to take it off. Frederick Pittser knew exactly where it had come from. I don't know how he knew, but he knew.

"The tiara belonged to my mother."

"And the bracelet. It's rather unusual."

"I don't recall," I replied. "It's one of those pieces of jewelry that I've had for a long time."

"And yet, you were seen wearing it a lot last year."

"I like it," I replied, feeling sick. With every second that passed, I was waiting for him to tell the whole of Thalia about Cynder. His questions about the bracelet were a warning, but I didn't know what he wanted me to do except stop the Magi coming back, and I wasn't prepared to do that.

Thankfully, King Theron began to chat about how proud he was of Luca. As Theron was a big talker, he chatted about the upcoming wedding for the rest of the interview, saving me from having to speak further. As soon as the small red light on top of the cameras went off, I dashed out of the studio to the nearest bathroom and was sick. A minute or so later, I heard a knock on the cubicle door.

"Charmaine? Are you ok?" It was Seraphia.

"I'm fine," I lied. "Just a bit tired."

I opened the door to find her concerned face looking at me.

"I'm not surprised. You had a long journey to get here, and we all drank a little too much last night."

I wanted to tell her that I wasn't suffering from a hangover. I'd not really drunk much at all, but then I realized it was better than the truth.

"I think I just need a nap."

"If we head back now, you'll have time to nap before the ball."

I'd forgotten about the ball that had been organized for me. It was a way for the lords and ladies of Thalia to meet me. As it wasn't scheduled for hours, maybe Seraphia was right, and I'd be able to fit in a nap. I just wanted to block everything out, and a nap was the perfect way to do it; but first, I had to find out what was going on in Silverwood. Frederick Pittser had said that both the Magi and the Anti-Magi had been involved in riots, but I'd not see the Magi demonstrating in Silverwood for over half a year.

I found Luca waiting for me just outside the bathroom.

"Are you ok? You dashed off pretty quickly."

"I'm fine. Do you know anything about the riots?"

"No. That's the weird thing. When I questioned the news team about it, they had no knowledge of any riots, nor has anything been reported here about them. I asked the station manager to call one of his royal reporters near your palace, but all he could tell him was that a whole bundle of fabric had arrived for the bridesmaid dresses. I was going to ask that ass Pittser about it, but he skedaddled quick as a flash once the interview was over."

"What about the rest of Silverwood? Any riots anywhere?"

"No. Nothing at all. Pittser was obviously a moron with bad information. Don't worry about it."

But I did worry. If Luca was correct and Pittser was making it all up, he was playing a game with me, and I didn't know the rules.

There were still thousands of flag-waving people lining the streets as we left the studio. I tried to smile, but my heart wasn't in it. As soon as we got back to the palace, I bounded up the stairs to my room, desperate to have some time on my own to figure out what it was that Pittser was up to.

I opened the door to find someone on my bed.

It was Cynder.

Two Men, Two Kisses

I stood staring at him, not sure if I was just so tired that I'd hallucinated him.

"Cynder?"

He was as beautiful as I remembered him and now all those months of dreams had crystallized into reality, I could barely breathe. In that second I knew that I'd not gone looking for him earlier to tell him I was sorry, but to look into his eyes just one more time. I couldn't deny it to myself any longer.

"I heard that someone came down to the kitchen last night and scared the kitchen maid so much she broke all the dishes."

"I was looking for you," I whispered, knowing that him just being here was wrong.

"I figured."

It wasn't the meeting I'd imagined so many times. In my head, I'd run into his open arms and kissed him. There was never anything after that. Just an endless kiss. However, I was standing shell-shocked by my door, and Cynder was making no move to come towards me. We just stared at each other as if there was an invisible barrier between us and that barrier was my engagement to Luca.

Neither of us had moved when the door opened behind me. I turned quickly to see Luca walking through it.

"Are you ok?" he said, turning to me. "You've looked pretty down since the interview, and then you rushed off so quickly when we got home."

"I...I..." I stammered, not knowing what to say. Cynder was laying on the bed right behind me. Luca only had to glance over my shoulder to see him.

"The interviewer was unbelievable," he continued "Are you sure you are ok?"

I stood stock still, barely breathing. Luca took my hand and led me to the bed. He sat down mere inches from Cynder's leg. He'd still not noticed him. How was that even possible?

Luca patted the bed next to him, and I sat too, being careful not to sit on Cynder. I glanced his way for a second and noticed he had a sly grin on his face.

Luca moved forward and kissed me. I nearly passed out with the sheer adrenaline and fear of the situation. I tried pulling back, but Luca was insistent, following me.

Seconds later there was a loud smashing sound behind Luca. A light bulb had fallen out of its socket and smashed on the floor.

"What the..." Luca got up and checked the socket. "How strange. It just fell out. I'll get someone to come up and clean the mess up."

"Don't...worry," I stammered, glancing at Cynder. His wand was out, and he had a curious expression on his face. I turned back to Luca. He was looking straight at me now. I was inches from Cynder, but it was obvious that he didn't see him. "I'm really tired," I said "I need a nap. I'll get someone up to tidy it later." I just needed Luca to be gone so I could breathe again. Being caught between the man I was betrothed to and the man that held my heart, was both terrifying and electrifying. I felt the blood draining from my face.

"Ok, if you are sure. You are looking a little peaky. Perhaps a nap would be the best thing.

Just don't stand on that glass in bare feet. We have a lot of dancing to do tonight."

I got up and walked him to the door. As he left, he pecked my cheek.

"I love you, Charmaine."

I kissed him back quickly to save me from answering. I'd never felt more wretched in my life. When he left I locked the door behind him and took a deep breath. I waited until I heard his footsteps walking away along the corridor outside before I spoke.

"He didn't see you."

"Did you forget I'm a Mage?" Cynder wiggled his wand and then returned it to his pocket.

"Why were you caught last year if you could just make yourself invisible like that?"

"I wasn't invisible, you could see me. I just made it so that Luca couldn't. If he was expecting me to be here, he'd have seen me. I tricked his mind that's all. The people who captured me knew what they were looking for. They were experienced Magi hunters. That little trick wouldn't have worked on them for a second."

"Oh," I sighed, trying to bring my heart rate back down to an acceptable level.

"What was Luca saying about an interviewer? I didn't see the broadcast."

I shrugged my shoulders. "There is an interviewer who threatened me last week at the palace in Silverwood. He said that I have to stop my crusade for Magi rights. He followed me here to Thalia and somehow managed to get a job at the local news network."

Cynder sat up on the bed, interested in the information. "What do you mean 'threatened you?' Did he hurt you?" I could see the anger in his face. I was ashamed to admit it to myself, but it made me happy. It meant he still cared about me.

"He bruised my arm, but it was nothing I couldn't handle," I lied.

Cynder looked thoughtful for a moment. "A lot of people don't want to live in peace with the Magi. You know that. He'll be some crazy fanatic. I'm sure Luca will get him fired, and he'll crawl back under the rock he came from."

I sighed and straightened up on the bed. "He knows about us."

"What?" Cynder sat up straight, matching my own posture.

"He told me when he bruised my arm. He said that if I don't stop what I'm doing, he'll tell the world about you and me."

"How can he know?"

"I don't know. I told Elise and Leo about us, but no one else."

"What do you know about Leo? Could he have told someone?"

"No. It's not possible. Leo is as fanatical about Magi rights as the interviewer is against them. Besides, he's a good friend, not to mention my new brother in law."

"What's this guy's name? I'll ask around and see what I can dig up about him."

"Pittser. Frederick Pittser."

Cynder's hand went up to his chin. I could still see the faint scars along his jawline where he had been beaten. I wanted nothing more than to kiss them, but I held back.

He got up from the bed and walked over to me. I could feel my heart rate increasing with each step he took. I should have stopped him. I should have said no, but I didn't.

When he kissed me, I felt like my heart might explode. His kiss was soft and sweet and way too short.

He pulled away leaving me breathless and desperate for more. Even though Luca kissed with such passion, it was nothing compared to the utter abandonment of my senses that Cynder made me feel. When I kissed him, I could feel my blood rushing through my veins, my body more alive than ever before. I never wanted it to end. It also made me feel like the most wretched woman in existence. I pulled back quickly, my rational side taking over a fraction too late.

"This can't happen. I'm engaged to someone else, someone who will be good for the kingdom."

"That's why you are marrying him? Because he'll be good for the kingdom? What about you? Will he be good for you?"

I looked into his eyes. I could see him searching right into my soul. I wanted to tell him that I loved him only, but what was the point? I'd only end up hurting Luca and destroying the tiny bit of credibility I'd managed to build up among the people. I'd promised myself that Luca was the way forward for me, so why was it so hard to answer Cynder's question.

Because you are going to have to lie to him, that's why.

"He's a good man. He cares for me, and I care for him."

"Do you love him?"

"Does it matter? You and I can't be together. It's impossible. Luca will help me make

Silverwood a better place for the Magi, a better place for you."

"And I couldn't, right? I'm just a kitchen hand, and he's a prince! I get it. You'd be a fool to choose me."

He brought his wand out and casually flicked it so the broken glass on the floor rearranged itself back into the light bulb it once was. I watched as it rose up and fixed back into place.

"That's not it at all. You know I don't care if you are a kitchen hand."

"But you care that I'm a Mage. Despite all your words to the people of your kingdom, you don't have the guts to stand up there and tell them about me. You are scared that some interviewer will tell the world and what would it look like? The new queen having an affair with a piece of scum Mage?"

"Stop it!" I cried. "You know that's not the truth. I made a promise to Luca and to my people. You being a Mage has nothing to do with that. Luca will help me make Silverwood safe again for the Magi. You'll be able to come home."

Cynder laughed mirthlessly. "There is nothing for me in Silverwood now. Everything I wanted has gone."

"I'm sorry. I never expected things to work out this way."

"I came to say goodbye. I'm happy for you. I'm glad that you are happy. You'll make a wonderful queen."

He kissed my cheek and unlocked the door. Without another word, he was gone. The weight of Cynder's words was etched into my brain, and the feel of his lips would stay burned on my own for a long time to come.

The Ball

couldn't sleep after Cynder left. I just lay on the bed, going over everything over and over again in my mind. I'd made a conscious decision to spend my life with Luca, and in my head, I'd done it for all the right reasons, so why did I feel so lost and wretched? In the end, I decided to get up and speak to Seraphia. If I was going to make Silverwood a stronger, more tolerant kingdom, I was going to need some help.

I knocked on her bedroom door. Tomas answered. A tall reedy man, he clearly took after his mother just as Luca had, although, unlike his brother, his hair was thinning slightly in places and he didn't quite have the same sex appeal. He seemed surprised to see me there. He was already in his royal attire for the ball and looked thoroughly harassed. I suppressed the urge to straighten his tie that looked like it had been put on in a rush and was now hanging at least twenty degrees to the left of where it should have been.

"I'm here to see Seraphia if she's available."

"Thank goodness you are here. She can't decide what to wear, and she keeps asking me as if I know what color shoes match a scarlet dress like I'm supposed to know."

I almost laughed at his expression. He looked hopelessly lost.

"I'll help her. Why don't you go and see if Luca wants some company?"

"Brilliant idea."

He strode past me, seemingly relieved not to have to talk about clothes anymore. I wandered into the royal chambers to find Seraphia looking exasperated on the bed, surrounded by dresses and shoes and jewelry.

"Charmaine! I'm so glad you are here. Does this go with this?" She held up a pair of red velvet shoes and a red dress.

"I'm no expert on fashion. I usually have someone else to dress me," I replied. "But the shoes are a different shade of red."

"You are right. I didn't want to wear the red in the first place, but Tomas said he liked it. I don't know why I get myself into such a fluster over these events."

She could have worn a paper bag and still looked stunningly beautiful. With her long dark hair and pretty face, it didn't really matter what she wore. I picked up a pretty pale pink dress and held it up.

"This is nice. It would go with those shoes," I said, pointing to a pair on the floor.

"Great idea. That was my first choice too." She took the dress from me and pulled her robe off, quickly throwing the pink gown over her perfect body. She looked adorable and sexy at the same time. They were not two words I'd usually put together in the same sentence, but she somehow managed it. I wondered for a second how easy life would be if I was as effortlessly beautiful as she was.

"How are you feeling now? Did you have a nice nap?" she asked, looking at me through her reflection in the mirror.

"I couldn't sleep," I replied honestly, although I didn't tell her the reason why. My stomach was wound up so tight that physical pain was shooting through my body.

"Don't let the media people get to you. There are always going to be haters. When I first started dating Tomas, there was an uproar. It was in all the papers and magazines how I was going to try and take over the kingdom. As if. I can hardly pick the right dress to wear for a ball."

"I didn't realize there was anti-Magi prejudice here as well."

"There isn't so much anymore, but there used to be. It was never as bad as it is in Silverwood. There were never laws here to prevent the Magi doing the same things as anyone else, but a lot of people didn't like it."

"You said Luca didn't like it," I said, remembering what she'd told me last night. It was hard to imagine Luca not caring about the Magi. He was as passionate as I was about their rights.

"Did I say that?" She asked, blushing. "I guess I had a little too much to drink. When I first started dating Tomas, he really hated me because of what I was. I think he was jealous of Tomas too, the fact that Tomas was going to get the throne because he was the elder son."

I remembered Luca telling me he envied his brother's chance to rule a kingdom. Seraphia turned round to speak to me rather than my reflection.

"I think he was mad that a Mage would help rule Thalia one day," she continued. "I remember the arguments he had with Tomas, with Theron and Sarina. It took him a few years to come round to the idea, but then early last year things began to change. I don't know what prompted it, but he came to me to apologize. He asked what he could do to help with Magi rights. Since then, he's really turned over a new leaf. It's been great watching how interested he's been in the Magi, even more so since being with you. You are having a great effect on him. Other people haven't been so nice, but I guess that's true for any princess. It's a lot better now than it was a few years ago."

She turned back to her mirror and started to apply her makeup.

"How did you get over that?"

"Theron and Sarina welcomed me with open arms and have always been on my side. They let me have free rein talking about my life as a Mage to the media. With their backing, I set up support groups, mixers and promoted Magi rights whenever I could. I was lucky that the people ignored the press and came to love me. The press had to follow suit if they wanted to sell their papers. There are still some that don't like the Magi, but you can't change everyone's mind."

I watched as she applied powder to her cheeks making them glimmer. I don't know how she did it. I was lost without Xavi and her helpers. She looked every inch the princess she was. I resisted the urge to glance at my own reflection in the mirror behind her. I didn't want to look at a traitor, and that's exactly how I felt about myself.

"I want Silverwood to be like that," I replied, sitting down on the bed between her dresses, "but I'm fighting against years of prejudice. Most of the Magi won't come out of hiding and those that have, still hate me for the years they were persecuted under my father's rule. I can't win whatever I do. Neither side likes me very much at the moment. My mother seems to think that if I wear the prettiest dresses and have my hair perfect, then people will forget about the years of hate and about what my father did."

"You've got it hard, but not impossible. You need people to stand behind you and back you up. Strength in numbers I always say."

"Well, I have Luca, of course. He's with me a hundred percent. I also have Leo and my friends Daniel and Dean. That's about it. No one else wants to come forward and help."

I didn't mention Cynder. She would have only asked me questions to which I had no answer.

"I'm here too. I'll happily come to Silverwood to give talks if you want me to."

I wanted her to come so badly, but I was afraid for her safety. There were too many people that hated the Magi in Silverwood.

"It's not really safe at the moment," I said, sadly. I hated the fact that she couldn't even come to my coronation. "I hope to make things better by the time of the wedding because I'd hate for you to miss it."

"I'll do what I can from here," she said. "I can speak to the media. I know Silverwood broadcasts Thalian channels. Maybe it will help?"

"Thanks, Seraphia. It can't hurt. I just don't think it's going to be enough. There are demonstrations in the streets, and the police are turning a blind eye to them. Last year, when it was the Magi demonstrating, the police were using tear gas. I thought that now I am queen, the police would listen to me, but the head of police is still fiercely loyal to my father. It constantly feels like we are on the brink of civil war. The anti-Magi hate the Magi, the Magi hate the anti-Magi and both sides hate me."

Seraphia moved away from the mirror and gave me a hug. "I'm sure that's not true. You are ruling a kingdom that is recovering from a brutal regime, and while it was great for the anti-Magi who got all the best jobs and university places, it sucked for people like me. You need to keep working on the Magi. Keep promoting Silverwood as a place with a future for them."

Cynder's words came back to me. *There is no future for me there.*

Seraphia carried on. "Those against the magi will be harder, but I know you can do it."

"I'm scared. There aren't enough Magi in the kingdom to step forward. I've created jobs and opened up the universities to them. I've made it a law that everyone should be treated equally, but the reality is, the law isn't so easy to enforce, especially when the police force doesn't want to enforce it."

"It sounds like you need a new police force. Have you considered advertising the police to the Magi?"

"I've mentioned it to the chief, but having him actually do it is another matter. I guess I have a lot of work to do."

"You need to get ready for the ball before you do anything to save your kingdom. It starts soon."

"Do you think you'll be able to help me with my make-up?" I asked. "When I do it, it looks like a four-year-old has been scribbling on my face."

Seraphia laughed. "Sure thing."

She followed me back to my room. I'd already picked a gown to wear. Thanks to Xavi and her notes, I also knew which shoes and which items of jewelry to go with it. The dress was a pale blue color which nipped in tightly at the waist and ruffled out. It was not my style at all, but I really couldn't be bothered to figure out something else. I only had enough dress clothes for certain events so if I didn't wear it now, I'd have to wear it for some other occasion, and if there is one thing I've learned about fashion and royalty, it's that you can't wear the same dress in public twice. This was the only ball I was aware of being planned for me. After today, I could wear something much more casual. I couldn't wait.

Once I was dressed, and Seraphia had made a much better job of my makeup than I could ever hope to achieve, we both made our way down to the large palace ballroom. It was magnificently decorated with swathes of the royal purple velvet hung around the edge of the ceiling and giant flower arrangements in the same color to match. Here, purple signified royalty. In Silverwood, it was solely worn by the Magi.

Unlike the way we did things at home, there was no formal announcement of royalty entering the room. People were already dancing, and no one batted an eye as we walked in. It calmed my nerves somewhat. I'd not been looking forward to it, but now that I could hide amongst the crowd, I felt better about it. A waiter appeared at our side and offered us a glass of champagne. My heart did an involuntary leap for a second as I caught the waiter's uniform, but it wasn't Cynder. I wasn't sure if I wanted to see him or not. If he kept away for the rest of my trip, it would give my heart time to heal.

But then you might never see him again.

I shushed the voice in my head and looked around for Luca instead.

"I really must go and find Tomas," Seraphia said. "He tends to hide at the back of the room for these things, and I love to dance."

Seraphia glided into the crowd. I was wrong about people not noticing us. I saw some very appreciative stares as she cut through the crowd. It had nothing to do with her royal title and everything to do with how stunning she looked. A young man I'd never met before walked up to me and held out his hand.

"May I have this dance?"

He looked so earnest and a little flushed as if it had taken a great deal of courage to ask me. I wanted to say yes to him, the dancing looked like such fun, but it wouldn't look good if the new queen danced with someone who wasn't her prince.

"I'm sorry. I've only just picked up my champagne," I said, holding up the glass." He looked dejected as he moved back into the crowd.

"You should have danced with him." A voice to my left made me jump. It was Luca.

"And how would that have looked? I didn't want to insult you."

"Last year, you were dating three other men, and I survived. I think I'm past being jealous of other men by now."

I wondered if he'd feel the same way if he knew about Cynder.

"Besides," he continued. "It's customary here to dance with as many people as possible. Dancing with other people is not an insult. If you look, you'll see that people swap partners all the time. It's how the dances work."

I watched, and he was right. Every so often, the people would swap partners and dance with someone else. I saw Theron dancing with a buxom lady who looked half his age. I couldn't tell who was happier about the situation, him or her. I gazed around to see if Sarina was bothered that her husband was currently nose deep in another woman's cleavage, and found her dancing with a very distinguished grey-haired gentleman.

"There is very little infidelity here in Theron. I think it's because people here have trust in each other."

My cheeks colored and I went back to feeling terrible. I'd not cheated on Luca in any way but in the heart. Except for the kiss I'd shared with Cynder in my room earlier. The kiss I could still feel branded on my lips. I could argue with myself that Cynder had instigated it, and it had only lasted a couple of seconds, but I knew I'd wanted it.

"I'll dance with all the men then," I quipped, trying to hide my shame.

"Oh no, you don't. I've got you now."

I hastily placed my glass down as he whisked me out onto the dance floor and spun me around in the same way the other couples were doing. I didn't know the dance at all, my dance teacher Stephan hadn't taught it to me, but it was pretty easy to follow. Spin, spin, bow, hold hands, spin again, etc. etc. After a few minutes, I was spun around very fast and caught by the man next to me. When I looked back, I saw

Luca dancing with an older lady. He turned and winked before spinning out of view. The man I'd ended up with was not the best dancer, and for a change, I was the better partner of the two. Neither of us was brilliant, but we managed a few spins without either of us stepping on the other's toes.

I danced for hours, enjoying it more than I thought I would. My feet were killing me, but the endless champagne breaks helped. Every so often, I'd end up dancing with Luca. We'd chat for a few minutes before I'd end up in another man's arms. It felt so strange, especially when I ended up paired with Theron for a while, but it was enough to take my mind off everything that was bothering me. I'd been dancing almost solidly for two hours, only stopping now and again to get a glass of champagne, and I was getting exhausted. I could smell the delicious aromas coming from the banquet hall next door. I couldn't help but think it would have been better to feed us all first as I was beginning to feel light-headed with the exertion and the alcohol on my empty stomach. I'd barely eaten all day, and I was starving.

I looked around to see if I could see Luca. I wanted to ask him what time dinner would be served. As he was so tall, he was pretty easy to spot above the others. He was dancing with a stunning blonde woman who was wearing a skin-tight black dress, which was wholly inappropriate for the event. My first thought was that Xavi would pitch a fit if she saw what she was wearing. As I watched, she laid her head on Luca's shoulder. I'd seen him dancing with many women this evening, and it hadn't bothered me, but there was something about the way they danced together. They looked a little too comfortable in each other's arms. There was a familiarity between them as if they'd danced together like this before. I hated that I felt a pang of jealousy, especially after what I'd done that day, but I didn't like the way they looked together. I was just about to walk over to them when the music changed and the partners did too.

Someone took me in his arms, and I barely noticed. I was too busy watching the fact that Luca and the blonde hadn't changed partners as they were supposed to.

I was pulled close to my new partner and his hand fit into the curve of my spine. I closed my eyes. I already knew who it was. I could feel it. The way he moved, the smell of his cologne. I didn't need to see him to know it was Cynder. Dancing with him had always been a kind of magic that no one else could perform, not even the most powerful Magi. It was sensuous and breathtaking. I knew if I opened my eyes, the spell would break. I couldn't be dancing with Cynder. He was one of the servants. I felt his breath on my ear, sending goosebumps down my arm. It was like we'd never stopped dancing. He whispered something, and the spell was broken.

"What?" I asked in alarm, unsure if I'd heard him right.

"You are in danger. This place isn't safe for you anymore. We have to go now!"

The Escape

We have to go now."

I looked into his eyes. I could see the fear in them, making me feel nervous. He'd been in such awful situations before, but I'd never seen him look so scared.

"I'm not going anywhere with you." I whispered, "I thought I made it clear earlier. I'm with Luca now."

"This isn't about that. It's about your safety," he urged.

"What is it? I need to warn everyone." Thoughts of the bomb at my own palace flittered through my head and I could feel the panic starting to rise.

"No time," urged Cynder. I noticed that in the few moments we were dancing before he spoke to me, he'd been leading me quickly and quietly towards the exit. To me it had been a wonderful dance, for him, it was a way to get me away without being noticed. He pulled me through a door and into a corridor. There was another door open, and by the cold breeze coming through it, I guessed we were heading outside. A small woman in a chef's outfit handed me a warm woolen shawl as I was pulled through the door. I stumbled as we ran down some stone steps. One of my shoes fell off as we ran. The cold stone against the heel of my foot jolted me back to reality. I turned. If I was in danger, so was everybody else. I couldn't leave them.

"I have to warn the others," I said steadfastly. "I'm not going anywhere until Luca knows what's going on.

"They aren't after the others. They are after you."

Cynder pulled me onwards ignoring my protests. I could barely keep up with my one heeled foot and one bare.

A black stallion was waiting for us.

"I can't go with you," I cried. "Whatever the danger is, I need to tell Luca's family."

A noise rattled past my ear.

"Gunshots!" hissed Cynder, picking me up and practically throwing me on the horse. Knowing we were being shot at was enough to bring me to my senses. I moved back to give Cynder room to jump on. Within seconds we were riding at breakneck speed into the night. I heard another gunshot, but it missed. We were too far away.

"Turn around!" I shouted loudly after ten minutes had passed and we were well out of view of the gunman.

"No can do. You might have made a promise to marry the prince, but I made a promise to protect you. If I turned around now, I'd be breaking that promise." His voice was whipped up into the howling wind, and I had to strain my ears to hear him. I had no choice but to cling to him and see where it was that we ended up.

We rode like the wind for what felt like hours. I clutched onto Cynder's waist tightly, afraid that if I let go, I'd fall. Despite the shawl, I was freezing. The wind whipped my hair and rain that had begun to fall was drenching my face. My bare foot felt like ice, and even though my other shoe would probably be useless wherever we were going, it was still better than none. Losing my shoe on the palace steps took me back to last year when Cynder had done the exact same thing. Dropping my shoe at the ball when a bomb went off. It was that action that had made him the prime suspect. No one had ever traced the shoe back to me. They would this time though. I was gone, but my shoe would be still sitting on the steps of the palace, waiting for someone to discover it.

The horse slowed down slightly, so I took the opportunity to look around me. I'd spent most of the journey with my face buried in Cynder's back and my eyes closed. The lights of Thalia's capital city twinkled below us, Luca's parents' castle easily recognizable in the center. The moon shone out between the grey clouds bathing it in a dull light. I recognized where I was. I'd been here not long before. Cynder had brought me to the mountains between Silverwood and Thalia. This was where I'd been so fearful of my life just days before. How ironic I was back here for my safety. Cynder veered off the road onto a rocky track I'd not seen on the journey here. A sheer cliff fell to one side into a canyon so deep I could barely make out the bottom in the darkness. Eventually, we stopped at a rocky outcrop. Behind a couple of bushes, I could make out the mouth of a cave. Cynder waved his wand, and a fire appeared. The light from it illuminated the cave. It was shallow but had ample cover from the elements. There were two thick blankets and pillows near the front.

Helping me down from the horse, he led me to the cave. Once inside he waved his wand again. My dress transformed from the beautiful gown into a plain green tunic and pants and on my feet were the warmest pair of slippers I'd ever encountered. He picked up a large fur-lined coat from the floor of the cave and wrapped it around me. Immediately I felt warm and dry.

"People are going to wonder where I am," I said. "I don't even know myself. Why are we here?" Cynder sat beside the fire and waved his wand for a third time. A couple of sandwiches appeared out of thin air. He handed one to me as I sat beside him.

"I can't make food, but I can transport it here. Someone close by must have made these. I'm sorry I don't have anything better."

"You shouldn't have taken me. What if there was a bomb?" I asked, ignoring the sandwich.

On his face, he wore a look of resignation.

"I had to take you. They wouldn't stop until they found you and then you'd be dead. There was no bomb. I already told you that they are after you, not the Thalian Royal Family."

"Who are 'they'? Why do they want me dead?" My stomach growled, but my sandwich went uneaten. "Is this something to do with the MDS?"

Cynder sighed. "There is a lot you don't know."

I sat up straight now. I could tell by the way he was looking at me that this was going to be important. I was ready to hear the full truth.

He began to talk, his voice low and even. "I've always been a big supporter of Magi rights as you know, but I'm very involved in certain groups."

"I know that you attended demonstrations," I replied.

"I didn't just attend. I organized some of them, back before it all got so dangerous and before I had to go on the run. There is a group of militant anti-Magi, and we were working to overcome them."

"Everyone is anti-Magi in Silverwood it seems,"

"It seems that way at the moment," Cynder replied with a sigh. "I should start at the beginning."

I noticed he twiddled his thumbs as he spoke. It reminded me of my own habit of fiddling with things when I was nervous. "My parents grew up here in Thalia. My mother was the head chef at a hotel, and my father was the pastry chef."

"So that's where you learned your cooking skills," I interjected.

"Yes. I'd often go into the kitchens and help them. I loved it there, but when I was seven, a job opportunity came up in Silverwood. There was a restaurant for sale. It was cheap because the previous owners weren't very good at cooking. My parents snapped it up and bought one of the apartments above it. The restaurant was just outside the palace making it a prime spot."

I knew where he was referring to. I'd been in his parents' apartment a couple of times. I'd not noticed a restaurant on the ground floor though. Not that I'd really been paying attention. I'd always been too eager to get to Cynder.

"The restaurant was a great success. Word began to spread quickly, and within a few months of opening, we were fully booked every night. Things couldn't have been better. Even at my young age, I was allowed to help out in the kitchens, and I loved it."

"It sounds like quite the exciting childhood." The only thing I'd been doing at seven years of age was climbing trees and scraping my knees.

To think that we had grown up just a few hundred feet from each other, with only a wall separating us.

"It was except for one thing. Anti Magi feelings were high even then. My mother reminded me every night that I was not to tell anyone that I was a Mage. I was forbidden to use my magic anywhere except in the apartment. For a few years, everything was great, but I got careless. We were so busy in the restaurant, and I was just a kid. I thought it would be ok to use my magic. I chopped up some carrots using my wand. The door between the kitchen and the restaurant opened, and someone saw me. Instead of keeping it to themselves, they told the local newspapers. People stopped coming to the restaurant. The people that we considered regulars just stopped coming back. The rumors started. People said we conjured up all our food and it wasn't even real."

"That's ridiculous," I interjected. I'd seen Cynder cooking on enough occasions to know he was an excellent chef.

"It's what the people thought. No one believed that we did it all by hand. Things just got worse. We were targeted for attacks. People threw eggs at us, smashed our windows, that kind of thing. A couple of months after the newspaper went out we had to close the restaurant. It was our last night of opening. My parents had long since stopped me working there."

"They blamed you for what happened?"

"No. They never blamed me. It just wasn't a safe environment anymore. We were threatened all the time. I don't know why my parents kept it open as long as they did, but I think they were trying to close it down with some dignity. They were also trying to save just a few more pennies to move back to Thalia where it was safe. That night, there was a fire. The fire brigade managed to evacuate the apartments above, but the restaurant was gutted. My parents never got out. The official cause was a fire in the kitchen. A magical fire the newspapers reported. I saw the truth though. Someone had barricaded the exit. I could smell petrol. Someone had done it on purpose. My parents were murdered for being Magi. Next to the door, someone had painted the letters MDS."

My hand flew to my mouth "Oh, Cynder!"

I desperately wanted to comfort him, but I sensed he wanted to keep talking. My heart went out to the little boy watching his parents die in the most horrific way.

"The MDS," I said, remembering what Frederick Pittser had said to me on the day of my coronation. "Frederick Pittser is one of them."

"It stands for Magi Death Squad and basically means death to Magi. They've been around for a long time, but since your father died, they have been a lot more open with their actions. You are right about Pittser. I'm pretty sure it was him shooting at us back at the castle. If not him, it was one of his lackeys. They probably heard about me sniffing around for information and decided to kill the pair of us in one go."

I took it all in. From the little I'd seen of the MDS, my death was becoming a priority, probably thanks to my public work on behalf of the Magi.

"What happened to you after your parents were killed?" I asked.

"The authorities wanted to take me in. I was ten years old."

I slipped my hand in his, but he barely noticed. He was lost in the past. The best thing I could do was listen, so I did.

"I was shipped from foster family to foster family. Basically, anyone willing to take in a Magi, but I never lasted very long. Most families took away my wand and told me not to use magic as it was against the law. The last family I was with were the opposite. They pretty much made me their slave. I spent every hour of every day cleaning their house with magic. They were important and powerful enough not to have to worry about getting caught by the law. I guess it was good training to become a dishwasher. At fifteen I finally had enough and ran away. Luckily, I was found living on the streets by a Magi family. They lived in a rundown shack, constantly starving because they were not allowed to use their wands. Even then, jobs were incredibly hard to get for people like us."

I thought back to the magi family I'd met when out with Leo. They'd lived in the most horrific conditions. I could imagine quite well how he lived.

"Many people visited the house," Cynder continued. "It was always full. At first, I didn't understand who they all were, but as I got older, I realized they were fighting a war. A war against the MDS... and your father."

The Cave and the Truth

I could see how hard it was for him to tell me that he was in a group fighting my father although I could hardly blame him after everything my father had done. I squeezed his hand lightly to encourage him to continue. "I thought the Magi weren't fighters."

"We aren't as such. Not that we would stand a chance if we were. There aren't enough of us to openly fight. If your father had found out about us, we'd all have been locked up years ago."

"So what did you do if you weren't fighting?"

"We fought in our own way. Secretly. Our successes were small but undetected. We spent years recruiting new members. There are more Magi in Silverwood than you know, or, at least, there used to be. Most are masquerading as non-Magi and have been for years. We

111

recruited from Laidys and Thalia. It was the beginnings of a group we named the Freedom of Magic."

"But what have you actually done?" Recruiting people and hiding them in plain sight was one thing, actually doing something was another entirely.

"Actually, the last few years have been wasted somewhat. We'd spent years getting our people into your palace, thinking if we overthrew the king, the MDS wouldn't have anyone to hide them. A lot of the Magi that worked there were part of our group."

I stared at him open-mouthed. "You had a part in the riots last year?"

"No," Cynder assured me. "In the end, your father's own actions prevented us from having to do anything. I already told you that we didn't want to use force. The riots happened exactly as you were told. At the time of your wedding, I was still on the run, but I know we had nothing to do with it. A lot of Magi were killed in the riots too. It wasn't what we wanted at all. We only ever wanted peace. What last year taught us was that our plans and intelligence were severely lacking. We didn't know about Xavier, and we didn't know what your father was planning. All that time we'd spent getting access to the palace, and we realized we knew nothing."

"My father had most of the palace bugged," I told him. "If there were talks to overthrow my father, he would have known."

"We were discreet, although there is every chance your father found us out. Not that it really matters now. Your father had already managed to fire all the Magi by the time of the riots."

My brain was going double time, trying to wrap itself around everything Cynder was telling me. They'd spent so long trying to infiltrate the palace only to all be fired at the same time.

"If you weren't planning to hurt him, what exactly were you planning to do?"

Cynder laughed without any humor. "Through years of spying on him, we'd managed to find out quite a few things. We planned on telling the media and exposing his secrets. We were almost set to do it before the events of last year unfolded."

"What secrets?" I asked. I could well imagine my father having a few. He'd managed to keep the fact he had a cousin a secret.

"The fact that he was a member of the MDS, or, at least, he knew about them and actively encouraged their activities. My parents weren't the only Magi to die at their hands during your father's reign, but none or the murders were ever investigated."

I didn't know what to say. I should have been more surprised, but for a man who thrived on lies, it wasn't the shock it could have been.

I had so many questions, but I couldn't decide which to ask first. Eventually, I spoke again.

"So what now? I've opened up the palace to the Magi, but no one is interested. If you want to overthrow the monarchy, why are you even telling me this?"

"We don't want to overthrow the monarchy. Not anymore. We want to work alongside you." Cynder shifted his position so he was looking right at me instead of the fire. His face was pink with the heat.

"How?" I asked.

"Our main objective at the moment is to keep you safe. We still have a member of staff who has access to the palace. He's there almost every day watching over you."

I racked my brain to think who was left. My father had succeeded in emptying the palace of all magi, and despite my best efforts at recruitment, none had come back.

"There are no Magi left in the palace."

"There is one. Daniel is a Mage."

I'd heard a lot of crazy things over the course of the past six months, and I'd heard a lot more in the last ten minutes, but this was something I couldn't comprehend.

"Daniel can't be a Mage."

"He can be, and he is. He's been protecting you ever since things began to get bad at the palace. He wanted to tell you a number of times what he was, but we asked him not to break his cover."

"You don't even know Daniel!"

"Daniel is one of the Freedom of Magic. I wouldn't call him a close friend, but I do know him."

I thought back to my friend. He'd been spending a lot of his time at the palace, but he'd never actually lived there. Unlike the other bachelors, he had his own place in town. Could it be true? Not once, had I seen him use magic. He'd kept truths from me before though. I only found out he was gay when we were going to announce our wedding. I wondered if Cynder knew about that. I guessed not.

"No Magi were invited to the ball," I said, feeling confused. "My mother said so in an interview."

"Your mother believed so. Actually, there were quite a few, thanks to me and my magic wand. We hoped you would pick one or more of them out. It was a gamble, but with a little help and pushing, you picked him. The others left after the ball. A couple were injured in the explosion."

I thought back to my reason for picking Daniel out of the hundred men at the ball. He was good-looking for a start, but that wasn't it. He'd made me laugh. At the back of my mind, I knew there was another reason, but it took me a few moments to realize what it was.

"Jenny told me to pick him. Don't tell me Jenny is a Mage too?"

I couldn't bear the thought of someone else I trusted keeping secrets from me. First, there was my father, then Cynder, then Daniel. Was no one who I thought they were?

"Jenny isn't a Mage, but a friend of hers is, not that Jenny knows that. This friend told Jenny that Daniel was her son and asked her to push for him a bit. Jenny thought she was doing her friend a favor, that's all."

I remembered now. I don't know how I'd not noticed before, but Daniel never spoke about his mother. It was always his father.

"What about Leo and Luca?" Could my own fiancé be lying to me? It seemed everyone else was.

"No. I've never met either of them, but when we found out who you picked, we looked into them. Leo has helped a lot with Magi rights. You already know that. At one point we thought about telling him our secret but decided it was too risky. Luca is exactly who he says he is. An all-around good guy."

Cynder said the last few words as though it was a bad thing. I suddenly felt very defensive.

"Luca has been good to me, and he'll be good for the kingdom."

"I'm sure he has," answered Cynder with the same disdain as before.

"What is it? What do you have on him?" I suddenly worried that I'd find out something I didn't want to know about Luca.

"I don't have anything on him," replied Cynder testily. He stood up and began to pace the cave floor. "It's what he has that bothers me."

"Oh," I shouted, suddenly feeling annoyed. "and what is that?"

"He has you."

Cynder pulled a hood over his head and stepped out into the storm. A second later and he was swallowed by the thick rain. I stood up and ran to the mouth of the cave. I could just see him heading off down the mountain trail.

Fine. If he was angry, so was I. My family had lied to me, my friends had lied to me, and Cynder had lied to me. Ok, so he'd not lied exactly, but he'd not told me the full truth either.

I stomped around the cave, feeling angry. Angry at my father, angry at the people who'd hurt Cynder, and angry with Cynder himself for keeping this from me for so long. Most of all I was angry at myself. I had no idea how to deal with the situation I had found myself in. I was a queen. I shouldn't be stuck in a cave in the middle of nowhere. I should have been more firm and stayed in Thalia. I should have stayed with Luca.

It was an hour before Cynder came back and my anger had dissipated as I realized that there was no way I could have stayed with Luca without putting him danger too. Cynder might have saved me from a bullet, but in taking me away, he'd saved Luca and his family too.

"I'm sorry," he said, handing me a bottle of water as he walked back into the cave. "I'm having difficulty handling my feelings." He pointed his wand at the fire that had almost died out, and the flames roared back to life. "Before last year, I didn't believe I could find love. I've lived a lonely existence, and when I helped found the Freedom of Magic group, I swore to myself that I'd be loyal to it. I had no time for girlfriends, and, truth be told, I didn't care. I began work at your palace last year. I was one of the last Magi to enter the workforce there. Before that, we'd spent a good couple of years holding peaceful demonstrations, trying to get somewhere, but we never did. It was infuriating. The more time we spent organizing demonstrations, the worse it all seemed to get. The MDS have people in high places all over Silverwood, and no matter what we did, we could never win."

"It was looking bad for us. I felt hopeless, but then I met you."

"I don't see what I did."

"You changed everything. For the first time ever, a non-Magi was willing to listen to me. Not only did you listen, you were in a position of power. The first night you came to the kitchen, I realized what an asset to the cause you could be."

"I was an asset to you?"

"I told the Freedom of Magic that things had changed. We made a new plan. I've already told you that Daniel was coming to the ball."

"I was an asset?" I repeated, my heart spiraling downwards as he spoke.

"You kept coming down to see me, and my feelings began to change. By the time the ball came around, I didn't care about what you could do to help the Magi anymore. I didn't care what your father had done, or how bad it was for people like me. My biggest fear on the night of the ball was that you'd pick someone to marry. Someone that wasn't me. I fell in love with you, not because you were an asset, I fell in love with you because you were you. Since then, everything else has been secondary. "When you picked Luca and announced your engagement, I knew that I had to leave you alone. I gave up on the Freedom of Magic and moved to Thalia. The king and queen gave me a job straight away."

I've spent the last six months trying to get over you. When I saw you in the royal dining room, I realized it hadn't worked. I still love you. I'm not sure I know how to turn that off."

"I don't know how to either," I whispered.

He took my hand. Just the slightest touch from him made my pulse race. It always had.

"I have to marry Luca," I said. "It's the only way I can think to help the Magi. It wouldn't be fair to him to break it off either."

"I know."

"I'm not sure I want to marry him," I said, verbalizing for the first time what had long since been at the back of my mind.

"I know that too."

"I love you."

"I know," he replied almost silently.

"Is there anything you don't know?"

"I don't know how I'm going to be able to let you go."

I closed my eyes, letting the tears fall. It was exactly what I wanted to hear and didn't want to hear at the same time. I felt his lips as he kissed away my tears.

"What now?" I asked, opening my eyes.

"Tomorrow, I take you home. It's a day away from here. You'll be safe there. Daniel will look after you, and you'll have the best security."

"I go home? What if I stay here with you?"

He looked around him at the cave.

"You have a country to lead and a man who will be worried about you. I know you well enough to know that Silverwood will thrive in your hands. You told me before that marrying Luca will provide stability for the Magi of Silverwood. It's what I used to dream about."

"And what do you dream about now?"

"I dream about something I can never have. Come on, it's late, and you need to sleep."

Pittser's Revenge

enny woke me from my slumber so early, it was still dark outside. While it was not an official job of hers, it was something she was wont to do every so often when there was something she deemed an emergency.

I'd gotten home late the previous evening. Cynder had left me a couple of streets away from the palace so no one would see us. He took off on the horse, back to Thalia, leaving me to battle through the hundreds of reporters that were waiting at the back gates. I told them nothing, of course. A member of my guards saw me, and with his help, I was escorted through the throng and safely into the palace.

After spending an hour being fussed over by my mother, Jenny, and Elise, and after I'd given them a diluted account of what had happened in the previous two days, I'd finally fallen into bed after having a long hot bath.

"Please don't tell me you are waking me to help you with the wedding plans. I've already told mother I'm too busy, and I don't want to go over what happened in the last two days again. I already told all of you everything."

"Get up and get dressed. We have a problem."

My eyes flicked open immediately. Her tone left me in no doubt that something had happened, something serious. My mind flashed to Cynder, but I'd left him safe and sound.

"What is it? Have the anti-Magi been protesting again?"

I sat up and rubbed my eyes as Jenny roughly pulled out a plain dress and threw it on my bed.

"Why didn't you tell me?" she demanded, although she left me no clue to what exactly I hadn't told her.

"Tell you what?" I sat up on the bed and pulled the dress towards me. I'd never seen Jenny look so upset.

"I've been in your life since the day you were born, and I never thought you'd do something as deplorable as this. There are hundreds of TV crews outside. Leo is out there right now trying to calm the situation, but they want an official statement from you."

I pulled the dress over my head quickly and jumped out of bed. "What are you talking about? What have I done?"

"It's in all the papers this morning. That odious creep Frederick Pittser has been broadcasting it all over every channel."

My heart sank like a stone. If Pittser was involved, it wasn't going to be good.

"What, exactly, is he saying?"

"He's saying that you are having an affair with a kitchen hand. It's a huge scandal. I don't know how you are going to recover from it. I wouldn't have believed it if you'd not told me yourself last night that it was a kitchen hand that helped you escape" She wrung her hands as she fretted, dancing from one foot to another. Ever my nanny, she abandoned her hand-wringing long enough to hand me a hairbrush.

I brushed through my knotted tangle of hair, wishing I'd had a chance to brush it before getting into bed the night before. "I'm not having an affair with anyone," I replied, making sure not to look her in the face as I said it. Ok, so technically I was speaking the truth. I'd

124

made it very clear to Cynder that nothing could happen between us, but she would see right past my words right into my heart.

"You were seen in his company, Charmaine. Someone saw the pair of you ride off from the Thalian palace together on a black horse."

"I told you I was in his company. Had I not been, I'd probably be lying dead in a morgue in Thalia right now. Did they also see the man who shot at me as Cynder was saving my life, because I'm pretty sure it was Pittser. The man is a high up member of a group called the Magi Death Squad whose main ambition in life is to see me dead."

Jenny's hands flew up to her mouth. "Did someone really shoot at you? I thought you were just so exhausted from the journey back that you were delirious. Then when I saw the news this morning...well I thought that it might be true."

"Thanks for your vote of confidence," I replied, pulling a pair of shoes on. "What exactly is the press making of it all?"

Jenny answered by running up to me and hugging me tightly, almost suffocating me in her massive cleavage.

"I knew you wouldn't have hurt poor Luca. Oh, I hope you get the chance to see him before he hears any more from the press."

In my exhaustion and haste to get to bed the previous night, I'd completely forgotten about Luca. There was no doubt in my mind that he'd be on his way back to Silverwood right now and any hope that he'd not see the papers or TV was ridiculous. If Jenny was right and it was all over the news, it would be broadcast in Thalia too. If he'd not already seen it, he soon would.

"I'm having a shower. Can you round up all the papers you can find including any from Thalia if you can get them and then set up a press conference for this afternoon at one pm? Tell them not to send Frederick Pittser."

"You're going to talk to them?" asked Jenny in astonishment.

"Do I really have any choice? You'd better instruct Xavi to be ready for me in thirty minutes. I'm going to need her help."

Jenny raised her eyebrows but didn't argue. "I hope you know what you are doing, child."

"So do I, Jenny. So do I."

At one pm precisely, I stepped out onto a hastily built stage that had been erected in the front garden. Hundreds of reporters and photographers had turned up to get a glimpse of the queen who had managed to mess up so badly in her first week. Although the grounds weren't opened to the public for the occasion, I could still see hundreds of people standing outside the gates watching from afar. It reminded me of last year when I was constantly being brought in front of the cameras to pick a husband, except now, I didn't hear cheers from the crowd. Instead, there was a collective boo as I made my way onto the stage. I could hear them shouting, and I was thankful I was too far away to hear what it was they had to say.

I'd asked that Frederick Pittser not be allowed onto the grounds, and, to my relief, I couldn't see him anywhere. Instead, Jenny had picked a woman to do the main interview. The bespectacled lady stood to greet me as I walked across the makeshift stage. Her hair was a nutty brown color with a hint of grey at the temples, and she had a warm smile. She dressed in the same smart way all interviewers did, but she wore a large red bloom in her lapel. There was no malice in her expression at all. I warmed to her immediately as she shook my hand.

"Welcome, Your Majesty, and thank you for agreeing to speak to us today. I'm guessing that this is going to be a difficult interview for you, so I just want you to take your time, ok?" She reminded me of a kindly old lady, although she looked to only be in her early fifties.

"No doubt, you've seen the news this morning," she began. "The people of the kingdom of Silverwood want to know if there is any truth to it."

"I have seen the news, and I have to admit to being very saddened by it. There was a time that the papers had to print facts, not conjecture. Sensationalist stories have always sold papers, but this is the first time I've seen them sold on total gossip and fabrication."

"So you are saying that you aren't having an affair?"

"I chose Prince Luca of Thalia to be my husband last year, and nothing has changed in that respect. You all saw him walking me down the cathedral aisle last week at my coronation, and you'll see him do the same at our wedding. The man that is in the papers was a member of staff here in the palace for a while before he moved to Thalia last year to begin a job there. I can honestly say I had no knowledge of him working there before I went to visit."

"So, you are admitting you know him?"

"Yes. I know all my staff. It doesn't mean I'm having an affair with them."

I tried to make a joke, but no one laughed.

"But not all of your staff were seen running away on a horse with you from the Thalian royal palace," she pointed out.

"Cynder saw that I was in danger. He did the only thing he could and rescued me. I was being shot at by a member of a group known as the Magi Death Squad. It seems that they don't like me much because of my involvement with Magi rights."

"It's been said that Cynder is a Mage also. Is there any truth in that?"

I sighed. Why was it a big issue? Why did it matter? It was then I realized that it wasn't the fact that I was having an affair that bothered people, but the fact I might be having an affair with a person of magic.

"Cynder is a Mage, yes."

I could almost hear the collective breathing in of shock from the gathered reporters. I guess not many of them knew. I watched as they scribbled furiously in their notepads. From outside the gates, I could hear the jeers even more loudly. I wouldn't have been surprised if most of them were the same people who demonstrated outside the palace daily. Hopefully, my outing their disgusting group on national TV would give them something to think about.

"A reliable source has been quoted as saying that you and Cynder started up an affair while he was working here in the palace, and that you only agreed to marry Prince Luca to get access to his parents' castle when you knew Cynder was working there."

"I've already stated that I didn't know Cynder was working at the Thalian royal castle, so that is preposterous. I went with Prince Luca to spend some time with his family and to meet his brother, the Crown Prince Tomas and the lovely Princess Seraphia, who is also a Mage."

The last part was completely irrelevant, but I felt the need to get it in there.

"May I ask you a question?" I said to the interviewer. I wished I'd gotten her name before coming on stage.

"Go ahead."

"Who is this reliable source?"

"Excuse me?"

"The source you spoke of. Someone broke this story, and it seems he broke it to every paper and news station in the land." I hesitated for a second, wondering if what I was about to say was wise. I decided I didn't care anymore. "Was it a Mr. Frederick Pittser, by any chance?" Of course, I already knew it was, but I wanted her to confirm it.

She looked nervous as if she didn't know how to respond. "Actually, it was," she admitted.

I already knew it was. I'd seen his smarmy face and his name in most of the papers. He was making sure I knew who had tried to bring me down. Well, let him try.

"You all know Frederick Pittser as a long time member of the Silverwood Press. He even interviewed me here in the palace last week after my coronation. What you don't know is that he assaulted me in my own palace. Then he followed Prince Luca and I to Thalia where he was once again, put in front of me to interview me and dispense his own Anti-Mage views. Now I'm not saying he had anything to do with the shooting, but it's a coincidence that less than a week after being threatened by him, I was being shot at."

"Did he threaten to shoot you?" asked the woman, aghast at my claim.

"No. He threatened to tell the world I was having an affair if I didn't cave in to his demands. He wanted me to block the Magi from coming back to Silverwood. Well, as you can see, he kept to his word which means that I didn't back down because it just isn't true about Cynder and I. I have no intention of closing the borders with Thalia or any of the other kingdoms that border ours. They were closed last year because of my father, and in my lifetime, I'll see that they aren't closed again. I've said it before, and I'll say it again. The Magi, as with anyone else, will always be welcomed with open arms to Silverwood."

"Wow, that's quite a statement. It could be said that Frederick Pittser's plan backfired then."

"I won't be blackmailed into doing the wrong thing."

"Especially, now that the Magi are flooding back into Silverwood. You must be happy about that, at least?"

"What?" I'd not heard anything about the Magi returning.

"Yes. They have been pouring back through the borders since the story broke this morning. Haven't you heard? It's been on the news all day."

I'd read all the papers to get the gist of what was being said about me, but I'd not thought to turn the TV on.

"I've not heard anything about it. That's wonderful."

"The gambling houses that were taking bets on who you'd pick to marry last year have all reopened."

"What do you mean?"

"They think you are going to marry Cynder. They are here because they think there is finally going to be a Mage Prince."

The Magi Return

After the interview, I'd hoped to go straight to the TV to see if what she said was true, but I was apprehended by Monty Grenfall before I even got to the palace.

"You can't accuse an innocent man of shooting you on live TV!" he hissed.

"If you have something to say to me, I suggest you do it inside," I said. There were still a lot of reporters around, and the last thing I wanted was them overhearing.

A couple of guards walked over when they saw how close the chief was getting to me, but I shook my head. They backed off as I led him to the sitting room where we conducted most of our interactions with the media, or had done before my life had turned into the plot of a soap opera, and we had to hold them outside to fit everyone in.

As soon as the door shut behind him, he began to yell.

"Frederick Pittser is a well-respected member of the press," Grenfall yelled. He was a good two inches shorter than me, but that didn't stop him from trying to stare me down. "He will be well within his rights to sue you for slander."

"If he does, can you let him know I'm pressing charges against him for assault, and while you are at it, I'd like you to get your best men started looking into my shooting. If he comes to you to help sue me, it will save you from having to go search for him. You can start by interviewing him and finding out where he was that night. You might also want to look into his history. He's a high up member of the Magi Death Squad. Remember, I asked you about the MDS? You said you hadn't heard of them, but I have reason to believe that they are hiding in Silverwood's top institutions, including your very own police force."

I had no way of knowing that, but I wanted to see Grenfall's reaction. As I suspected, he looked nervous for a second before covering up his expression with one of fury.

"Now, I know you say there is no law against peaceful demonstrations," I continued. "but I think you'll find that shooting at a queen is very much against the law."

I tried not to smile as I caught the look on his face. His mouth was open in shock. He was clearly not used to being told what to do. Well, neither was I. I was way past being intimidated by this toad of a man. I couldn't resist adding some words before sending him on his way.

"Oh, and by the way. Now that there are high numbers of Magi coming into the country, I'm creating an initiative for them to join the police force. There wasn't a single Magi police officer when I last checked, and I think that it's about time that there was."

"I'm not having any Magi in my force!" he bellowed.

"I thought you might say that, which is why I'm going to hire a Mage to lead the police jointly with you."

I turned on my heel and left the room, leaving a startled Grenfall with his mouth hanging open. I instructed the guard outside the door to escort Mr. Grenfall off the property.

I couldn't feel bad. He deserved everything he got. It would do him some good to be dropped down a peg or two. I'd make sure to check on whether he was doing his job with respect to

Frederick Pittser too. It was he that had shot at me. I was sure of it. If it wasn't him pulling the trigger, I was in no doubt that he had something to do with it. I headed down to the cinema room to meet with Jenny and my advisors. I'd asked that they all meet me down there so we could all watch the day's news and make plans together.

I was surprised to see Elise, Leo, Daniel, and Dean there too. Even my mother had shown up.

It took a few minutes for a member of the palace staff to hook up the projector to the TV. Someone squeezed my hand. I saw that it was Daniel and smiled. I'd not had the chance to speak to him since coming home, but I knew I needed to. I wanted to speak to Leo too. Leo might not know about Cynder and Daniel working for the Freedom of Magic, but he should. He was on our side, and the quicker everything was out in the open, the better. For now, though, it was nice to feel the support.

I found a place to sit as the cinema screen was brought to life. I almost wished I'd remembered to bring popcorn. As the footage filmed just half an hour before was shown, I felt better than I had all day. I was on every channel talking to the interviewer who it turns out was called Marybelle Foster. I watched as I told her about

Pittser and then about how Cynder was a Mage.

The scene cut to the crowd outside the palace where they jeered and called me names I'd certainly not heard in the live version. I sighed. I didn't think it was possible to make the monarchy less popular than it already was, but I'd somehow managed it in just one week.

The scene cut again to one of our borders. I couldn't tell which one it was. It wasn't the border between Thalia and Silverwood that was for sure, it was too flat. It was probably one of Silverwood's southern borders. In any case, people were hiking back through. Hundreds of them. It was amazing to see. The reporter thrust his microphone into the face of one of them, a young man with hope on his face, and began to question him.

I sat up straight, desperate to hear what was going on.

"Why are you coming back to Silverwood?"

The young man grinned. "It's my home. I was born here and grew up here. I left last year because I had to, but when we got the news of the queen dating a Mage, we knew it was safe to return."

"The queen has been very open about wanting the Magi to come back. Long before her coronation, she invited you all back. Why are you only listening now?"

"We always listened, but it was never safe for us. Many of us were born and raised here. A lot of us lost our jobs last year under the king's regime. Granted, they were only menial jobs, but it's hard to feed your family when there is no support. We've wanted to come back right from the start, but words have never meant much to me. The queen has shown with actions that she wants us back. If she can date a Mage, then all Magi will have to be safe, won't they?"

"You are aware that the queen has emphatically denied dating the Mage known as Cynder. She says she plans to marry Prince Luca."

"Yeah, well, she says that, but she was pushed into it by her tyrant father, wasn't she. She had to pick a husband and decide to marry him in only a few short months. Now, I believe in love at first sight, but I think the likelihood is that she picked someone that she was forced to. A lot of the Magi believe she was already in love with this Cynder guy. He worked in the palace, so there is no way she wouldn't have known him. She might say she is marrying the prince, but I, like the other Magi, believe the wedding will never happen."

"Interesting theory," replied the reporter. "There is a rumor that bets are being taken on who she will end up with."

"Too right! The polls have opened again, and this time there is a Mage involved. I, for one, will be putting my money on Cynder."

"What happens if she goes ahead and marries Prince Luca?"

"Not gonna happen, mate."

"Surely, that's for her to decide?" asked the interviewer.

"Well, if she does marry the prince, I guess I'll have to pack up and move back to Ramsden."

Ramsden was our southernmost border. It was a small country, – even smaller than Silverwood, but it was more progressive than here.

I watched riveted as the reporter spoke to Mage after Mage. The theme was the same among all of them. One of hope and of happiness at finally being able to come home.

Yes, they'd all come home, with one caveat— that I marry Cynder.

When the reporter cut back to the studio, and they began to analyze the reports, a great cheer went up in the cinema. Many of the people there had not been interested in Magi rights this time last year, but they'd seen me work tirelessly to promote equality, and the fight had become their own. They all crushed around me, hugging me and cheering. I wasn't sure whether to feel happy or nervous. The Magi expected me to marry Cynder, but it wasn't going to happen. Would they all leave when they realized that nothing had really changed? It was going to take an awful lot of work to persuade them to stay. The lights went up. In the cinema doorway stood a lone man watching us with a sad expression on his face. It was Luca. He'd finally gotten here.

Luca

When everyone saw Luca standing in the doorway, they all became suddenly quiet. The jubilation of just a few seconds ago died down as they took in the expression on Luca's face.

"Excuse me, everyone." I disentangled myself from the group of people and walked over to him. His expression didn't change, and it frightened me. I'd managed to mess up again and hurt someone I cared about. In all the drama of the day, I'd given little thought to Luca, but now that he was here, I knew that he should have been my main priority.

We walked along the corridor in silence, neither of us knowing what to say. Behind us, I could hear the others filing out of the cinema room. I needed to find somewhere quiet to speak with him. Somewhere where no one would interrupt us. Even though my father was no longer around to listen in to private conversations, I still felt his presence whenever I had something important to say, something that I wouldn't want him to hear. Last year, I often retreated to the gardens to whisper secrets. It felt like as good a place as any.

Outside, the grass was slightly damp as if we'd just missed a light drizzle. The camera crews and the rest of the media had long since left, but there were still a number of workmen taking the stage down. I directed Luca around the side of the house and into the expansive back garden where we would finally be able to speak in peace.

"Is it true?" he asked.

"Did you see my interview today? I spoke the truth there. I told the world that I had picked you to marry, and in a few months, I would become your wife."

"I didn't see the interview. I was too busy rushing here, but that wasn't the question I asked you. I asked if it was true. Are you having an affair with a member of my parents' staff?"

My brain and my heart were at war with each other. While I could technically say no and be telling the truth, I knew it would not be fair. I had to either be completely honest with him or not at all. I couldn't go into a marriage with lies of any kind, even lies of omission.

"Before the ball last year, before I even met you, I met Cynder. He was working in our kitchen. I found him dancing around the kitchen one night, so in my fear of having two left feet, I asked him to teach me to dance."

I didn't dare look at Luca's face as I spoke. Nor could I look toward the apartment where Cynder and I once spent a night together. Instead, I concentrated on a bird that was pecking away on the lawn, playing tug of war with a worm that had come up for the rain.

"I came to have feelings for him. After the ball, he was accused of planting the bomb. He had to go on the run. I missed him terribly. I did everything I could to try to find him."

"I see," replied Luca, not seeing at all.

"At the time, I was still getting to know you. I'd barely spent any time with you at all. I was dating four men, one of which, I was being pressured into choosing as a husband. I'm not going to lie to you. I didn't immediately fall for you. It took time. I had the kingdom to think about as well as myself."

"So you picked me because I was right for the kingdom?" he spat.

The bird won the war and flew off, the worm dangling in its beak.

"At first, yes. You were the obvious choice. You were a similar age to me and held my ideals. Then as I got to know you, I realized you were a great person to be around. I began to think of you as more than someone that would be good for the country, but as someone who would be good for me too. When I asked you to marry me, it wasn't just out of duty, although that did come into it partly, it was because I could see a future for us together. I can honestly tell you that before the other night, I'd not seen Cynder for over six months. I'd had no contact with him at all. I'd chosen you, and I was happy. What happened the other night was not a secret tryst or a romantic excursion. Cynder didn't know I'd come to Thalia. He'd gotten a job there to put the past behind him, just as I had. The problem was, the past came back to haunt him. He was a member of a group of Mages that had spent years trying to bring about the downfall of my father. Unfortunately, when I arrived in Thalia, I managed to bring Frederick Pittser with me."

"Who?"

"Frederick Pittser, the reporter that spoke to us at the TV studios in Thalia, remember? I thought he was nothing more than an outspoken anti-Mage, but Cynder found out

144

that he was actually high up in an underground anti-Mage group who were plotting to kill me. He took me from your palace to save me. In doing that he saved a lot of other people too."

"How so?"

"Pittser or one of his cronies tried to shoot me as I escaped with Cynder. If I'd still been at the ball, he would have come for me there, shooting anyone in his path until I was dead. It's ironic that last year it was the Magi who were trying to bring down the monarchy, but this year it's the anti-Magi."

"So you and he..."

"Nothing happened. I promise. I've chosen to marry you, and I will. Cynder dropped me off in Silverwood and left. He's on his way back to Thalia."

I heard him sigh in relief as though I'd alleviated all his fears. Part of me still felt bad that I'd left out the most important part—that my heart still beat for Cynder, but there was no future with him. He was on his way back to Thalia, and the likelihood was I'd never see him again, or if I did, it would only be on the occasions he was either serving me dinner or maybe in a few years, cooking it at the Thalian palace.

"Hmm."

"What?" I asked.

"These past few days, I've been wanting to kill him, but it seems I should be thanking him."

"He's gone back to Thalia. I think the best way to thank him would be to get word to your parents to tell them not to fire him. He's a great chef. He'd be an asset to their kitchen team."

"I'll do that. If he's there, that means he's not here near you. I understand now why he took you, but that doesn't stop me feeling jealous."

I looked up at his gorgeous face. It was almost comical how someone could be so utterly beautiful could be jealous of someone like me, and yet, I could see the pain in his expression.

He was quiet for a moment, so for the first time since he'd been home, I touched him. I put my hand to his face which softened immediately. He looked so relieved and so handsome. When he leaned forward to kiss me, I moved forward to meet him in the middle. This time, there was no hesitancy on my part. I'd made the decision to be with Luca, and the flutters I thought I'd lost long ago came back. Luca was the most wonderful kisser. The way his lips moved against mine as we explored each other made the flutters turn into tingles then great earthquakes that shot up my spine. His tongue found mine as I pressed my whole body into his, matching his passion. I was ready for him and everything he had to give.

Somewhere a flash erupted. Luca pulled back, and we both looked to the high wall that encircled the palace grounds. A photographer dipped quickly below the top of the wall, and we heard him jump from his ladder and run away.

Luca and I laughed, which broke the tension that had been between us even more than the kiss had.

The very same thing had happened to us last year. It had been our very first kiss and had taken me by surprise. The photographer that had caught us then had left me in the worst position possible, and it was only because Jenny had woven her magic with the press, that we'd managed to stop the photo being published. Now, it didn't matter. I'd picked Luca, and he'd picked me, and it didn't matter if the whole world knew about it. After the nightmare of the day so far, having a photo of us kissing would only cement the words I had said earlier.

Luca took my hand, and we headed back into the palace.

The group we'd left behind had migrated to the parlor where they were all drinking champagne. My advisors had retired for the

147

night, but my mother, Jenny, Elise, Leo, Daniel, and Dean were still there drinking.

When they saw us walk in hand in hand, they came bounding over and continued the group hug they'd started earlier. Someone passed me a glass of champagne and one to Luca. For the first time in a long time, I stopped worrying about the state of the kingdom and decided to celebrate my small victory. The Magi were coming back, Luca was by my side, and the people of Silverwood were finally beginning to believe me.

I took a swallow of champagne, feeling the bubbles tickling my throat.

I tried not to think of Cynder. He would be halfway home now on his horse. If Luca was true to his word, Cynder would have a job to go back to. I still had a very long way to go to pull Silverwood together, but hiring a Mage chief of police to work alongside Grenfall, was a stroke of genius. With any luck, Grenfall would quit his job, saving me from having to fire him. Either that, or he'd become more tolerant. Either way, it was a win-win situation.

I sipped my champagne and felt at peace. Looking over at Luca, confidently chatting with Leo and Elise, I knew I'd made the right decision. Someone tapped me lightly on the arm, and I turned to find Daniel. I hugged him tightly.

"Hey, you'll crease the shirt," he quipped and then a moment later, "Can we talk?"

He led me to the quieter side of the room, and we sat on the long ornamental sofa.

"I guess you know about me, huh?"

"Cynder told me everything," I admitted.

"I'm sorry to have deceived you. I hated myself for doing it. Right after our first date, I wanted to back out, but I saw that you needed me more than ever. I came in here with the intention of pulling your father down, but when I met you, I realized it would mean I'd end up pulling you down with him. You were so sweet and fearless that I couldn't bring myself to do it."

I smiled at his words. "I was anything but fearless. I spent most of last year quivering under my clothes."

"If that's the case, you hid it well. I saw that you could become the leader we always imagined. The Magi wanted the royalty to be gone completely, but when I met you, I saw another path."

"Oh yes?"

"I saw you as queen. I knew even then you'd do a much better job of it than your father or

149

your grandfather or any of your ancestors before you. Instead of greed and prejudice, you looked around you and saw what needed to be done. It's no surprise to me that Silverwood is a small country with little going for it. For years, its subjects have been so busy warring amongst each other that we've wasted energy we could have put into building it into a respected kingdom. A kingdom that prospers and is equal to those around it."

It might have been the champagne talking, but I was feeling bold. "That doesn't sound like much of an ambition. Why not make it a kingdom that has no equal?"

Daniel grinned and held up his glass. "And that's why I know you'll make a great queen."

"Thank you, Daniel." I took a sip of my champagne and looked over my shoulder to where the others stood. They were all so busy chatting and laughing and drinking that they wouldn't hear me.

"I know that you and Cynder knew each other and I know why you came to the palace. I'm wondering..." I trailed off

"You are wondering why I stayed?"

"Yes," I admitted. "You got what you wanted. My father died. I became the queen. You live outside the palace, but you are here all the time. You and Dean may as well move in here."

"Just because the Magi are now free, doesn't mean you are."

"What do you mean?" I asked.

"You got shot at the other night. Your father might be dead, but there are still people that want to kill you. The Magi Death Squad will not stop until we overwhelm them. Thanks to you, there are hundreds of Magi coming back into Silverwood. You've provided opportunities for us that we couldn't hope to have as recently as last year. Just as the Magi wanted one of theirs in power instead of a king or queen, the anti-Magi want the same thing now except with one of their kind. You have no heirs. It's possible that Elise could take over, but if they kill you, there's nothing to stop them going for her too. They'll already have someone in mind to take over when you die."

"Frederick Pittser?"

"No. He's high up, but there will be people above him. I've been given word that there is a man they call The Regent, but I don't know who he is. Whoever he is, he's ready to become the new ruler when the time comes. With all our intelligence, we are still no closer to finding out who he is so all we can do is protect you and let you continue to spread your voice to the people. The best thing you can do for your safety is to promote Magi rights to the point where the Magi are so ingrained into society that no one even notices or cares about whether someone has magical ability or not."

"But that could take years," I pointed out.

"It will take years. It's likely that it won't even happen in your lifetime, but you are setting the groundwork for a Silverwood that can live together in harmony. Your children and your children's children will continue that legacy I hope. Until then, I'll be here as long as you need me to protect you."

"Does Dean know?"

"That I'm a Mage or that I'm here to protect you?"

"Both...either."

"No. I've not told him."

"Do you love him?"

"I love him more than I ever believed possible."

"Then tell him the truth. He deserves your honesty."

Daniel came over to my side and hugged me.

I grinned. "You know, now that I know you are a Mage, I might have to get you to do more around the palace."

"For you, Mi'lady, anything. Just call me your fairy godmother."

I gave him a playful swipe and grinned.

I felt so safe in his arms. I truly was the luckiest girl in the world to have all these men looking out for me.

A New Competition

I went to bed with a smile on my face. Thanks to the champagne and the long, long day, I slept better than I had in months.

It really felt like a new beginning. A new start. I woke up with plans on how to accommodate the new Magi and what I could do to help them settle back into their lives. The first job would be to round up my advisors and make a plan. I pulled on some trousers and a sweater and fixed my hair into a plain ponytail. Today was not a day to be a pretty princess, it was a day to be a ruthless queen!

In the breakfast room, the table had been set out for the five of us as usual. Mother, Elise, Leo, Luca, and I.

In the middle were the day's newspapers waiting for me to read them as I always did. I was surprised to find myself alone until I saw the time on the ornate carriage clock on the mantelpiece. It was 6.00am. I'd slept so well, I'd woken up way earlier than usual. No wonder no one else was down yet. I seated myself in the usual place and poured myself a glass of juice that had been left out in a crystal jug. After taking a sip, I picked up the first paper.

I never made it to my second sip of juice. I couldn't. I was too busy trying to comprehend what I was seeing on the front page. I picked up the next paper. It said the same as did all of them.

I read through, hoping I'd somehow mistaken the headline but no. I'd read it correctly. The people on the news report had said as much the night before, but it had not really registered. I'd just been so happy to have the Magi coming back.

Someone came into the room and kissed my cheek from behind, by bending over my shoulder.

"Luca, have you seen this?"

I didn't ask him why he was up so early. In light of the news, it didn't matter. Luca took the paper from my hands and sat next to me. I watched his face, fearful as to what he might think as he read the article through, but his expression didn't change.

"The people think you are choosing again. They want another chance for you to pick your husband."

"I know," I replied, "I read it."

The gist of the articles was that the Magi had come back with the understanding I would be marrying Cynder. As yesterday's newspapers had reported I was embroiled in a torrid love affair with him, it was an easy assumption for them to make. The Magi expected me to marry Cynder, the non-Magi expected me to carry on with my wedding plans and marry Luca, and the media wanted me to choose again. They wanted to put me in the same position I was in last year where I spent the summer being filmed eliminating the men one by one.

"The papers are doing this to sell more copies," I said. "I'm not choosing Cynder. I meant what I said last night."

Luca shook his head thoughtfully. "The Magi will leave if you don't."

"They can't leave. Why does it matter to them who I marry? I've stated time and time again that I'm on their side."

"But it obviously does matter. Perhaps they think that if they had a Magi prince, things would be better for them."

"Are you suggesting we break off our engagement and I marry Cynder?"

"What's happening? Why would you even say that?" I turned to find Jenny bustling in, a look of shock on her face as she caught my last words.

"Why are you up so early?" I asked wearily, not wanting to have to repeat the situation to her.

"I'm always up at this time to make sure everything is ready for your breakfast. What's going on?"

I handed her one of the papers and rubbed my temples.

"I'm not suggesting you marry Cynder, of course not," said Luca "I believed you when you spoke to me last night. I trust you."

"So what then?"

"Just because you aren't going to marry him doesn't mean they have to know that. Why not do as the media asks and hold another competition? Him versus me. It will be great publicity for the cause, and while everyone is fixated on who you will marry, we can be working on getting the kingdom in a fit state for the Magi. It would be a great opportunity for us to work on bringing the people together."

"Or kill each other!" I replied incredulously.

"Think of a football match," continued Luca. "Both sides jeer at each other, but the game is the common cause. While they might not want the other side to win, anything is better than the match being canceled."

"You're serious, aren't you?"

"It makes sense."

"No, it doesn't. It makes no sense at all. Why would Cynder even want to come back here? He has a job at your parents' palace. You promised me that you'll call the king and queen and get them to let him keep his job."

"Sure, and I will, but think about it. He's going to be hounded by the press over there. My parents aren't equipped to deal with that level of scrutiny. It would mean hiring more guards to watch over him. None of them would get a moment's peace, let alone Cynder. If he came back here, you could make him head chef if you liked. You've said yourself he's a great cook and the one you hired to replace the guy who got sent to prison is mediocre at best. We can keep an eye on him here. There are plenty of rooms for him along the servant's wing."

I just stared at him with an open mouth. How could he suggest such a thing? It had nearly killed me giving up Cynder, and I'd had to do it on more occasions than I'd like to remember. Now, I was being asked to live alongside him and pretend to not know who to choose, him or Luca. It made sense to someone who didn't know that in reality, it wouldn't be pretense at all.

"What happened to yesterday when you said you wanted him to keep away?"

"I do, obviously, but I thought about it last night and realized I have to trust you. You are going to be my wife very soon, and there will be men who find you attractive. I can't send them all to work in my parents' kitchen."

My mother, Elise, and Leo chose that moment to walk into the room. Why was everyone up so early? I glanced at the clock and saw that it was now half past six. Perhaps it wasn't so early after all. I wanted to go back to bed. The enthusiasm I'd woken up with had been torn from me, leaving me exhausted.

A couple of servants bustled in with dishes of hot food while Luca passed them the papers and let them digest the content.

I picked at a piece of bacon, remembering back to when Cynder had brought me a bacon sandwich to my bedroom last year. It had seemed so simple then. How had everything gotten so complicated?

Over breakfast, my family argued over whether to back down to the media or to fight them. I sat silently listening to their points of view while eating the little food I could get into my churning stomach. Even Jenny had pulled up a seat and was joining in the debate while tucking into great piles of eggs and bacon.

I wanted to get away and speak to someone, but who? Elise and Leo knew about my feelings for Cynder, but they were both being strangely tight-lipped about the whole thing, while Luca, my mother, and Jenny were anything but.

"I'm going out for a bit," I said, but no one noticed. They were too busy debating what to do next.

I left the room, wondering where to go from here. Calling my advisors had seemed like such a good idea this morning, but now I couldn't bear the thought of it. I decided I'd speak to Daniel. Now that everything was out in the open with him, he was the best person to talk to. The fact he was a Mage and knew Cynder was a bonus.

I could have gone out of the palace grounds to see him in his home, but I knew that if I showed my face outside for even a second, the paparazzi would be on me like flies. Instead, I sent one of the guards to deliver a message asking him to come.

Half an hour later he met me in a downstairs sitting room. It was a room I rarely ventured into which meant that I was confident that we'd be left alone.

"What is it?" he panted as he walked through the door. He had sawdust all over him that sweat from his brow made little rivers through. "I ran. Is everything ok?"

"Not really," I said, handing him the nearest piece of cloth which happened to be an old-fashioned sofa protector. He ran it over his brow and came to sit beside me. I could smell the wood shavings on him. "Sorry if I pulled you away from work."

"It's no problem. My father can handle it by himself for a few hours."

"Why do you not use magic?" I asked. I'd never even seen him with a wand. "In your work I mean, or do you?"

"I don't use magic because I'm not supposed to be a Mage, remember. No one in Silverwood knows except you and Dean."

"So you told him then?"

"I did. He didn't care at all. I was so scared to tell him, but when I saw how brave you've been, I thought I could try to be as brave. I'm so glad you talked me into it."

I smiled wistfully, glad that things had turned out well for him.

"As for why I don't use a wand at work, it's because I love the feel of the wood between my hands. I like making something out of nothing. I wouldn't get the same satisfaction from waving a wand and magicking something up. Is that what you wanted to see me about?"

"No," I sighed. "Have you seen the papers today?"

"No, I've been too busy. Why, what's happened?"

I told him about everything the papers said and about how Luca seemed to think it was a good idea to bring Cynder back. He listened carefully without interrupting right up to the point where I told him that my whole family was now debating it upstairs.

"Maybe this is just the thing you need. It's quite brilliant really. You've been asking people to listen to you for the past six months, and no one cared. Now you've got your chance to shine."

"But it's so unfair to Luca...and Cynder."

"Not really. So you all pretend for a while. Luca can be the big brave guy whose fiancée can't decide who she wants. Cynder can be the hero underdog. By the time the wedding rolls around, and you marry Luca, you'll have all the Magi in jobs and schools. Cynder will be able to go back to Thalia a hero and everybody's happy."

I gazed at Daniel, trying to keep the tears in. Always perceptive, he noticed right away.

"Everybody isn't happy, are they?" He paused for a moment before the realization hit him. "You know, last year, I could see that you were in love with someone else. Even when you proposed to me, I knew that you didn't really want me. I could see the light shining in your eyes, and it wasn't for me. When you announced you were marrying Luca, I thought it might have been him, but I was wrong, wasn't I?"

I nodded slowly.

"Does Cynder know you are in love with him...please tell me the stories of you two having an affair aren't true?"

"No. Nothing happened between us on the journey back from Thalia. I told him I was marrying Luca, and he respected that."

"But you wanted something to happen. Oh, honey."

He took me in his arms as I wept into his shoulder.

"You know you don't have to do it, right? You can go out there and make a statement about how you are marrying Luca, and that's the end of it. Cynder can stay in Thalia, and you'll never have to see him again if you don't want to. You'll get over him eventually. You do want to marry Luca, right?"

"Of course, I do. I had a little crush on Cynder, that's all." I lied. Daniel saw through me straight away.

"I know when something's more than a little crush. Do you want me to tell your family that it's a bad idea?"

"How can I do that? They'll wonder why I think it's a bad idea. They'll figure it out, just like you did."

"They won't. You are a good actress. You've had me fooled for quite a while. I never guessed that you were in love with Cynder."

"But what about the Magi? They are counting on me. If I go out and say it's not happening, they'll all leave."

"Not all of them will. You've made it illegal to show any prejudice against them. Go on TV and carry on promoting their rights. Keep on doing what you've been doing. People will come around eventually."

"Do you really think so?"

"I know so. If anyone can do it, you can. I have every faith in you. Besides, I think you need to do this for your own sanity. I was in love with

Dean for a long time before I felt brave enough to tell him. It nearly killed me." He grabbed the other sofa protector and handed it to me. I gave him a small smile and wiped my eyes before hugging him again.

"Hey, get your hands off my fiancé," said Luca playfully as he bounded through the door. "It's a good thing I know you have a boyfriend, or I'd be worried."

I pulled back from Daniel and blinked a couple of times. I didn't want Luca to know I'd been crying.

"I've been looking all over for you," he said, turning back to me. "I've called my father and told him to send Cynder back straight away. Apparently, he'd managed to get back already. I guess that's the power of magic."

"Magi can't teleport," I said, remembering what Cynder had told me the year before.

"The power of trains!" said Daniel.

"Yes, well, anyway. He's on his way back," replied Luca. "Father said he seemed eager to come and help us out. Jenny's calling the news stations as we speak, setting up a big announcement."

I stared at him open-mouthed.

"I haven't agreed to any of this. Why did you do that without asking me? I don't want to go through the same charade as last year. I'm done." I could feel my voice rising. How could he go behind my back? "I thought I'd put my view about the matter across this morning."

"I know you said you didn't want to, but I thought you were just a bit nervous. I know you hate having to wear all those dresses and give those interviews, but you'll be fine. I've already asked Xavi to come up with a nice outfit for you to wear this afternoon."

"This afternoon?" I repeated.

"Yes. When we tell the world that you are once again going to have to pick a prince. Well, in this case between a prince and a kitchen hand, but you know what I mean."

I didn't know what to say. There were no words. Once again, I'd become trapped in a situation I had no control over. I barged past Luca without saying another word and ran straight to my room, locking the door behind me.

The Announcement

Hours later, I found myself right back where I'd been just six months before. The news crews were positioned ready to begin filming, and Marybelle was back. She had a big grin on her face, and who could blame her. She was getting more coverage than any other interviewer in Silverwood. My terrible life was becoming great for her burgeoning career. I didn't hate her, although I wanted to. She was just another cog in the wheel of the media. Fed by the public's bizarre desperation for sensationalized stories, she was nothing more than a way to get the news out to the public. She had her job to do, and so did I. I'd spent the earlier part of the afternoon getting primped by Xavi and her crew. If I was going to go through with this, I might as well do it looking good. So much for my plans to wear sweatpants and quietly run the kingdom for the next few weeks.

Marybelle brushed her newly dyed blonde hair and straightened the pretty silk scarf around her neck in preparation for the interview. Her glasses had also been dispensed with. She knew as well as I did that this would be viewed by hundreds of thousands of people. Gone was the kindly old granny she had been just yesterday. Now she was a blonde bombshell. She must have spent all night at the beautician's.

Thankfully, due to the lateness in setting the event up, there wasn't much of a crowd, even though the public, as always had not been allowed onto the grounds. I watched as they filled up the space behind the barriers slowly.

I didn't want to do this. Choosing Luca over Cynder had broken my heart into tiny pieces already. No good could come of putting myself through it again. I was quite frankly astounded that Cynder had agreed to come back. There was no reason for him to. At least I was doing it for a good cause.

Why, oh why, did Cynder say yes?

"Because he's in love with you," whispered a voice from behind me. I turned quickly to find Daniel standing there.

"I didn't realize I said that out loud," I replied, mortified. I looked back to see if any of the TV crew had picked up what I'd said. Apparently not. They were all still setting up. Thank goodness, I'd not been fitted with a microphone yet!

I stood and pulled Daniel to the side of the stage where no one would overhear us.

"I can't do this, Daniel. I can't choose again."

"Because you don't want to go through the public scrutiny, or because you don't know if you'll pick the same man?"

Daniel could read me like a book.

"I'm picking Luca!" I said with as much force as I could muster. "I have to pick Luca." I looked down at the floor of the stage, scared to look into his eyes. He already knew more about me than I knew about myself. I couldn't bear him knowing more truths.

"No one is going to force you to make any other choice. It's up to you..." He put two fingers under my chin and slowly raised my head so that I had no choice but to look at him. I could feel tears pricking at the corner of my eyes. Xavi would kill me if I let them fall and ruin the perfect mascara. "If that's what you really want."

"Hey, not interrupting anything improper am I?" Luca quipped as he bounded over. "This is becoming quite a habit, me turning up and finding you two huddled together."

"I think you know you've got nothing to fear," said Daniel. "From me," he added almost inaudibly.

If Luca picked up on it, he didn't say so. If anything he seemed in high spirits as he bounded across the stage to shake hands with Marybelle.

I saw the flush on Marybelle's face as he took her hand and turned on the charm. I don't know what it was about him that could make women weak in the knees. Ok, his stunningly beautiful looks didn't hurt. I reminded myself that it was good to feel jealous of him talking to other women. It meant I'd made the right decision in picking him. When Marybelle began to giggle, I moved towards them and took Luca's hand. He kissed my cheek playfully, and we both sat on the sofa provided for us.

The crowd was already cheering at our presence, so I gave them a small wave. They were, after all, the reason we were all here.

Marybelle came over and gave us a brief rundown of the interview. She was going to introduce us (Like we needed any introduction – we'd been headlining the papers for the best part of a year now!) then she'd interview us as a couple. I wondered aloud if it might be better if I was interviewed alone as Cynder wasn't here to tell his side of the story, but she assured me that we'd get more ratings her way. She looked at Luca as she said this. He gave her a wink, so I gripped his hand harder.

"Cynder will get the chance to tell his side of the story tomorrow," said Marybelle, turning cherry red again. I bit my tongue so as not to tell her she could do with more powder on her face.

Someone called out 'Places' and Marybelle ran to the center of the stage. Patting her, now perfect hair she held the microphone up and fixed her smile in position. Someone ran over and quickly slipped a small microphone on Luca and another one on me. The words I'd been wanting to have with him would have to wait for another time.

I wasn't nervous anymore. Over the past year, I'd become accustomed to standing on the stage and sharing my life with the world, but this was the first time I really didn't want to be here. All I could think about was Cynder as Marybelle began her introductions. He would be here tonight or tomorrow morning. I was looking forward to it and dreading it at the same time.

The screams from the crowd made me jump, and, for a second, I thought maybe there had been another bomb scare or shooting, but it was just the excitement of the people as we were introduced. I plastered a fake smile on my face and waved at them. Luca stood and took a bow. The crowd went wild. They loved him.

He was enough for them. Why couldn't they see that? But as I looked out over the hoards of screaming women (because they were mostly women with only a few men dotted around here and there) I noticed that none of them were Magi. Even though I'd abolished the rule of the Magi having to wear purple, I'd noticed that many of those that came back across the border still wore it. It surprised me at the time, but they were probably making a statement. The mark of the Magi had been one of repression, but now they were wearing it for a show of force.

Marybelle came over with her microphone and sat in the chair opposite us. Her blond curls bobbed up and down as she walked.

"So, Your Majesty. It seems that four men weren't enough for you to choose from, and you've added another into the mix."

I gritted my teeth. This girl must have taken lessons from Sadie on how to make the most of an interview.

172

"It's not like that, Marybelle. I've already chosen the man I'm going to marry, and he's sitting right here next to me..." Luca squeezed my hand tightly. I wasn't playing the game. "...However, some people think it wasn't a fair choice, so I've elected to open up the rounds again. I'll date Luca and Cynder equally, and a month before the wedding I'll pick the man who will become my husband."

"How thrilling! Prince Luca. You must be devastated to know that the queen's heart might belong to someone else."

"Marybelle! I know Charmaine will pick me again. After all, if she picked me out of a hundred men, I feel confident that I can win out of the two of us."

"What are your thoughts on Cynder. He's a Mage."

The crowd booed at his name making me squirm in my seat. This was not how I wanted things to go.

"I know he's a Mage." Luca's voice rose above the crowd. "His magical abilities don't worry me half as much as his ability to woo women."

He grinned, and I sighed. This was quite possibly the most embarrassed I'd ever felt in my whole life. Luca was playing up to the crowd something dreadful, and they were lapping up every word. At least, they weren't booing anymore.

Marybelle smiled widely back. She was lapping it up too.

It was my turn to squeeze Luca's hand. He got the message.

"Actually, Marybelle, the fact he is a Mage is the reason we are doing this. I'm not worried that Queen Charmaine will choose anyone else. What we both are worried about is that the Magi feel underrepresented here in Silverwood. In the first round of selections last year, the Magi weren't represented at all. This was not the fault of the queen. She had no choice in picking the hundred bachelors to attend the ball, but if she had, you can be confident that she would have made sure that there was a fair selection."

I didn't enlighten him that Daniel was a Mage. I hadn't known myself when he came to the ball.

Luca continued. "I feel confident, though, that no matter who the queen would have chosen, the end result would have been the same, and it would still be me she ended up with. I know that at the end of this current contest, things will not have changed. I love the queen, and I know she loves me."

The crowd broke out into the biggest cheer yet.

Marybelle stood and faced the camera.

"What more is there to say? Prince Luca and Queen Charmaine are inseparable. Can Cynder the Mage come between them? It seems unlikely..."

The camera panned back to us. We were both holding hands still.

"We'll hear his side tomorrow, so tune in then. Same time, same place. Until then, this is Marybelle Foster signing off."

I stood up quickly and left the stage, my head full of anger and confusion. Luca quickly caught up with me.

"I thought that went pretty well, don't you?" he said, not noticing how upset I was with the whole thing.

I didn't answer. The crowds were behind us now, but we could still be seen. I waited until we were back in the palace before I told him what I thought.

"I don't like this. I'm done with choosing people. Why can't I just have a normal life? Meet someone and get to know them before they propose to me? This, what we are doing, is ridiculous. It's demeaning for all of us."

"I'm sorry you didn't have the proposal of your dreams but think of the ratings. You saw the crowd. Quite a lot of people turned out even though it was so last minute. There'll be more tomorrow."

"They were booing the Magi! They were booing Cynder."

"You think the Magi won't be out in force tomorrow? It will be different then, just you wait and see."

As usual, Luca didn't understand what it was that was upsetting me. This was his chance to be in the spotlight, and he was going to make the most of it.

The Photo

My head buzzed as I returned to my room that night. Cynder still hadn't arrived at the palace, and no one seemed to know where he was. That concerned me as the papers and TV stations seemed to know everything else about him.

I'd instructed the guards at the gates to come and wake me as soon as he arrived, but it didn't stop me from lying awake for hours. By the next morning, he still hadn't shown, and I wasn't sure if I was glad or not. I didn't want to go through the ridiculous charade again, and it would give me great pleasure to get up on the stage and announce that it was all over. On the other hand, I knew that if he didn't come, I'd probably never see him ever again and I didn't think I could bear it.

I wearily went down to breakfast the next morning with my insides warring with each other. I was exhausted and could hardly keep my eyes open, but at the same time, alert for any mention of Cynder.

Everyone was already there at the breakfast table including Jenny who had taken to eating with us, rather than helping serve us now. Not that anyone seemed to notice or mind. I sat next to her, and she heaped my plate with bacon and eggs. At least something was going well.

I desperately wanted to ask if Cynder had turned up in the night, but with Luca there, I didn't want to come across as too eager. They would tell me if they knew.

One of the footmen walked over to me casually and whispered in my ear. Cynder was sleeping in one of the guesthouses outside. He'd turned up in the early hours and requested that I not be awakened.

Nodding my head slightly, I carried on eating as if nothing had happened. I couldn't be seen to be rushing off midway through breakfast, but I wolfed down that bacon in double-quick time and made my excuses shortly thereafter.

Following a quick detour to the kitchen, where I had them quickly cook up some more bacon and put it in between two slices of bread, I hurried out of the palace and down to the guesthouse that had been reserved for Cynder—the one next door to Luca's.

I knocked impatiently, knowing full well that the paparazzi could get a photo of me from this angle if they chose to climb the outer wall, which they had on a number of occasions.

When the door opened, I thrust the bacon sandwich at Cynder, and marched past him, shutting the door quickly behind me.

"This is a turnabout for the books," he grinned, taking a bite of the sandwich.

He looked as exhausted as I felt, and he was dirty. His clothes were the same he'd been wearing the last time I saw him.

"What do you mean?" I asked, sitting on the nearest sofa. I needed to keep my distance from him, or I'd launch myself at him.

"It's usually me who brings you bacon sandwiches."

"I thought it was about time I repaid the favor," I answered, waiting for him to sit down. I could already feel the electricity between us. Apparently, filthy clothes and a half-eaten bacon sandwich were not enough to quell my heart racing whenever he was near. Would anything ever be enough?

"I only got in an hour or so ago. I'm sorry I look like this. I'll go take a shower."

"Do you have any clean clothes at all?"

"No." He looked ashamed as he said it, but he could hardly be blamed. He'd not been home in more than a week and hadn't anticipated coming back here to the palace.

"I'd use my magic to change, but I'm too tired. It takes a lot of energy. I'm sorry."

"Eat up. You are coming with me."

His eyebrows shot up as I practically dragged him from the guesthouse. He was due to go on stage in a matter of hours, and I couldn't let him do it in filthy clothes. In stark contrast to Luca's finery, I'd never seen Cynder in anything more special than a palace uniform. I knew he had one in his bag. The uniform of the Castle in Thalia, but I didn't want the public's first glimpse of him to be anything less than Luca. He might not be a prince, but that didn't mean he couldn't dress like one.

"Are you going to tell me where we are going because people might begin to ask questions if they see me like this and you like that."

I looked down. In my haste to see Cynder, I was still in my nightclothes. I'd not even noticed. At least, I was wearing a robe over the top, but he was right. This would not look good on the front cover of the papers. I led him straight to the huge dressing room in the hopes that Xavi would already be there.

She was poring over a wedding magazine as we entered. As she took in the sight of us, she frowned.

"I'm going to have to get the whole team in, aren't I?" she asked in a resigned voice, wrinkling her nose at Cynder's messy attire to really put the point across.

"I want Cynder to get the full works. He needs to look like a prince for the interview this afternoon."

Xavi arched an eyebrow as she made her way over to us. Taking a lock of Cynder's hair in between her fingers, she grimaced.

"At least, you are a good-looking chap. All hope is not lost."

"Thanks, I guess," replied Cynder, casting his eyes over to me. I shrugged. I should have warned him about Xavi. Between her and her team, she could make a prince or princess out of anyone. After all, she'd performed miracles on me, but she did it without grace. When she thought you looked a mess, she'd certainly make it known.

"And do you want us to dress you up today?" she enquired as though, dressing me would make her day infinitely harder.

"Just give me the same look the same as yesterday, please." Let them work on Cynder. The public had seen enough of me already. I'd been dominating the front pages for the best part of a year, but this was the first time they were going to see Cynder, and I wanted them to take him seriously.

I wanted them to love him, I thought to myself. I didn't need to add the 'as much as I do.'

Xavi ushered him into the marble room for a thorough wash. Heaven knew he needed it.

Xavi clapped her hands, and like magic, her whole team came running into the room and lined up as they always did. I often wondered if Xavi was actually a Mage, the way she got her staff to just appear like that, but perhaps they were all waiting outside the door for her command.

I was given three of the twenty staff, while the rest worked on Cynder.

A plain, but smart, blue dress was handed to me. I used the third room at the end to get dressed in. Usually, I had no embarrassment in getting changed in the main dressing room in front of all the staff, but as Cynder could come back into the main room at any moment, I didn't think it would be the best idea. My helpers lowered the dress over my head and let me twirl in front of the ornate gold-framed mirror. I looked very plain. Perfect. Cynder couldn't shine if they decorated me in diamonds to stand beside him.

"What clothes do we have for men?" I asked, glancing down the rows and rows of fancy dresses, all hanging, waiting for the right occasion to be worn. On a shelving unit at the end, hundreds of pairs of shoes filled the walls, and next to that, was the jewelry. The most expensive jewelry was kept in the vault down in the basement, but there was plenty here to choose from. Rows and rows of tiaras featuring every color of jewel imaginable twinkled in the dim light as did the countless necklaces, bracelets, and pairs of earrings. I hated to think just how much money they all cost when there were people still struggling to feed their children outside the palace walls.

My eyes skipped over all the pretty dresses, to see if there were any mens' clothes. I couldn't see any at all.

"Your father kept his clothes in a wardrobe in his room, Your Majesty," replied one of the dressing staff.

"What about clothes that didn't belong to my father?" I asked. My father's clothes wouldn't have fit the slim body of Cynder in a million years. While my father had enjoyed substantial meals throughout his life and had a portly stomach to reflect this, Cynder had to forage where he could. As a result, he was skinnier than he should have been. If there was one thing that made me happy about Cynder being here in the palace, it was that he was going to be fed well.

The young dressing maid shrugged her shoulders.

After having the full Xavi treatment, I couldn't let Cynder wear his filthy clothes for the interview. I thought of all the men in the castle who were a similar size to him. There were two I could choose from.

I thanked the dressers and ran out of the room, forgetting to choose a pair of shoes. As it was, my plain blue dress was currently matched with a pair of old, fluffy, pink slippers.

I found Luca still at breakfast, chatting with my mother. He was discussing the upcoming interview whereas she was talking about the wedding. Neither was actually listening to the other. The day's newspapers were spread out on the table, but I ignored them. Whatever they had to say could wait. Dressing Cynder could not.

"So there you are, sweet pea," Luca kissed my cheek and dropped the newspaper he was holding. "I wondered where you had rushed off to. I was just telling your mother that you might have run off with that Cynder chap. I take it he's arrived?"

"He has. He's just getting ready for the interview now, but he has no clothes to wear."

"Surely, he had some clothes with him when he left Thalia?"

"That was days ago now. They are all dirty. I don't think he packed much. We left in rather a hurry, if you remember?"

"Can't he conjure something up?" Luca asked irritably.

"No. Magic doesn't work like that. To conjure a suit, he'd have to make it disappear from somewhere else. He isn't a thief."

"I never said he was," replied Luca defensively. I realized I'd gone too far.

"I was hoping he could borrow something of yours."

"He can't wear my clothes. The public would know."

"So?"

"So. I am a prince, he is a servant. They would know in a second that he was wearing my things."

"He's telling the truth there," piped up my mother who had suddenly started to take an interest. "It wouldn't be right for him to be wearing Luca's clothes. If you like, I could ring down to the servant's quarters and see if we have any of his old uniforms?"

"No," I sighed. That's exactly what I wanted to get away from.

I pondered over it and then remembered there was another man in the house. A man who always dressed smartly, no matter what the occasion.

I searched the whole palace before finding Leo in the Library. He was sitting in one of the leather-backed chairs, with his nose in a book."

He seemed surprised to see me as I ran through the library door.

"Charmaine! What a pleasant surprise. I've barely had a chance to see you in the past few weeks what with everything going on. How are you doing?"

"I need to borrow one of your suits," I replied, out of breath from running up and down the palace corridors.

"Ok," he said without even asking why. "Go to my room and take one, but first I need you to look at this."

He handed me an old photo. The young man in the center of it was undeniably Cynder. Beside him were two women. Both were dressed in the finest clothes money could buy, but despite this, they managed to look extremely unattractive. The photo was old, probably taken about five years or so ago. Cynder looked so young in it.

"What is this? Where did you find it?" I asked.

"I've been keeping an eye on things for a while now. When this whole thing with Cynder cropped up, I thought I'd look into him. I found out that he was the member of The Freedom of Magic group. They are a group of Magi, who have been trying to overthrow the monarchy for a number of years now."

"I already know. He's told me all about it. Actually, I've been meaning to talk to you about everything, but it's been so hectic these past couple of days. I'll have to make time to have a meeting with you and bring you up to speed." I turned to leave, desperate to get back.

Leo grabbed my arm to stop me.

"What is it?" I asked, noticing the serious look on his face for the first time.

"Did he also tell you he is already married? That's his wife."

The Revelation

I looked down at the photo again. I wanted to ask which one, but it didn't really matter.

"Who is she?"

"As far as I can tell, she's one of the daughters of the Countess Bloom. The other woman is her sister."

I barely heard him. Cynder was married. He'd kept his involvement with the Freedom of Magic group from me, and I'd forgiven him for that, but this? Not once had he mentioned having a girlfriend, let alone a wife.

He looked so young in the picture; he couldn't have been more than sixteen years old. Neither woman was holding his hand. They both pouted into the camera while he stood in the middle looking sullen. Nothing about the photo shouted out that he and one of them was a married couple. They looked quite a few years older than him for a start. It didn't add up at all, and yet, when had Leo ever been wrong? He had friends in high places, and when they couldn't help him, he used money to do the talking. Not once, had he steered me wrong, and what reason would he have to lie about it?

"Are you ok?" Leo asked in concern. "I thought that if you knew about him, it would make it easier for you. Both Elise and I thought having Cynder back was a mistake. Elise is really worried about you."

"I'm fine," I lied. I was anything but. Leo was right though. Knowing Cynder had lied to me, or at least not told me the truth about having a wife, would make this ridiculous competition a whole lot easier for me. I'd do what I had to do and when the time came to pick, I'd not have a problem choosing Luca again. Maybe I'd even show the photo of Cynder and his wife to the public. They'd understand then, why I couldn't marry him. No one would blame me, and maybe the Magi would stay.

"What else do you know about her?" I asked, fingering the corner of the photo between my fingernails. I had to resist the urge to rip it into shreds.

"Not so much. The Countess Bloom is a very wealthy woman, and her two daughters have been trying to marry into royalty for years. I'm not sure what prompted Drusilla to end up with Cynder when her taste in men, much like her sister's, is one of position, power, and money, of which, Cynder has none. Her sister, the one on the right is still unmarried as far as I'm aware."

I looked down at the photo again, this time, focusing on the woman to Cynder's left. She was so unattractive and overly made-up that I couldn't see what Cynder saw in her. I knew I was being shallow, but I was feeling angry.

"Can I keep this?" I asked Leo.

"Sure. Listen, I'll find out what I can for you. I'm sure this is all for the best in the circumstances."

"Yes, you are probably right," I sighed. I slipped the photo into my pocket and headed upstairs to get Cynder a suit.

Elise was in her room as Leo had said.

"Charmaine!" she squealed as she opened the door. I put the photo to the back of my mind as I took in the scene before me.

Her bed was covered in hundreds of tiny pink silk roses, and she had a needle and thread in her hands.

"I've been sewing these for the wedding. Do you think there are enough?"

"What exactly are they for?" I answered with a question of my own.

"I'm not exactly sure," she laughed. "I just thought they might come in handy. Maybe we could sew them onto the wedding gown?"

"If they are for my dress, then there are too many!" I replied, filled with horror at the thought of it.

"Well, I guess we could use them for the tablecloths instead," mused Elise. "What can I do for you? I'm surprised you aren't spending time with Cynder. I can't wait to meet him."

I tried not to show how much my stomach churned at the thought of it. Elise knew how I felt about him. To her, Cynder was a wonderful fairytale. If only she knew that not all fairytales have a happy ending.

"Actually, I just saw Leo in the library, and he told me I could borrow one of his suits if you don't mind getting one for me. A nice one."

"All of Leo's suits are nice. So, can I meet Cynder?"

"He's having the Xavi treatment, but I'll introduce you to him before the interview if you like." No point telling her the truth. Perhaps, Leo would tell her, saving me a job.

She grabbed a suit out of the closet and handed it to me, managing to hug me at the same time. "I'm so excited!"

She jumped up and down on her feet like a child who's just been told they can have candy.

Were we really sisters? We were so different personality-wise, and she was much prettier than I could ever hope to be. With her, it was effortless.

I said a quick thanks and bounded back down the corridor to the dressing room. I'd already been gone more than half an hour. Xavi would be waiting impatiently for the suit.

I rushed through the door to find Cynder sitting in a chair having his hair cut, and wearing nothing but a towel around his waist. I couldn't help the flush that rose to my cheeks as I handed the suit to Xavi.

"About time!" she admonished. "The poor boy's freezing."

I looked over at him. He appeared perfectly content to be sitting there with Jon washing his hair. Alezis would take over soon to cut it into a style.

"He's very cute, though," Xavi carried on under her breath, before winking at me.

I'd never seen her lose her cool once, so to see her blushing over a man, was strange, to say the least. Not that I could blame her. He was way too skinny for his height, but his lean body had muscles in all the right places. His washboard stomach rippled with the hint of a six-pack, and his arms were much thicker than I had expected them to be. He was still way too thin, though, and would benefit from a good meal or two. I made a mental note to tell the kitchen to give him extra portions at every meal. He might have been married, and a liar to boot, but I couldn't bear the thought of him starving.

I took a spare chair and watched as Alezis played with Cynder's hair for way too long. Just as he had done with mine, he examined every part of it in great detail before even beginning with the first cut. I was used to him by now. A haircut, even a simple trim could take upwards of two hours, but I could see Cynder getting impatient.

I walked over to the two men. Almost without thinking, I rested my hand on Cynder's bare shoulder. The thrill that ran through me was not entirely unexpected, but the intensity of it took me by surprise. How could that happen when I was so angry at him? I tried to ignore it as I spoke to Alezis.

"Please, can you work a little faster? The interview is in a couple of hours, and we still have to fit in lunch."

Alezis hated to be rushed, but he sniffed and nodded his head.

"I will do it, but don't expect my usual excellence if you are going to rush me."

"I know whatever you do will be a work of art, Alezis," I said, laying it on thickly. "It always is. Just don't cut too much off. I like his curls."

He brought his hand to his chest in mock horror. "I wouldn't dream of cutting off these gorgeous curls!"

I smiled as I went back to my seat. I had a feeling that Alezis might have developed a crush on Cynder.

Once I was finished with makeup, and someone had brought me a pair of blue shoes to match the dress. I found myself waiting for time with Alezis. He didn't seem to notice me waiting as he continued his conversation with Cynder. As far as I was aware, he'd not chopped a single hair on Cynder's head, although I noticed he was spending quite a lot of time running his fingers through it.

Cynder saw me through the mirror in front of him and gave a small cough. "I think Her Majesty is waiting for you?" he said to Alezis.

With great reluctance, he let Cynder up from his chair. Both Alezis and I let our eyes fall to the towel. Cynder was whisked away to the room with the dresses in it where he would no doubt be getting dressed in Leo's suit.

As Alezis had taken so much time with Cynder, I had to be content with a quick style. He pulled my hair up and loosely put it up into a high bun. It was not what I was used to with him—Alezis liked extravagance, but I liked it. I looked a little like a smart secretary with my smart suit.

I glanced at my watch and noticed how late it actually was. We would miss lunch if we weren't careful.

Cynder appeared from the dressing room. I heard Alezis gasp as he took in the sight of Cynder in a suit. He looked breathtaking. The suit was a little too large for him as Leo was slightly more muscular, but it made such a difference to see him in something so smart and distinct from the uniforms and rags I was used to seeing him in.

"Purple flower or not?" asked Xavi.

"Sorry?"

"The suit is black. Do you want him to wear a purple flower to mark him as a Mage?"

"No!" I hated that the Magi were marked in some way. It was a practice I wanted to get away from.

"I'll wear the flower," smiled Cynder, plucking the dyed rose from Xavi's hand. I could practically feel her melt next to me. This guy had more magic than he knew. The whole of Xavi's team was mesmerized by him. He turned to me. "Showing the kingdom I'm a Mage is what this is all about right?"

I nodded.

"I'm going to need some socks and shoes too," he said. I looked down at his bare feet. He wiggled his toes.

"I forgot, sorry," I said, feeling flustered. "I'll take you to Leo and Elise's room to get some."

Much to the disappointment of the team, I took Cynder's arm and pulled him from the room.

"I don't have any underwear either," he whispered, causing my blush to deepen. I could hear the amusement in his voice. He knew exactly what he was doing to me, and for the first time, I was beginning to hate him for it.

The Siren

After managing to find a pair of shoes and socks that not only fit but matched the suit, the two of us headed to lunch, the photo still burning a hole in my pocket. I wanted to ask him why he'd lied to me, but I decided to wait until after his interview in the afternoon. If I talked to him now about it, I was going to be angry, and the last thing the public needed to see right now was the pair of us arguing. I also couldn't begin to formulate the words needed anyway. My head was way too messed up with the whole situation.

Even though I'd spent practically the whole morning with him, we'd barely spoken. I felt more nervous than I probably should have as we walked into the dining hall. My heart thumped as we opened the door and I made sure not to be standing too close to him.

My mother stood and came running over to us. She shook Cynder warmly by the hand.

"I never had a thing against the Magi, you know. I just picked out the best men for the ball."

I knew my mother was referring to a TV interview she had been part of the previous year where the interviewer had pointed out how no Magi had been invited to my ball despite there being a hundred men to choose from. I tried not to smile. My mother had always been a woman of the people and hated to upset anyone. I'd be extremely surprised if Cynder had even seen the TV interview in question.

"It's fine, Your Royal Highness. I'm sure you picked the best men in the land, and who wouldn't want the best for Her Majesty? She deserves the best."

If my mother blushed, it was nothing compared to the flaming red color my cheeks felt likely to be.

"Good thing she found the best then, really," said Luca strolling over and clapping Cynder on the back a little too strongly. I began to wonder if Luca's motivation for inviting Cynder was what he told me it was.

Elise ran over and hugged Cynder so hard, she almost knocked him over with her enthusiasm, and Leo shook his hand although I noticed he was hesitant to do so.

If Cynder was nervous, he didn't show it. Even when the waiters came in to serve our food, he sat back and waited patiently until it was his turn as though it hadn't been him on the other side just days before.

When I looked at my plate, I was surprised to find that I had chicken, whereas everyone else had salmon. I was just about to inquire as to why when I noticed a sly grin on Cynder's face as he quickly hid his wand under his jacket. He'd made it a point to serve me plain chicken last year when I told him I preferred it to the lobster and pheasant that were being served at the ball. He'd remembered.

As he was seated at the further end of the table from me, any conversation I had with him would have been heard by everyone else around the table, so I turned to Leo instead, while Cynder chatted with my mother and Elise.

"I've not found out anything else yet, but I have someone looking into it," whispered Leo. "What did he say? Did he deny it?"

I sighed. "I've not asked him. I'm worried if this all comes out before the interview, it will mess everything up. I was going to speak to him about it later."

Leo opened his mouth to reply when the palace sirens went off. I'd not heard them since the day of my wedding to Xavier, and that had signaled a riot where a lot of people died. Before that, we'd been sent to the safe room because someone had set off a bomb. My family jumped up, leaving their food half-eaten, and Luca took my hand. I let him guide me to the entrance to the basement in the hallway, but as one of the guards opened the door, I halted.

"You go in. I'm going to find out what this is all about."

"Don't be ridiculous. If there is a threat, let the guards deal with it," hissed Luca, trying to pull me to the stairway.

"The sirens have gone off over nothing before," I replied, remembering a couple of times last year when they went off just because there was a demonstration outside the palace. On that occasion, my father had stayed out to find out what was going on. As much as I hated most of what he stood for, I always admired his bravery in times like this and I was damned if I wasn't going to equal that bravery.

"You don't know that it's nothing! Come down, I'll stay out in your place and let you know."

"I'm the queen! Let me go." I pulled my hand from his roughly. He responded by picking me up, putting me over his shoulder, and carrying me down the basement steps. Behind us, the basement door closed.

The others headed past the shelves of antiques to the small living space at the end while Luca finally let me down.

"How dare you!" I hissed, under my breath. "I'm the queen! You've completely embarrassed me in front of my family, not to mention the staff."

"Not to mention Cynder is more like it."

"What?"

"I didn't expect you to be spending the whole morning with him."

"Is that what this is about? You picking me up was your way of showing him that you own me? Some male dominance thing?"

"No. I picked you up because I care about you and don't want you getting shot or blown up." He raised his voice. "If you remember, it was only a few days ago that someone tried to assassinate you outside my parents' castle."

He didn't give me time to argue back; he stormed off towards the others who were all watching.

I felt ashamed, but angry at the same time. I needed to get away and find out what was going on, no matter what Luca said.

At the top of the stairs, the guard let me out. I instructed him not to let any of the others follow me. The last thing I needed was Luca pulling me back down the stairs again.

The entrance hall was empty, leaving me unsure of what to do. It hadn't occurred to me before, but a meeting with the head of the guards was something I should have done a long time ago.

I heard someone barking orders and followed the sound until I found Turner, our current head of the household guards, in the main hall.

"Turner, can you tell me what the siren is going off for?"

"You need to be downstairs Your Majesty. It's not safe up here for you."

"You would always speak with my father during an emergency," I pointed out. "I'm asking you to do the same for me."

Turner sighed as though I was some stupid little girl, which irritated me further.

"The Magi have turned up outside wanting to be let into the grounds."

"And?" I waited for him to elaborate. Judging by the rather surprised look on his face, he wasn't going to. "People are coming onto the grounds to see the show. There are barriers set up. The same ones as yesterday. I don't understand what the problem is. Has something happened?"

"Your Majesty. We can't just let them in with the normal people."

"They *are* normal people. Do you mean to tell me, that the guards are not letting them in and that the sirens have been set off because of this?"

If I sounded angry, it's because I was. I was livid. With everything I'd been trying to change, I couldn't believe that this was happening with my own staff in my own palace.

Ignoring Turner's protestations, I turned on my heel and headed for the main doors. The walk down the long driveway scared me. I could hear the crowd shouting which only got louder as I got to the front gates.

Behind them, I could see thousands of people. Some were wearing the purple color of the Magi, many were not. All looked angry.

My plan had been to just open the gates, but there were too many people pushing forward with anger in their voices for it to be safe. Instead, I headed to the stage area. The news crews were still setting up in their own section, but Marybelle was on stage, having her makeup retouched by a make-up artist. She seemed quite surprised to see me on stage so early.

"Your Majesty. We don't go on for half an hour."

"Where is the sound guy?"

She pointed to a thickset man who was fiddling with a tangle of wires.

I thanked her and walked over to him. He bowed deeply and dropped all the wires on the floor when he saw who it was who had come to speak to him.

"Do you have a microphone I could use that will make my voice loud enough for the people on the other side of the gates to hear me?" I enquired.

"I could run you a microphone to the speakers, yes." He bowed again appearing nervous.

"Please, could you do that for me, right away?" I asked, trying to sound as pleasant as possible.

He nodded his head and ran to the other side of the stage, where he began sifting through another pile of wires. A minute later, he was back with a microphone.

"Just turn it on and talk," he said showing me the button on the side.

"Thank you. Do you think you could ask someone to project me onto the screens too, please?"

The screens were set up so that the people in the crowd, as well as people watching on their TV's back home, could see, but they were currently turned off.

I didn't wait for his answer.

"Hello, fellow people of Silverwood," I began. My voice boomed out across the grounds. Almost immediately a thousand eyes turned towards me. "The gates will be open shortly for the interview. I'm grateful to you all for coming out to see me today and to support both Cynder and Luca. I appreciate that tension is high, but the aim of this is so that we can all live together in peace. I'm going to instruct the guards to open the gates now, and I would appreciate it if you could all make your way to the stage area calmly." I pointed to the barriered section below me, just behind the area for the media. "There is enough space for everyone and those at the back can see us all on the big screens." I turned to the huge screen behind me that turned on as if by magic as I spoke.

"Please leave your differences behind as you come through the gates and let's have a wonderful afternoon together."

I nodded my head to the guards at the gates. They pulled back the lock, and the gates opened. I held my breath to see if my words had gotten through to them. At first, there seemed to be a massive rush, but as the area within the barriers filled up, I noticed that people were being kind to each other. Pushing was at a minimum, and there was plenty of purple mixed in with the other colors being worn. I'd done it. There was no fighting, no riot, just a large group of people out to see their royal family. I gave a huge smile as hope flooded my chest. It was a small step to the unification of the kingdom, but it was a start.

I felt a little better as I made my way back up the driveway. The crowds behind me were still noisy, but it was cheering as opposed to the aggravated tones they were using earlier. Not only were the Magi and non-Magi standing together peacefully, they were doing it because of me. I couldn't help but give myself a little grin as I entered the palace. Unfortunately, I came face to face with two extremely angry men.

"What do you think you were doing?" Luca hissed. "You could have been killed. Turner told me that you disobeyed him."

"Disobeyed him? I'm the queen, and I'm the one who gives orders to Turner, not the other way around."

"When it's a question of your safety, Turner is in charge. Do you hear me?"

I'd never seen Luca so angry before. I wanted to argue with him, but we were due to head down to the stage at any minute.

"I'll talk to you later about it!" I replied, using the same tone he had with me. Luca glared at me and stormed past me to the front door. I'd wanted to walk down the driveway with my hand in his, but so much for that idea.

"Are you ready to go?" I asked Cynder, who was standing just behind Luca. I was concerned that he would be nervous. Unlike Luca and I, he was not accustomed to standing up and speaking in front of such a huge group of people. I hated that I still felt nervous for him after what Leo had told me, but it was a habit I couldn't seem to shake.

"The guard wouldn't let me out until the sirens were shut off," he said. His voice wasn't as angry as Luca's had been, but I could sense the frustration in it.

"I was fine," I protested.

"I wasn't able to protect you. Do you know how that makes me feel?"

He walked past me and followed Luca down the driveway. Now I had both men angry with me, not to mention Turner who was standing silently by the wall but glaring at me sullenly all the while.

Tears pricked the corners of my eyes, but I refused to let anyone see. I dabbed at them carefully so as not to mess up the make-up and headed down the driveway to the stage by myself.

The Interview

oth men were standing at the side of the stage when I got down there. Neither was speaking to me, and yet, they kept a healthy distance from each other too. Luca's jealousy infuriated me. I knew it was going to happen. How could it not, but he was the one that started all this. He'd invited Cynder to stay here. I was also angry with Cynder, but couldn't show it in front of everyone. With the current high level of emotions between us, it was certainly going to make an interesting interview.

Marybelle was already on stage warming up the crowd. The screen showed highlights of the competition last year and the interview when I said that I was going to marry Luca, no matter what.

I watched Cynder's reaction to it, but he remained stoic. Not a trace of nerves showed on his face as he watched Marybelle and my "story so far" as it was being called. A quick glance out into the crowd told me that, so far, everyone was behaving. I'd already ordered extra security for the event, but so far, it wasn't needed. That, at least, gave me peace of mind. This show was probably the most important of all those that had come before. Everything else was to get the people involved in the royal life and to increase our popularity, but this was to mend old wounds and bring a new peace within the kingdom.

Marybelle had the crowd worked up well. There were equal amounts of cheers and boos at the mention of both men, but, at least, they were in good spirits. I was reminded of a time when I was a child that I was taken to a pantomime, and we were encouraged to cheer for the good guy and boo for the bad. Only in this case, there was no good or bad guy, just two men thrust into an awkward situation which they were both enduring for the sake of their land and people.

Marybelle continued until she'd whipped up the crowd into a complete frenzy and then she announced my name. I pulled myself up straight and walked right past Luca and Cynder onto the stage.

The cheers rang out immediately, although I noticed the people booing were louder than normal. I suppressed a sigh and smiled and waved as I was supposed to do. I read some of the banners as I made my way over to Marybelle. "Cynder is our king!" and "No royal Magi!" At least both sides of the argument were covered. I'd instructed the guards to throw out anyone causing problems, but I'd forgotten to be specific on banners. Technically, the people holding them were not doing anything wrong, but it wouldn't look good to all the people watching at home. Still, it was too late now.

"Good morning, Your Majesty," Marybelle smiled as I walked out onto the stage.

"Good morning, Marybelle, and to everyone out there who made the effort to come and see us today. It's quite a turnout."

"Yes, it is," she agreed. "Estimates have it at ten times the turnout for Prince Luca's interview. I think Cynder is going to be a popular choice."

I didn't glance to the side of the stage. I could already imagine Luca's expression.

"That's a little unfair, Marybelle," I began, trying to sound diplomatic. "The prince's interview was at very short notice and not really advertised. This time, everyone knows. It makes sense that more people would turn up."

"Some would say that it's because the Magi are trying to take over. It's been said that it's a conspiracy to get a Mage into the royal family."

A fresh round of boos went up, probably from both sides.

"There is no conspiracy, Marybelle," I laughed lightly to cover how annoyed I was with this particular line of questioning. "I've already chosen who I'm going to marry. However, I want to keep things fair. As it has been noted on many occasions, no Magi were invited to my ball last summer. Both Luca and I agreed that to build a stronger future for Silverwood, we would open it up just this one time. Both Luca and Cynder are very fine men, and it would be an honor to be a wife to either of them."

"But it sounds like Cynder doesn't have a chance if you've already picked. Wouldn't you say that this contest is already over before it's even begun?"

I took a deep breath. There was no way to get out of this line of questioning without either upsetting the people or one of the men. Cynder knew we could never be together, and he also knew that it had nothing to do with him being a Mage. If I chose Cynder at this stage, I'd look like an adulteress and lose the tiny bit of respect I'd won. I couldn't really win no matter what I said. Not that it mattered anyway. Cynder already had a wife!

"How about we take a seat and let the boys speak for themselves?" I said in an attempt to wiggle my way out of it.

I sat in one of the four oversized chairs that had been set out for us. Each had our name taped to the cushion. Luca and Cynder had been placed on each end with Marybelle and me in the middle. I wondered for a second if it was done that way on purpose to put me closer to Cynder. I ignored the sign, and, instead, I sat on the seat designated for Luca. Now the two boys would have to sit next to each other, and I couldn't be called out for favoritism.

Marybelle took it in her stride. She turned back to the crowd and invited Luca onto the stage.

Luca gave Marybelle a quick peck on the cheek and sat in the seat next to me. So much for trying to manipulate things! Marybelle took the seat next to him leaving the one on the end for Cynder.

"So, Your Highness," Marybelle began, speaking to Luca first. "How do you feel now that Cynder is here?"

"I've said it before, and I'll say it again. The queen and I have a very tight relationship. I have to admit to being a little taken aback when I first saw him. He's a good-looking fellow, but I'm confident that I'm the one who holds the queen's heart."

"Well, there you have it, folks. Prince Luca is a man you don't want to go up against. Well, we've waited long enough. It's now time to introduce the man of the moment. Please put your hands together for Cynder."

The crowd went wild. Half were screaming and clapping, while the other half jeered. Cynder walked onto the stage and waved to the crowd. He held his own well, but I could see his nerves just under the surface. This had to be difficult for him. He sat in the last remaining seat and grinned shyly. Behind my back, I crossed my fingers. This had to go well. I knew both men would play their parts well. Maybe Cynder's shyness would work in all our favors, but it didn't stop me feeling nervous about the whole thing.

"So, Cynder. Tell us about yourself."

'Yeah,' I thought. 'Tell us about yourself, such as how you met your wife!' A mixture of nerves for him and anger at him surged through me. Before today, I'd not known it was possible to feel two completely different emotions about one person.

"There's not much to tell," began Cynder. "I worked in the palace here for a long time."

"And what did you do?" Marybelle interrupted.

"I was the kitchen hand. I washed the dishes."

"That's not all," I interjected. "He served us our food on big occasions. He's also an excellent cook and is in training to be a chef at Prince Luca's palace in Thalia."

Urgh. I hated myself. I was sticking up for him now and why? Despite my anger at him, I didn't want him looking like a fool on stage.

Luca gave me a strange look and Marybelle commented.

"It sounds like you have a big fan here, Cynder."

I'd gone too far again. In trying to speak up for the men, I was inadvertently showing favoritism. Something I really shouldn't be seen to do.

"I hope so. I'm a big fan of hers." He looked me right in the eyes as he spoke, and I had to look away to stop my heart from fluttering wildly in case, by some weird miracle, the people could see how he made me feel. Luca grabbed my hand—another act of ownership. I wanted to yank my hand away, but a hundred thousand people would see, so I had to smile and pretend I didn't care.

"How did you and the queen first meet?" asked Marybelle, not picking up on the tensions between the three of us.

"She was preparing for the ball last year and had been working so hard that she missed dinner. She came down to the kitchen to get some food, only to find me dancing around the kitchen doing the dishes. I made her something to eat."

"Ok, so she missed dinner one night, and she was hungry. We all get that, but why did she keep coming down? Word has it that this is when you began an illicit affair."

My insides squirmed, but I couldn't butt in now. The raucous crowd quietened considerably, both sides eager to hear what he had to say. I held my breath as he spoke.

"Yes, I can't deny it! We began a torrid love affair."

I could hear the crowd's collective intake of breath. My heart hammered in my chest as I took in what he was saying, and I almost didn't notice Luca's hand gripping mine so tightly it was cutting off circulation.

Even Marybelle seemed lost for words.

"Really?" she squeaked.

"No, of course not. She came down for my cooking. She's already told everyone what happened."

I breathed out in relief, and Luca finally let go of my hand that had turned purple.

Marybelle's expression changed from one of pure excitement to one of acceptance. She'd just lost the scoop of the century. Served her right.

"Surely, she could have eaten dinner with the rest of her family after that first time?" continued Marybelle, trying to eke some juicy morsel of gossip out of him.

"She said she liked my cooking. The head chef that worked in the palace at the time made a lot of very rich foods and the queen, or Princess Charmaine as she was then known, wanted something a bit different. With me, she could pick what she wanted rather than what was on the official menu."

"She came down for the food? Every night?"

"Every night until the ball."

"What else did you two do when you were down in the kitchen alone?"

"We danced."

Marybelle perked up considerably at these words. "You danced?"

My heart fell at how this would sound. I'd not coached Cynder on what to say, so I couldn't blame him, but I was hoping our dancing wouldn't come up at all. To feed me meals was one thing, but for a kitchen servant to be dancing with the future queen was something else entirely. It proved a closeness I didn't want to admit to publicly.

"Can you show us what you danced like?"

"I don't think so. We've both been out of practice for a while now."

"Come on. The people want to see, don't you?"

A loud cheer went up. At least, they were all on the same side about something.

I was just about to jump in and say no when the whole crowd began to chant in unison.

"Dance dance dance."

My heart dropped as I realized it was not something I was going to be able to avoid. They were chanting as one, their voices in unison. It was the first time I'd ever heard Magi and non-Magi come together over anything before.

Cynder stood up and crossed the stage to me. He held out his hand. I could see that he was as nervous as I felt. This could go so badly wrong, and we both knew it.

"I guess a few steps can't hurt," I said aloud, giving a quick smile to Marybelle. A few quick

219

steps would be enough to make the crowd and Marybelle happy without giving the appearance of closeness.

I shrugged quickly at Luca, hoping he would understand I'd once again been backed into a corner by the media. His expression was unreadable.

Every time I'd ever danced with Cynder had been a magical experience, and yet now, I felt sick with nerves. I remembered a quaint little dance my old dance teacher had taught me and which Cynder and I had practiced for a short time. It involved little to no touching and was perfect. I whispered the name of it quickly to Cynder, and he nodded.

He held my hand in preparation, but before either of us had the chance to move, slow music began to flow from the speakers.

Slow music which would be impossible to dance this particular dance to.

I gulped as Cynder pulled me closely to him. The crowd cheered, but I could hardly hear them over the sound of my heart thumping. Just like that, we were back in the kitchen again, just the two of us. I rested my head on his shoulder without even thinking and our fingers entwined. I knew these steps without thinking. There was no name for this dance, but it was ingrained within me. I could dance this way with Cynder in my sleep. He twirled me slowly around the stage while a battle raged within me. I knew I needed to stop what we were doing, but as always, when dancing with Cynder, I was spirited away to a magical place, and I couldn't stop. Eventually, the piece of music came to a close and Cynder pulled back, breaking the spell. Before I knew it, Luca was in front of me, his face like thunder. In front of a hundred thousand people, I'd messed up in the worse possible way. Again!

Elise

"Start the music again," Luca barked to the sound technician at the edge of the stage. Another melody came on, different from the last, but equally as slow. Luca took me in his arms and began to twirl me around the stage.

"What are you doing?" I hissed into his ear as quietly as I could so as not to pick it up on my microphone.

"I'm dancing. What does it look like?"

I wanted to tell him that it looked like he was desperate and jealous, but I didn't want to anger him further, so we danced. Luca was a good dancer. Years of lessons with the leading dance teachers meant that he was much better than I was, but because of that, he was able to lead me well. I closed my eyes and tried to enjoy it. After all, I was dancing with the man I would soon be marrying. What was not to enjoy? And yet we both knew this was a charade. We were doing it because he was jealous and the people of the kingdom expected it. Because of that, my old fear of dancing in public was rearing its head again, and I became concerned that I was going to trip over and fall flat on my face.

To my relief, the music finally stopped. The ordeal was over. We'd satisfied the crowds and Marybelle, and any damage I'd caused between Luca and I could be fixed. However much I hated having to play out our romance through the media, and with it, the jealousy that this new chapter was bringing, I knew that Luca was a good guy who deserved better. In his position, wouldn't I have acted out of jealousy too? Of course, I would. I thought back to the ball at his parent's castle when he'd been dancing with that girl. I'd been jealous then. What if the media had put them together the way they had Cynder and me? I would have hated it.

I quickly sat down in my seat, glad that the nightmare was over.

The noise from the crowd was unbearable as they chanted the names of Cynder and Luca, each side trying to outdo the other.

223

"Wow," said Marybelle, facing Luca. "You sure love your bride to be!"

"I really do," he shouted back, trying to be heard over the noise of the crowd. They quietened down slightly as he spoke, eager to hear what he had to say. "I've never hidden my feelings with regards to Charmaine. I loved her from the first moment I saw her. When she picked me as one of the men to sit with at the ball, I honestly couldn't believe my luck, and when one by one, the other men left, I tried not to get my hopes up. Yet as the days went by and I fell in love with her more and more, I thought I began to see a spark in her. I hoped she was beginning to fall in love with me. Did you know that of all the men, it was I she kissed first?"

"No," replied Marybelle, sitting forward in her chair. "Tell us about it."

"We were in the garden, and a paparazzo scaled the outer wall and took a photo of us. Her Majesty was so worried as she'd not officially picked me yet. I guess she couldn't resist."

I thought back to the day he was talking about. He'd kissed me, taking me by surprise. I'd not expected it, and yet, I'd fallen right into it. He was a great kisser. Afterwards, I'd been terrified that it would be on the front page of

224

every newspaper until Jenny managed to keep it quiet. No one knew about it until now.

Marybelle nodded and turned to me. "Was this at the same time you were dancing with Cynder in the kitchen?"

"No. I didn't see Cynder from the day of the ball to the day he rescued me from Luca's castle when I was being shot at."

I lied because I had to. I had seen Cynder on a number of occasions between those times. We'd even slept next to each other in his parent's old apartment. Oh, how times had changed. Even then, I'd known it wasn't innocent, although we did nothing beyond kissing. I'd wanted to, though, and if Cynder's neighbor hadn't come up to warn us that the police were looking for us, who knows where it might have led? I looked over at Cynder who was staring down at his feet. Luca wasn't the only one that this was hard on. It had gone beyond pleasing the people and was now a real contest between the two men. A contest neither of them deserved to be in.

I stood up and walked to the front of the stage. I had to do something drastic to salvage this. I'd spoken to the people earlier, and, by some miracle, it had worked. As far as I could see, there had been no violence. Both sides had come together over a common, if opposing, goal. The Magi wanted me to pick Cynder, the non-Magi, Luca. Either way, both sides needed me to pick.

"Behind me are two men," I began. "Two wonderful men who have put themselves before you at the people's request. They've done it for the same reason I stand before you. To bring our land together, so that the Magi and non-Magi can be able to be together as you are today without the fear of getting hurt or being persecuted. Look at the people standing beside you. I see people in purple and people not wearing purple, but beyond the color of your clothing, it's people I see. To me, you are all the same. No matter who I pick between Luca and Cynder, my love for you all and for everyone else in my kingdom will not change. I will pick the man I love the most, and my decision will rest solely on that. His magical ability or lack of it will not have any effect on my decision. Only love will."

A roar went up in the crowd as they listened to my words. I felt someone take my left hand and then seconds later someone else took my right. Luca and Cynder stood on each side of me, supporting me equally. If it was difficult for me to be up there, I could only imagine how hard it was for both of them. I lifted my arms, taking theirs with me and the crowd went wild. Between us, we'd done it. We looked united. It was the best I could hope for. I knew I'd have to mend bridges with both of them later, but for now, we were a team, and we'd achieved everything we'd set out to do. I walked off stage, still hand in hand with both men, without giving Marybelle the chance to stop us. The people had been given enough of us today. They'd have to wait until next week after my first official date with Cynder to find out more. This week, my private life was going to be kept behind closed doors.

When I was sure we were out of view, I pulled off my microphone and stamped on it until it was crushed into a million pieces. It was childish, but I was emotionally spent and had had enough. The fight I expected to happen with Luca and the long talk with Cynder about his wife was in my immediate future, and I wasn't sure I had the energy for it now.

To my surprise, Luca held out his hand to Cynder. Cynder took it and shook it warmly before patting Luca on the back. He kissed me swiftly on the cheek and turned away from us to make his way up the driveway back to the house.

Luca pulled me into a hug. What was going on? Why wasn't he shouting at me? I'd seen the look he gave me after I danced with Cynder.

"I think we did a good job, don't you?" he said.

"What are you talking about? It was a nightmare. At one point, I thought you were going to get up and punch Cynder in the face."

"Oh, good!"

"Oh, good?" I repeated incredulously.

"Yeah, just before you got to the stage earlier, Cynder and I decided to act it up a little. You know, pretend we were enemies. We thought a little harmless rivalry wouldn't hurt. If you thought we were serious, that means the people watching must have."

I opened my mouth as if to speak, but no words came out.

"Come on!" He took me by the hand and led me up to the palace.

"Are you telling me the whole thing was an act? Your anger at me for not staying in the basement when the siren was going off, the dancing on stage?"

"I'm not happy that you ignored the siren, no. I was worried about you. I love you. I can't cope when you keep running off into danger. We live in dangerous times as it is without you actively seeking it out, but I understand why you did it. You are a born leader whether you realize it or not, and it wouldn't be my place to tell you what to do. I'm only mad at myself for not following you when you ran back up the stairs. I hope you'll forgive me."

I could barely believe what he was saying to me.

"What about the dancing?" I croaked.

"I didn't enjoy it, but I have to admit it was a stroke of genius. When I watched you dancing with Cynder, I almost believed you were really in love with him."

We'd reached the hallway of the palace, and Cynder was nowhere to be seen. Luca hugged me again.

"Go get ready for dinner. I'll see you there."

He left me in the middle of the entrance hall feeling more confused than ever. I'd ridden a rollercoaster of emotions from anger to confusion in the past few hours, and now I didn't know how to feel at all. Instead of looking for Cynder as I probably should have done, I decided to go to my room and have a couple of hours to myself to try and work out how I was supposed to be feeling.

I'd only lain on my bed for a couple of minutes before there was a knock at the door. It opened, and Elise walked in. She shut the door behind her and sat on the end of my bed.

"Oh, sorry, were you sleeping?" she said when she realized I was lying down.

"I was just about to have a nap. What's the matter?"

She seemed awfully quiet. Something was up. It was so unusual for her to not come bouncing into my room like an overexcited puppy. I'd not seen her at the interview either which was also strange. She'd made a point of coming to all the others. As I looked more closely, I noticed her eyes were red from crying.

She sat silently, playing with the hem of her shirt, a habit she'd undoubtedly picked up from me at some point.

I sat up and took her hand. She bit her lip as she spoke.

"I'm sorry!" The tears began to flow fully now. Whatever it was that was upsetting her was really bad. Elise didn't get sad. It just wasn't her nature.

"What is it?"

"I..."

Her tears came faster. I passed her a tissue but didn't speak. If she needed time to tell me, then so be it.

"I'm pregnant," she sniffed.

"Why are you crying? That's wonderful news." I sat up and took her hand.

"You aren't mad?"

"Mad? Why should I be mad? Unless it's Luca's or Cynder's, and then, you've got some serious explaining to do, young lady." I tried to put on a silly voice. She giggled and the Elise I knew began to shine through again.

"No. It's definitely Leo's. I thought you'd be upset because I know the media will jump on it and I didn't want to take the spotlight away from you. I know how much this all means to you. You are working so hard to get the Magi to come back."

"Oh, honey," I hugged her tightly. "Nothing would make me happier than you taking the spotlight away from me. I've had to deal with it for the best part of a year, and I need a break, especially after today's fiasco."

"What happened today? I'm sorry I didn't come down. I was trying to work up the courage to tell you."

I told her about the whole interview and about how angry I felt about being told what to do yet again. I told her how angry Luca had looked when I danced with Cynder and how the whole thing had been a setup between them both.

"Now, I'm not sure if I should be angry or relieved. Both men seem to be on the same side, and it's me that's the outsider."

Elise began to laugh. "What a predicament. Two men publically fighting over you but in real life, they are only pretending. No wonder you don't know whether to laugh or cry."

I began to laugh along with her. When she put it that way, it was rather amusing.

"Come on. Let's get ready for dinner. I'll order extra champagne. We have to toast the baby!"

Speaking to Cynder was going to have to wait.

The Pumpkin Carriage

The week between interviews flew by at such a pace, it was the day before the next one before I knew it. As I had the last time, I was expected to go on dates with both men and report back. In truth, I'd been keeping my distance from both men all week. Confusion filled me whenever I thought about either of them. I'd avoided Luca because I just wasn't sure how to deal with him. And if I spoke to Cynder, I'd have to ask about his wife, and I wasn't ready for that yet. I'd spoken to Leo to see if he'd found out anything else, but his informant hadn't come back to him yet. I knew I needed to broach the subject to him, but no matter how I put it in my head, it sounded wrong.

When the time came round for our official date, I'd still not spoken to him about it.

I decided to hold our date in the bowling alley on the ground floor of the palace. I'd had a date down there before with Daniel and enjoyed it, although that might have been because he'd gotten me drunk on mojitos and other cocktails. As it was so far out of the way from any of the other rooms in the palace, I knew we'd be able to talk without being overheard. I wasn't sure if I wanted anyone else to know he already had a wife yet. Leo had promised me he'd keep it a secret for now while I decided what to do. Once Cynder came clean about the whole thing, I'd have to make a decision whether to tell the public now or later. I'd also have to tell Luca who was sure to be happy about the whole thing.

I headed out of the palace to Cynder's guest house. I felt the nerves creeping up on me as I neared his door. It dawned on me that this would be our first real date. An official date! It felt strange after everything we'd already been through together. It felt stranger knowing he already had a wife out there somewhere. I was ready to hammer on his door angrily. The tension had been building up in me all week and had now reached a crescendo.

I marched right past the guest house that Luca was staying in and headed to Cynder's door. There was a small envelope pinned to the door. It had my name on it. I looked around to see if anyone was watching me, then pulled it down. It was one of the palace's official envelopes. He must have asked my mother if he could have one. I fingered the royal crest before ripping it open. Inside was one sheet of paper—another bit of palace stationery.

In neat handwriting were the words "My Lucky Charm. I still remember where we danced. 7pm."

I looked at my watch. It was only 4pm.

Where we had danced? The only place I could think about was the palace kitchen, but back then it had been late. At 7pm, the kitchen would be bustling with staff, getting dinner ready.

He surely didn't want to meet me there?

I walked back to the palace slowly, feeling perplexed. As I had a few hours to kill, I decided to take a walk around the grounds. The grass was wet with rain, but the skies had cleared, and it was unseasonably warm. As I walked around the palace, a thought occurred to me. There had been one other place we had danced. I let my eyes gaze up at the apartment that used to belong to Cynder's parents. It was still light out, so there was no illumination coming from the window, and yet, I knew I was right. Cynder was meeting me outside the palace. It was risky, but nothing compared to the last time. I'd managed to sneak out of the palace and meet him there twice last year. He'd been on the run from the police then. This time, I'd only have to worry about paparazzi spotting me.

Excitement flooded through me. The brief time I'd spent in his apartment classified as the happiest in my life.

He's married, you idiot!

Damn that little voice in my head!

I ran back inside and up to the dressing room. Xavi was ready and waiting for me. My guess was that she'd been waiting all day in the faint hope I'd show up, but not really expecting it. A broad smile passed her lips as she realized she'd have her chance to make me up after all.

My plan was to ask her to find me a nice, but understated, dress. Something simple.

"Before you say anything," said Xavi as I walked through the door I've already got a dress picked out for you."

I wanted to argue, but I was intrigued.

"Why have you picked me a dress? You don't even know what I'm doing for my date. I could have been going to the swimming pool."

"Cynder came up earlier and picked one out for you," she said, clicking her fingers.

Immediately two of her helpers ran into the huge closet at the back.

"Cynder picked a dress?" I asked, a small smile on my lips.

"Not quite." Xavi was obviously enjoying teasing me.

"So did he or didn't he?"

"He asked us to order it in. It came this morning."

The girls came back with a dress bag on a hanger. I watched as they unzipped and pulled it carefully out of the bag. The top half was a jeweled bodice with a thousand diamonds clustered around the prettiest purple stones. The bodice tapered off in a V shape at the back to a long flowing skirt. The second girl presented me with a pair of matching shoes. They were simply the most stunning shoes I'd ever seen with heels that defied gravity.

"You let him order this?" I asked, thinking of the cost. The shoes alone must have been worth thousands.

"He paid for it himself."

"He paid for this?"

Xavi smiled. "If you look closely, they aren't real diamonds. It cost a pretty penny, but nowhere near what you are thinking. Now normally, I wouldn't let you be seen dead in fake diamonds, but it is a pretty dress, and the poor boy was so insistent. I must insist that you wear these real diamond earrings to make up for it."

She handed me a pair of pear drop diamond earrings. Alezis swept my hair back from my face so the diamonds would show and the make-up girls did wonders with my face. I looked so much more sultry than I had ever done before with the deep purple eyeshadow they'd picked. As I twirled around in front of the mirror, I felt more than a little naughty. If anyone saw me, they couldn't say I wasn't dressed in a proper fashion. The dress reached down to the floor after all, but there was something decadent and sexy about it. The fact that it was the color of the Magi didn't get past me either. Xavi handed me a long purple cloak with a hood. "He said you might want to wear this too."

I looked down at my watch and realized it was half past six already. I kissed Xavi and thanked the others before taking off awkwardly down the palace corridor.

At the bottom of the stairs was Luca. I suspected he'd been waiting for me for a while, desperate to know what I had in mind for my date with Cynder. His eyes nearly popped out of his head as he took in my sultry makeup. Thank goodness, I'd already put on the cloak, and he couldn't see what was underneath. The crystals on the bodice part of the dress were sewn onto see-through material, and it was only the delicate positioning of the crystals that hid everything. This was not a dress you could wear a bra underneath.

"You look nice," He managed to get out. I felt bad for him. I made a mental note to dress up for my date with him next week.

"I'm having dinner out. I'll be back before midnight, I promise." I kissed him on the cheek, leaving a perfect print of my lips in the dark shade.

He looked like he was about to say something but then a voice behind me startled the both of us.

It was Daniel. Inexplicably, he was carrying a pumpkin and a cage of mice.

"Could you come and help me with something please, Charmaine?"

I turned to Luca and shrugged. Giving him another kiss, I followed Daniel out of the main entrance to the corridor that would lead us to the back part of the palace.

"Be home by midnight!" I heard Luca call as the door shut behind us.

"What's going on?" I asked as the pumpkin was thrust into my hands. "It's not Halloween yet," I pointed out.

"You'll see," said Daniel, taking me to the back door. This was the entrance the staff used to come in and out of the palace.

I glanced down at my watch again. It was a quarter to seven. "I'm sorry, Daniel. I'd like to help you, but it's going to have to wait. I'm going out with Cynder, and I'm going to be late."

"Could you put that pumpkin down just there at the bottom of the stairs?"

I looked down to where he was pointing. The long gravel driveway stretched right down to the bottom of the garden to the back entrance. The same entrance I'd sneaked out of so many times last year. I walked slowly down the steps, careful not to trip over my dress in my heels and put the pumpkin down.

Raising my eyebrow, I turned to Daniel.

"This ok?"

"Perfect!" He opened the cage and let the mice run free.

I was going to be late, but something about what he was doing fascinated me so much that I decided to hang around for a couple of more minutes to see what it was.

He pulled out a wand and pointed it at the mice. In a flash, they started to grow. The pumpkin, caught in the blast, did the same. Within a minute, in front of me stood a gleaming white carriage and six white horses. Daniel waved his wand again, and the horses became tethered to the carriage. Daniel held out his hand to help me up the step.

"This is for me?" I asked, astonished. Cynder had told me that Daniel was a Mage, but until now, he'd kept his powers to himself. It was strange to see him using them, especially in such a way.

"Milady, your carriage awaits."

I grinned at his formality.

He helped me into the carriage, which had orange upholstery and smelled faintly of pumpkin. It clashed horribly with my purple dress, but anything was better than trying to navigate the gravel path in the shoes I was wearing. A slight movement of the carriage told me that Daniel had boarded the carriage at the front, and a moment later we were off. I marveled at the clippety-clop sound coming from the hooves of the horses or mice or whatever they were. Daniel had done an amazing job. There was no doubt in my mind that Cynder had put him up to this. Cynder had been planning this date ever since he got here, nearly a week before. He must have in order to have ordered the dress in time. Why was he doing this for me when he had a wife back home wherever that was?

The journey was a short one, leaving me little time to wonder where his wife was now. As far as I was aware, she wasn't working at the Castle in Thalia. Maybe they had separated long ago which would explain why I'd never seen or heard of her. It didn't explain why he'd not told me about her, though.

I couldn't decide whether I was more sad or angry with Cynder, or whether I was mistaking either of those emotions for excitement. I hated myself for thinking it, but I was excited about our date, even though I knew it was going to end almost as soon as it had begun.

I'd only just popped my head out of the carriage's window to tell the guards to let us pass when we were practically there. The door opened, and Daniel stood there to help me to the ground.

I took a few moments to look at the restaurant on the ground floor. I'd not really paid attention to it before now, but after hearing Cynder's story about his parents, I couldn't help but think back to how it must have been all those years ago. Of course, there was no hint of the fire that had once gutted it entirely. The current owners had done an excellent job of having it completely refurbished. I watched a couple in the window make a toast. They looked so happy and at ease. I envied them for a second, before realizing that for the first time, I'd be heading up to Cynder's apartment without having to keep an eye out for police. The last time, I had sneaked out of the palace, and Cynder was a criminal on the run. How things had changed.

The steps that led to the apartments above the restaurant were covered in purple petals.

"Follow them!" urged Daniel. "I'll be here to take you home. What time do you plan on leaving?"

I remembered what I'd promised Luca.

"I'll be back down at ten to midnight," I said, wondering if it was true. I should have questioned Cynder about his wife before now, but I'd not expected him to go so overboard for our date. If the date finished early which I suspected it would, I could easily walk home. I turned and followed the petals right into the building.

I already knew where I was going, but it was so wonderful to follow the purple blanket of violets, delphiniums and hundreds of other different types of flower. I wondered if he'd bought them or got them here by magic. The scent of lavender filled the air as I walked up the stairs. When I came to the top floor, the carpet of flowers stopped. Not at the doorway to the apartment, but at the window.

Ignoring it, I knocked on Cynder's door, and when he didn't answer, I tried to open it.

"I think you'll find it's locked!"

I turned, expecting to find Cynder but instead came face to face with his neighbor from downstairs, Mr. Frost. I'd met him last year when he'd gotten me out of a sticky situation.

"Hi, Sam."

He was dressed smartly, just as Daniel had been. I guessed Cynder had something to do with that too.

"Your Highness," He bowed deeply. I ignored the royal protocol and hugged him, taking him by surprise.

"I'm here to escort you out of the window," Sam blustered, obviously embarrassed by my over-exuberance.

"The window?" I ran to it and opened it. In the distance, I could see the lights of the palace. I wondered if Luca was watching me right now. It was too far to see clearly without a telescope so I couldn't be sure.

"The fire escape Your Highness."

I looked down and saw that there was indeed, a small platform on which to stand. Metal stairs led both upwards and downwards. I climbed out, trying in vain not to get my dress snagged on anything and waited for Sam. The cool air was much keener at this height, so I pulled my cloak tighter. When I was sure Sam was fully out, I began to head down the steps, unsure of exactly where I was going.

"Not that way."

I looked at Sam. He was pointing up. Turning around. I headed up the stairs, my shoes clanging on every step.

At the top, I wasn't prepared for what I saw. A thousand fireflies lit up the roof which was covered in so many purple petals that I could barely see the floor of it. A string quartet played a slow melody, and there, next to a table set for two, was Cynder.

The Date with Cynder

Sam whispered goodbye and made his silent retreat, leaving us alone except for the musicians.

Cynder was dressed in an exceptionally smart suit which fitted him much better than the one he'd borrowed from Leo the week before. He saw my hesitation and walked over to me, taking my hand.

"I hope this is ok for you."

The way he was looking at me, I could see that he really wanted me to be happy with the surprise. In any other situation, I would have been blown away. It was so romantic, but I was still seething inside. How could he do something so amazing for one woman when he was married to another?

"Did you do this for your wife too?"

I folded my arms and glared. No amount of flowers and music would make up for the biggest lie he'd been hiding from me.

He took on an expression of confusion which surprised me. Surely he wasn't going to deny it.

"What are you talking about? I don't have a wife."

"Please, Cynder. I know about her." I pulled out the photo Leo had given me from a small clutch bag and handed it to him. He took it and began to laugh. It was not the reaction I expected.

"Why is this funny?" I demanded. The musicians began to falter as they watched the scene unfold in front of them.

"I don't know where you got your information, but I'm not married, and I'm certainly not married to Drusilla and Deirdre. They are my sisters."

"You never mentioned sisters," I replied unconvinced, pulling the photo back from him. They looked nothing like him. Like each other, sure, but they had nothing of the beauty Cynder possessed. There was no family resemblance at all.

"When my parents died, I told you, I ended up with a number of families. One of them was a countess called Anastasia Bloom. She asked that I call her stepmother. These two were my stepsisters although, they weren't really. They were her two daughters. They treated me like garbage, making me do all the work while they spent their time gossiping about princes and spending all their money on ridiculous fashions.

I didn't stay long, but the short time I did, I was forced to take on their surname."

"Cynder Bloom?"

"Don't remind me! I changed it back to York as soon as I left. Is that why you thought I was married to them? I'm only about fourteen in this picture."

"Not both of them," I said, feeling a mixture of relief and stupidity. I should have figured it out. I took the photo back and studied it. He did look young in it.

I needed to speak to Leo and tell him to stop snooping on Cynder. I could actually do with introducing them all properly. Cynder had met my family, but apart from the odd mealtime, he'd not spent much time in the palace.

"Is that why you've been ignoring me all week? I thought I'd done something wrong." He took my hand, and the ice in my heart melted. "Do you like all this? I wasn't sure what to do for you."

I looked around. The musicians picked their instruments back up now that the drama was over and began to play again.

"Ok? It's the most wonderful thing I've ever seen. You went to so much trouble."

"Most of it is magic," he admitted, before guiding me to one of the seats.

He took the seat opposite and almost immediately, out of thin air, a waiter came and placed a plate in front of me. He served Cynder next, who thanked him. When I looked around, he'd completely gone again.

"Was he magic too?" I whispered, not wanting to cause offense.

"He's a dog. The musicians are rats, and if Daniel brought you here, you already know that the horses were mice."

I gazed at the musicians. The four of them played beautifully and looked so smart in their finery. If it weren't for all of them having whiskers, I'd never have known, they weren't always human.

I stifled a giggle at the thought of it.

"Don't laugh, it's complicated magic!" but Cynder grinned too. "It's taken me ages to train Fido to bring the food up rather than eat it."

I burst out laughing, unable to control myself.

It diffused what I'd feared would be a difficult situation.

"It is really good!" I replied, taking a bite out of the starter. It was some kind of fish dish, quite unlike anything I'd ever tasted before. "You made this yourself, didn't you?"

"It's the Queen of Thalia's favorite. She lets me make it for her," admitted Cynder.

With everything that had been going on, I'd not thought much about Luca's parents. They'd lost a member of their staff because of me, and now I was out on a date with him instead of their son. I made a note to write to them the next day apologizing. They would have seen that it was Luca's idea to bring Cynder here, but that didn't stop me from feeling guilty about it.

When the first course was finished, we waited for Fido. The silence between us was palpable. Neither of us had said a word to each other throughout the whole course. As I was eating, I could pass this off as enjoying my meal too much to talk, but now that we had finished, the quietness stretched on too long. It had been so easy when I could hate him for lying to me about having a wife. Sure, I'd been upset, but it meant I could marry Luca without anything getting in my way. The fact that Cynder hadn't kept this hidden from me made things messy again. Messy, because I still wasn't sure that Luca was the man I wanted to marry. It wasn't helping that Cynder had organized the most romantic night I'd ever had in my life. I fished around in my brain for something to say.

"Why did you come back Cynder?" I asked. "You know I'm marrying Luca and you know that this whole charade is only for the media. Why put yourself through it?"

"I came back because I needed to. I knew I could help here a lot more than making food in the kitchens of Thalia. I've been waiting a long time for the chance to turn things around. Thank you."

"What for?" I asked.

"For giving me the opportunity."

I nodded, grateful that he could not see what I was thinking. I'd wanted him to give me an answer like that. It made everything less awkward, but now that he had, my heart ached. The truth was, I'd wanted just a small part of him to come back to see me. No matter how complicated it made everything. I shouldn't have wanted it, but right then, I knew I did.

'It's better this way!' I thought to myself as Fido took away our plates and replaced them with clean ones. A huge silver bowl was brought and laid between us, smelling delicious. Fido ladled the stew or whatever it was into my bowl. It was a spicy concoction with a creamy texture and quite unlike anything I'd tasted before.

Watching Cynder as he dipped a chunk of bread into the stew, I followed suit. It made me smile. There was no way he'd have gotten away with it at the palace. Jenny would have admonished him for not using the right cutlery. For some reason, it made the meal even more delicious.

After we'd finished, Cynder rose and took my hand.

"Let's dance."

"I can't. I'm sorry." It was clear that dancing was the reason he'd brought me up here in the first place. The whole of the rooftop was covered in petals, and I'd never seen a more romantic dance floor in my life, but that was the problem. If I danced with him, if we even spoke too much, or about the wrong things, I knew my heart wouldn't be able to take it. I had to be strong. It wasn't fair to Luca otherwise.

"Why not?"

"Because I'm scared. I'm scared that I'll forget who I am or you will. I'm scared that I'll do something to hurt Luca. I'm scared that if we start, I won't ever want to stop."

Cynder smiled down at me. "I'm not going to hurt you, Charm."

"Just being here with you hurts. Don't you know that? Why do you think I've avoided you this week? Because I fell in love with you a long time ago, and I don't know how to turn that off. I didn't want you to come back because I needed to get over you. When I thought you were married, it made things easier, but now..." I paused, unsure how to carry on. "How am I supposed to get over you when we have to go on dates like this? You have made this date the most perfect date I've ever been on. I may be a queen and used to such wonderful things, but you've still managed to make it more special than anything I could have imagined. I was just going to take you to the bowling alley in the palace. I never in my wildest dreams expected you'd do this for me. I love it, and I hate it all at the same time because as much as I want this date to be real, it can't be. You and I can never be together. You know that, and yet you still went to all this trouble for me. The dress, the food, the carriage. My plan was to make this the least romantic, most boring date ever."

I was babbling, and I knew it. Everything I'd tried to keep inside, spewed up to the surface. Cynder held up a finger to my lips.

"Shhh." Just that small touch was enough to have my blood burning through my veins.

"I'm an idiot, and I'm sorry. This is too much."

"You aren't an idiot..." I began.

"Yes, I am. I should have known how this would affect you. I've thought of nothing all week but planning this so I could win you back. I didn't come back for the Magi, I came back because I wanted to. Being apart from you has been hell. I was so happy when I found out that there was to be another competition. A chance to get you away from Luca. I've wanted nothing more than for you to come to me and tell me that it's over between you and him."

Tears began to spill over, and I made no attempt to stop them.

"I can't end things with Luca. I'm the queen. Can you imagine how it will look if the public finds out I'm with you? Yeah, they all think they want that. It makes great television. They love watching us go through these dates as if we are lab rats under scrutiny, but the truth of the matter is, if I really do break my engagement with Luca, they'll never trust me. Even the Magi. Yeah, they want you as their king, but if I dump Luca for you, they'll never want me for their queen."

"I know all that." He wiped a tear from my cheek with his thumb. We were only inches apart, and yet, it might as well have been hundreds of miles. "That's not the reason you can't be with me, though, is it?"

"No," I admitted. "I can't do that to Luca. He's stood by me through the worst time of my life. You weren't there..." I saw the look on his face and immediately felt bad. "Not that you could have been. I know you were hiding from the law. I'm not blaming you, it's just this is the way things are. I've promised my life to Luca. I can't go back on that promise."

Cynder nodded. "You are a true asset to your kingdom, my lucky Charm. Luca is a very lucky man. I wish you both well."

He stepped back, dropping his hand. I could still feel the warmth on my face.

"Please don't be like that. I don't want to hurt you either. I don't want anyone to hurt."

He turned and pointed his wand right at me. At first, I thought I'd hurt him so much that he was going to attack me. As I stepped back away from him, I felt something happening around my body. My dress began to move and became lower. What was going on?

When the strange movement finally stopped, I looked down at myself. The beautiful dress and the high heels were gone. Instead was a shabby pair of trousers and a dull brown tunic. Over the top, my beautiful cloak had turned a shoddy brown color and it had holes all over it. On my feet were a pair of brown boots.

When I looked up, I saw that the beautiful suit Cynder had been wearing now matched my own attire. We looked like a couple of street urchins.

"What are you doing?" I asked in shock.

"I've been selfish. This date was a date for a queen. Luca can give you that next week." He took my hand and led me to the stairwell. "Let's get out of here."

As we ran down the stairs into the night, I looked behind me. Four rats emerged from four suits and ran off into the darkness, their instruments hitting the ground.

As we got to the bottom floor, I pulled my earrings out. They really didn't go with my new outfit at all. Slipping them into my tunic pocket, I pulled the cloak hood up, to conceal my face.

"No one will recognize you," Cynder said, pulling the hood back down. He showed me my reflection in the restaurant window. My hair hung loosely over my shoulders, and my face was now free of make-up and filthy. I barely recognized myself. If Xavi saw me now, she would pitch a fit. I, on the other hand, felt strangely free.

"Come on," he said, pulling me with him.

"Where are we going?" I laughed as he took me down a street I'd never been down before.

"I'm taking you on the least romantic, most boring date you'll ever have. You are going to love it!"

The Least Romantic, Most Boring

Date

I laughed as we ran through the darkened streets. People passed us, barely giving us a second glance. Since I was a small child, every outing I'd ever been on had people gawping at me as though I was an exhibit in a zoo. The only time I'd managed to walk the streets without being seen was last year when I'd come out with Leo, and even then, I'd had to wear a cloak to cover my face and stick to the shadows. Now, I walked with Cynder through the streets with my face on full show, and not a single person recognized us. Without all the fancy clothes, the woman who had graced the cover of every magazine and paper for the last six months was almost invisible. I'd never felt so free in my life.

We walked for an hour until we came to a pretty little square surrounded by shops. In the center was an ice skating rink. So many people were out, enjoying the evening, eating hot food from the little wooden market stalls dotted around the edge of the square, and dining at the restaurants.

"Let's skate!" Cynder invited. "Do you have any money?"

"No. I don't carry money; I'm the queen." I reminded him, feeling foolish.

"Me neither. Wait here." I watched as he sneaked in the back entrance of the skate rental place. A second later, he came out carrying two pairs of skates.

"You stole them?" I whispered.

"They are for hire. We'll take them back. Technically, I only stole time with them. We are street rats now, remember?"

I took my pair and pulled them on my foot, leaving my boots to one side. Street rat or not, I'd make sure I sent one of the palace staff with some money tomorrow. Lacing up both skates, I headed out onto the ice where I promptly fell straight over onto my butt.

"You've never done this before, have you?" asked Cynder as he reached down to help me up.

"No," I admitted. "It looks so easy."

And it did. Couples skated around hand in hand, children chased each other at frightening speed across the slippery ice. No one but me seemed to have any problem with it.

"Hold my hand," instructed Cynder. "We'll take it slowly." I held onto him as he pulled me out onto the ice. Nerves about being in love with him were completely overshadowed by the fear of falling on my face and breaking my teeth. Ice skating, it seemed was a good choice.

I was never going to be a great skater, but with Cynder helping me, I managed to stay upright for the rest of the session. Speeding around on the ice left me feeling exhilarated and the cool night air colored my cheeks.

Even though it was early spring, the weather was still colder than average, and my hands were freezing by the time we dropped the skates off and put our boots back on.

Cynder took me to one of the small wooden huts that lined the picturesque square. The smell of cinnamon and chocolate filled the air.

"Cynder!" Greeted the rotund man in the window of the hut as if they were old friends.

"Long time no see. I've been watching you on the news. Crazy times, my friend." He glanced at me and whispered something in Cynder's ear that I didn't quite catch. Cynder grinned. "Can you spare us a couple of your finest doughnuts?"

"For you, my friend, anything. Here's a hot chocolate each too."

He handed us both a cup of thick creamy chocolate and a cinnamon doughnut each. I was still full from dinner, but it smelled so good, I wolfed it down anyway, licking the sugar from my lips for good measure.

"What did he whisper to you?" I asked as we walked away from the square, our hot chocolates still in hand.

"He said I should be careful stepping out with a pretty young thing like yourself when I am supposed to be courting the queen."

I snorted, blowing hot chocolate everywhere. It was amazing how people could look but not see what was right in front of them.

We walked until we came to a canal which was lit up prettily, not with the magic fireflies that Cynder had produced earlier, but with fairy lights. A boat was moored to the side, waiting for passengers to fill it for a short pleasure cruise.

"Don't worry. I'm not taking you on anything as romantic as that. This is a boring date. I've got something much more appropriate in mind." He handed me a pair of oars. "You can row."

I followed him down to a tiny rowboat that was tied to the canal's edge with a thick rope. I stepped in and put the oars in the correct position, but he took them out of my hands.

"I'll row there. You can row back," he said, pulling the oars through the black water.

"Where exactly are we going?" I wondered aloud.

"Nowhere."

The oars cut through the glasslike surface of the water, sending ripples all around us. The fairy lights continued all along the banks. I watched the people we passed. Couples out on a romantic nighttime stroll, a couple of teens walking their dog.

"Is this what life is like?" I asked, trailing my fingers through the frigid water.

"What do you mean?" replied Cynder.

"The freedom to walk along the canal, to eat a doughnut without being hounded by the press. Is this what life is like for people?"

"Some people. It's not like this for the Magi, or at least it hasn't been for a good many years."

"What's it like for the Magi?" I asked.

"You know how unsteady it's been for the last year, but before that, it wasn't much better. The Magi lived in squalor, unable to feed themselves."

I remembered back to when Leo had brought me out with him. He'd taken me to a house that was barely more than a few bits of wood thrown together. Its occupants weren't allowed to use magic and so were forced to rely on handouts. I wondered if I could make a difference.

As if they had known what we were saying, a couple of older teens started shouting from the side of the bank.

"Oy Magi! Show us some magic."

At first, I thought they were talking about Cynder, but as I watched, they pushed a small boy to the ground. He couldn't have been more than ten or eleven and was dressed worse than Cynder and I were.

"I can't!" the boy cried. "You took my wand. I can't do magic without it."

"Turn the boat," I said quietly, but I didn't need to. Cynder was already steering it in the direction of the boys.

We'd not quite reached the bank when there was a splash in the water right next to us. It was dark, but I clearly saw the blond hair of the child as he disappeared under the surface. Thinking, he'd swim right back up, we both waited a couple of seconds before we realized he wasn't going to. Without thinking, I dived into the pitch black water. A thousand needles hit me as I plunged beneath the icy surface. Opening my eyes, I tried to see the boy, but it was no use. It was too dark to see anything, so I dived down deeper with my arms out in front of me trying to feel my way to finding the boy. The water next to me moved, shocking me. I'd not thought to ask if any creatures inhabited the murky canal. Someone grabbed my wrist and pulled me back up to the surface. As we broke through the glassy surface, I saw it was Cynder who had pulled me back up. In his other arm was the boy. He coughed up some of the black water as we helped him into the boat. Cynder helped me back in and then pulled the boat to the side with the rope, before pulling himself out onto the bank. I had nothing to give the shivering boy to warm him up, so I pulled him close to me and wrapped him up in my arms. I'd been wrong, he was younger than I'd originally thought, roughly six or seven and he looked malnourished.

I looked around me, desperate to find anything that could warm him up while Cynder tied the boat to the bank. The poor kid was shivering so violently, he couldn't speak. My own teeth chattered in unison with his.

Spotting a police officer on duty, I called him over to us.

He came running over, but when he saw the pair of us, I saw his attitude change. His body stiffened.

"What's the problem?"

"What's the problem?" I replied. "Can't you see what the problem is? This boy is freezing. I'm freezing, and the two boys who threw this young man into the canal have run away, taking his wand with them."

The policeman looked down on us. "There's nothing I can do to help you. I suggest you go home and get dry, that's if you have a home to go to."

"Look here, Mr.," I said, letting go of the little boy and facing up to the policeman. "We need to go to the police station, and you need to write a statement. Those boys need to be caught and charged with attempted murder. While we are there, we all need a shower and a change of clothes. I'd also like a doctor brought in to give us all a checkup. Goodness only knows what germs are in that water. Then, I'd like you to provide a warm meal for this young man and find out where his parents live so that he can be reunited with them, do you understand?"

"Now, who do you think you are talking to?" barked the officer. "I'll arrest you if you talk to me like that again." He grabbed my arm and pulled out a set of handcuffs.

Cynder, having tied up the boat ran over to us. "I wouldn't do that if I were you." He pulled his wand out and suddenly I wasn't cold or wet anymore. Looking down, my drab clothes had magically turned themselves back into the beautiful dress I'd been wearing earlier. The small boy's eyes widened as he took in my magical change of appearance, but it was nothing compared to the shock in the police officer's eyes as he finally realized who I was.

"Your Highness! I'm so sorry, I didn't realize..."

"Can you take us to the station before you start apologizing for treating people like scum? It's freezing out here."

He nodded and beckoned us to follow him.

"Nicely done," whispered Cynder as we followed the officer through the night.

The small station was only a few blocks away, so it didn't take us long to get there. When the other officers saw me, they did everything I asked. Within an hour, we had all been offered a shower and a hot meal. The young lad had wolfed it down like there was no tomorrow. Cynder and I, already full, declined the meal although we both had a cup of coffee.

I was just about to sit down with a police officer to give my statement when I was asked to go into the back room. Following one of the female officers, I was surprised to see a familiar figure.

"Monty," I said, slipping into the seat in front of him.

"Your Majesty. I was called here to take your statement. The officers thought having a senior officer might make you feel more comfortable."

While Monty did little to make me feel comfortable, he was right that I wanted someone high up to deal with this.

"Thank you. A young boy was thrown into the canal just a couple of blocks from here—" I began

Monty cut me off.

"May I inquire as to what you were doing out by the canal at this hour?"

I looked at the clock on the wall. The time was eleven forty-five. I was never going to be able to get home by the time I promised.

"That's not really any concern of yours," I replied brusquely. "What should concern you is that a couple of anti-Magi thugs threw an innocent child into the water."

"Innocent? If they were anti-Magi, does that mean the boy in question is a Mage? Maybe he was doing magic on them, and they were defending themselves?"

"They were twice his size! The innocence of the child is not in question. However, the guilt of the older two boys is. I want them found and charged with attempted murder."

Monty's mustache twitched. "Now that's a bit harsh, don't you think? It was just a prank."

"The boy nearly drowned. If I'd not been there to save him, he would surely have perished."

"But he's just a..."

"A what?" I knew exactly what he was going to say, but I wanted to hear him say it. I wanted to hear him say the word Mage because then I could fire his sorry ass for flouting the law on prejudice."

"I know what you are thinking, Your Majesty, but the truth of the matter is, I can't arrest two young boys because they happen to throw a vagabond in the water. He's a Mage. He can fend for himself."

"I'm so glad you said that, Mr. Grenfall. Please take your things and leave."

"Excuse me?"

"I'm firing you. I said I was going to find a Mage to help you, but it seems to me that if you can't remember your own laws, then I'll just have to find someone to replace you."

"What law exactly do you think I've broken?"

"I made it quite clear that I would have no discrimination against the Magi. If you refuse to look for these boys because their victim is a Mage, then that is blatantly flouting that law."

"You can't do that. Your own father hired me. I've been on the force for over thirty years."

"Well, you'll be able to have a nice rest then, won't you?"

"If you replace me with a Mage, that's discrimination against the non-Magi. You are breaking your own law!" He crossed his arms and glared at me with a self-satisfied grin on his face.

"I actually said I was going to bring a Mage in to help you. I said nothing about a Mage replacing you. I'll hire the best person for the job, be they Mage or non-Mage."

I stood up, leaving him to simmer in his own outrage. Having him in charge of all the police in Silverwood was no good. It was about time we had some new blood. Some new magical blood.

By the time we finally left the police station, it was about two o'clock in the morning. Our statements had been taken, and the young boy's mother had been found and brought to the station. The earliness of the hour hadn't stopped the paparazzi from being out in force. Someone, I suspected Grenfall, had tipped them off and now there were hundreds of them camped outside the station waiting for us.

As Cynder and I walked down the station steps, hundreds of flashes from all the cameras dazzled us.

"Move aside!" A voice boomed out, causing them to part. In front of us stood Luca. Daniel was by his side. He took my hand, and we followed him to the pumpkin carriage Daniel had magicked up earlier. As we closed the carriage doors behind us, Luca wrapped his arms around me. His warmth filled me.

"So much for being back at midnight, huh?" Luca said. "The carriage turned back into a pumpkin, so Daniel was forced to use magic on it again. I don't think the mice were too happy. Did you know he was a Mage?"

"I'm sorry," I sighed, ignoring his question about Daniel.

"Don't be. I heard you were quite the hero. I'm proud of you. I have to thank you too, Cynder, for keeping her safe."

Once again, Luca surprised me by not being angry. I don't know why I thought he would be or why I was expecting it. Instead, he was being perfectly lovely.

"Did you two have a good time before all the excitement?" he asked.

"It was the least romantic, most boring date I've ever had the misfortune to go on," I said.

I noticed Cynder's mouth curl up at the edges before he turned his face away to look out of the carriage window.

Out in the Open

The next morning, I did something I should have done a long time before. I called a meeting of the household. As I'd slept in and missed breakfast, I asked the kitchen to send up some croissants and fruit.

A member of staff brought Daniel and Dean up to the palace, and I brought the rest of the men. Elise was in bed with a particularly nasty case of morning sickness, and my mother declined to come as she was too busy with some wedding issue or other that I had no interest in. The meeting ended up with just the boys and me. Luca sat on my right and Cynder on my left. Leo, Daniel, and Dean filled up the remaining spaces.

"Thank you all for coming," I said, standing up. As I did, Jenny walked in with a huge pot of coffee. "Jenny, you can stay too. I think it would be helpful for you to know what is going on."

Jenny blushed and sat between Leo and Dean. She grabbed a notepad and pen from her pocket and waited for me to begin.

"My reign has gotten off to a tumultuous start. I wasn't anticipating becoming a target for assassination so soon, and yet it happened. You all know that Cynder here saved me and brought me home. So far, the danger has not resurfaced, but the group behind the assassination attempt is still out there. They are called the Magi Death Squad. A man named Frederick Pittser is one of the members. You probably remember him as the man who told the media that Cynder and I were having an affair to stop me from inviting the Magi back into the kingdom. Unfortunately for him, his plan backfired. The Magi have been coming back in force over the last week or so, including people who weren't living in Silverwood originally."

You all know I've been forced into another round of competition for who will be my husband. It's not been easy, but I want to thank both Luca and Cynder for going through with it. It was not an easy decision to make for any of us, but as you have, no doubt, seen in the papers, the popularity for the monarchy has increased massively in the past week, ever since it was announced we were doing this. It's my belief that the competition is what's buoying that and bringing the Magi back. Furthermore, since Cynder arrived, I've had no reports of any attacks on any Magi, nor have I had word that there have been any further demonstrations. This competition, as ridiculous as it is, is uniting the kingdom."

"It's all good news then!" said Dean.

"Mostly, yes, but there are a few problems and a few things I want to clear up before we go any further. The people around this table are the people I trust most in the world. You've all proved yourself in one way or another, so I think it's time a few truths were known. Firstly, Daniel is a Mage."

I heard Jenny gasp. She stopped scribbling and looked over at Daniel. Dean took his hand.

"He knows I was going to tell you all and agreed to come out of the closet so to speak."

"Wouldn't be the first closet I've come out of this year," he quipped.

"But your mother..." said Jenny, trailing off. "Maggie was the one who asked me to put in a good word for you at the ball."

"I'm afraid my mother is dead and has been for a great many years. Maggie is a friend of mine. She agreed to lie to you to get me into the palace. I'm so sorry."

"But..."

"Jenny, that's why we are here," I said as kindly as I could. She hated being lied to as much as I did. "We are clearing the air."

"Ok." She picked up her pen again. I could see she wasn't happy but kept it to herself.

"Daniel and Cynder are in a group fighting the Magi Death Squad, called the Freedom of Magic. They have known each other for quite a while. Originally, this group was set up to bring down my father, but since he did a pretty good job of that himself, they decided to help the monarchy rather than fight it."

"We decided to help you," corrected Cynder.

"And I'm grateful. I think it's safe to say we all have a common cause here. To bring Silverwood together and to eliminate hate between the Magi and non-Magi. I was wondering if you both would tell everyone exactly what it is that the Freedom of Magic have been doing, and what it is they are doing now."

Cynder stood and cleared his throat. This wasn't going to be easy for him. He was going to have to tell the truth about the fact that the Freedom of Magic had originally intended to bring down the monarchy. I listened to him as he spoke, and gauged the reactions of the others. At first, I could see they were uncomfortable with what they were hearing, especially Jenny. But as he continued with how they had been helping us since my father died, she visibly relaxed. When he finished up with telling everyone how he had saved my life in Thalia, Jenny got up and gave him a hug. A huge honor indeed!

"I hope you all understand where Cynder is coming from," I said, taking over from him. "The Magi have been persecuted for years. I don't blame him or Daniel for trying to bring down my father, and I hope you won't either. The main thing is, they are on our side now, and we are all working together. Cynder, Daniel, would it be possible to bring some other members of The Freedom of Magic to the palace? I would like to talk to them all. If we are going to fight the Magi Death Squad, we need to all be on the same page."

"We could try," replied Daniel. "The police might try to stop that many Magi from getting into the palace. We all know that the MDS has people in high places including the police force."

"No, they won't. I'll say it's a garden party for Magi. All of Silverwood knows what I'm trying to do, whether they like it or not. They will just assume that I'm trying to mend fences. Also, that brings me to my next point. I fired the chief of police last night. The kingdom cannot run for long without someone running the police force, but I saw last night how corrupt our police force can be. Leo, I know you are a businessman and not a policeman, but I trust you. I'd like it if you can jump into the police chief's position for the next couple of weeks. Your detective skills are nothing short of amazing...except for a couple of little mistakes." I'd told him that morning that his informant was wrong about Cynder being married, a fact that embarrassed Leo no end. "I want you to organize and implement a recruitment drive for Magi police at all levels, and then when you think things are running smoothly, hire someone to take on the chief role."

"Whatever you need," replied Leo smoothly.

"I can help with that," butted in Dean.

I looked at him expectantly.

"I'm a policeman. I worked under Grenfall. I was so pleased to find out that you fired him this morning. It was the talk of the station."

"You are a policeman?" I'd just assumed he was a carpenter like Daniel.

"Yep."

"Perfect. Can you help Leo?" I thought for a second. Something I remembered came to mind. "Actually, I need someone to look into a guy known as The Regent. He's a high ranking member of the Magi Death Squad. The highest. He'll probably be someone already in power with a lot of money and a lot of influence. I need to know who he is. Do you think you can set up a squad to look into that?"

"I'm just a police officer. I'm not sure I'll be able to start an investigation on my own. I don't have the authority."

"I'll come into the headquarters tomorrow and let everyone know of the changes. I'll make it known that I'm looking for a new secret task force that has something to do with the anti-Magi sentiments. Then, between us, we can pick from those that look like a good fit. Until then, we'll keep the full reason for the task force quiet. I don't want everyone knowing we are looking for The Regent. He could even be a member of the force. Leo can help with that too."

"Sounds good!" replied Dean, looking like the cat that had got the cream.

After the meeting, I retired to my office. Jenny had already started making it a bit more liveable and less severe by adding a vase of flowers and some nice paintings of Silverwood on the walls. There was a long way to go to completely remove any trace of my father, but it was a start.

Now that the air had been cleared and everyone knew fully what was going on, it made me feel so much more at ease with everything that was happening.

Jenny had been instructed to organize the garden party-cum-meeting with the Freedom of Magic. Leo and Daniel were going to be sorting out the corruption within Silverwood's Police force. And Cynder and Luca were working with me to make sure that the competition to choose one of them didn't turn into the farce that last year's had.

For the first time in weeks, I finally felt like I had everything under control.

Of course, like everything else in my life, the feeling of control was short-lived.

The nightmare started when I pulled the first of the day's papers towards me. The front cover had a photo of Cynder and I coming out of the police station the night before. I'd expected as much, but the part that worried me was the fact that, thanks to our actions last night, Cynder was way up in the polls. Despite him being a Mage, he was beating Luca by a large margin. In fact, Luca's popularity was at an all-time low.

I sighed and pushed the paper to one side. I'd have to tell Luca to plan something special for our date, something the public would enjoy. Sitting in the movie theatre eating popcorn might be my idea of a good night, but it wouldn't be enough to win the public over.

I picked up the rest of the papers to read later. I wouldn't be showing them to Luca, and with some luck, he'd be too busy to read them. He didn't deserve to be so low in the ratings.

I found him chatting to Jenny about the upcoming garden party. It was due to take place the day of our date. It meant that the televised interview would have to take place the day after that which was fine with me. I hated the necessity of it all anyway.

"Luca, I know you are helping Jenny, but I've been thinking..."

"Yes?"

"Our date next week. I know I'm supposed to plan it, but I'm very busy. I was wondering if you could come up with something a bit special?"

He bounded over and gave me a kiss. "Absolutely, I've already got some ideas! It will be perfect, I promise."

I gave him a small smile and left them to it. I knew Jenny would help him too. With a party and a date to organize, she'd be in her element.

It wasn't until later that I brought myself to look at the other papers. If the first one was bad, the rest were infinitely worse. There on the front page of the first was the photo that Leo had shown me days before. The one of Cynder and his ugly stepsisters. Underneath the photo was the caption in large letters.

Kingdom in shock as Cynder's hidden wife is exposed.

The rest of the papers had led with the same story. Just as Leo had believed it, now the kingdom did. Everyone now believed that Cynder was married.

Wedding Proof

"I don't know anything about this." Leo sat opposite me in my office. I watched as he massaged his temples.

"What about your informant? Could they have gone to the press?"

"Yesterday, I would have said no. He's been my friend for years, and I trusted him completely. I guess I was wrong. I'm sorry."

The door opened, and Cynder walked in. I'd invited them both up here for an urgent meeting. Leo had beaten Cynder to it by a couple of minutes. I passed the paper to Cynder to let him digest the contents.

"I'm so sorry, Cynder," began Leo. "I was just looking out for Charmaine. I didn't know anything about you, and I was worried about a stranger coming into the palace. I didn't leak this to the press, but my informant must have. I'll deal with him, but I obviously can't take this back." He smacked his hand down at the paper. I'd never seen him mad before.

"Don't. There's a possibility it isn't your informant. If my ex-stepsisters got wind of him, there is a good chance they leaked this themselves. I'm actually amazed it took them so long."

"Are they anti-Magi?"

"No, they just like money and power. Seeing me living in the palace must be killing them. I haven't seen them in years, but that won't stop them. This is their one shot at fame, and they are going to make the most of it."

"What shall we do about it?" I asked.

Cynder thought for a minute. "Ignore it. It will go away on its own eventually."

"The people will want to know the truth," I reminded him. "They will expect a statement from me."

"Any statement you give will only add fuel to the fire. You don't know these women. They are power-hungry. You talk about them at all, and it will validate their claim. They'll say you are lying."

"But I'm not lying. They have no proof, no wedding certificate."

"They won't care. Even bad publicity is publicity to them, and they'll milk it for all they are worth. I honestly think it's better to leave it well alone and let the flames die out. If you don't bite back, they will get bored eventually."

I couldn't help but wonder what damage they'd do in the meantime, but I let Cynder have his way. I didn't know these women, and he did. If he said they were ruthless, then I believed him. I'd be monitoring the papers, though. I wasn't about to let two crazy women mess up everything I was working towards.

The next day, I headed to Silverwood's main police station with Leo and Daniel. The whole force knew we were coming and, apart from a few key staff members manning the reception desk, they had all crammed into the biggest conference room in the building. Even with the huge capacity, it was standing room only.

The second in command, who'd taken up the mantle in the two days since Grenfall had left was a jovial middle-aged man with the unlikely name of Copper. Jason Copper. I briefed him fully before seeing the rest of the staff, and he seemed more than happy, to have Leo come into the force. Jason was a man I took to straight away. With one of those faces that had a permanent smile, he was more than happy to accommodate us. Even better, was the fact that he agreed with us on a lot of key issues regarding the Magi. He told us how he'd repeatedly spoken to Grenfall over the past few years about the Magi and had been shot down at every turn. After an hour-long meeting with him, I decided that he and Leo should work together. If Leo liked him as much as I did, he'd eventually get the chief of police position to himself once Leo had finished what he was there to do.

I looked at the faces looking up at me with great expectation and knew that this was going to be one of the most important speeches I ever gave. These men and women were Silverwood's backbone. As they were on the front line, so to speak, they dealt with Magi and non-Magi and the problems between the two communities on a regular basis.

"Good morning," I began. "As you are no doubt aware, I terminated Mr. Grenfall from his position of Chief of Police a couple of days ago."

There was a cheer. It seemed that Grenfall was as unpopular with his staff as he was with me. That would make things easier.

"For the next few weeks, Your second in command, Sergeant Copper will be taking his place. His title from today onward will be

Acting Chief of Police. Alongside him will be Mr. Leo Halifax. As you are probably aware, Mr. Halifax is my brother-in-law, but he is also a trusted member of my staff.

"Mr. Copper and Mr. Halifax will be working together in the coming weeks to streamline the police force. I want to assure you that your jobs are all safe and there is no need to panic. If you are happy in your current position, then there is no need for that to change.

"However, we are looking for some people to step up for a new task force. This task force will be dealing with highly privileged information regarding Anti-Magi groups. I can't say any more than that now, but application forms will be left by the door for you to pick up if you think this is something you might be interested in. Anyone can apply, but only the best will be picked. There is a hefty bonus plan for those who get the job.

"Mr. Dean Wentworth, another of my advisors at the palace, will be in charge. Some of you may already know him. The positions that are left vacant by those moving up to the new task force will be filled with people from outside the force. A recruitment drive for Magi to join the force will be trialed starting this week. If there is anyone here who doesn't like that or will not be able to work alongside the Magi, please leave now. Take your coats as you won't be welcomed back."

I waited for someone to leave, but apart from a few grumbles, no one did.

I took a deep breath. So far so good! By the time the people cleared the conference room, I was feeling a whole lot more confident. No one had openly complained about me hiring Magi, and I'd even managed to find a couple of people who would look into Cynder's sisters for me. They'd been on the front of all the papers again, and despite Cynder's reassurance that it would just go away, I wasn't so sure.

Leaving Leo and Dean to begin their new jobs, I headed back to the palace. A quick session with Xavi and her crew had me ready for my interview with Marybelle. After the scandal with Cynder had broken overnight, I'd decided to cancel the big interview on the stage with all the leading newspaper reporters and TV stations, and just invite Marybelle into the palace. I didn't have the energy to deal with an excitable crowd on top of everything else, and so the palace gates would remain shut to the public this week. When I looked out of one of the front windows of the palace, I could see that, despite the cancellation, people had still turned up for the show.

"It will be ok," said Cynder, putting his hands on my shoulders behind me. I gave a huge sigh, and he kneaded the tension from my shoulders. As much as I hated to admit it, I welcomed his touch.

"I don't know if it will be. The monarchy is too frail to stand another scandal. Two days ago you were the kingdom's hero, and now they hate you. It's like every day there is something new. One day you are the favorite, the next it's Luca. The whole thing is madness."

Cynder stopped what he was doing and spun me around. Dropping the curtains I'd been holding open, I turned to face him. His hand went to my face, touching my skin. My body reacted immediately as it always did when he touched me. Heat flooded through me at his slightest touch.

"I promise it will be fine." He kissed me lightly on the lips, and despite myself, I closed my eyes, savoring it.

"Stop!" I said, but he already had. It was the kiss of a friend, no more. He smiled. "We stick to the plan. If the interviewer asks about my sisters , we say "no comment" and leave it at that."

If only it were so simple. I followed him out of the room up to the sitting room where I knew

Marybelle and her crew would be waiting. The "kiss of a friend" still burning on my lips.

"You've had quite the week," began Marybelle, not giving us time to prepare. I'd wanted to tell her not to speak about Cynder's sisters, but she'd gone straight into her interview, the second we'd both sat down.

"Yes, Marybelle, thank you." I pulled down the hem of my skirt and tried to look in control. "This week has been quite an adventure. Firstly, we rescued a young boy from drowning, and this morning I began the process of rolling out a new initiative at the police headquarters for Magi to join the police force. At the moment there is not a single Magi police officer in the whole of Silverwood. That's a startling statistic and one I'd like to see changed in the near future."

"Of course. What do you make of the rumors about Cynder here?" She turned to him, her newly blonde curls bobbing behind her. "Did the queen know you had a wife when she invited you to the palace?"

"No comment." Cynder crossed his arms defiantly.

"He's not married," I butted in. "It's a vicious rumor and no more. Cynder and I have already spoken about it, and neither of us has anything more to say on the matter."

"But surely you must be wondering if you can trust him, after all, his wife has provided evidence that they shared a last name and that they lived together."

I gripped the hem of my skirt and began to pick at a loose thread. How Cynder could sit there so calmly was beyond me. While part of me wanted to scream out that she was once his foster sister, I knew it would do no good. Cynder didn't want his past raked through by the media, and I could understand that. The beginnings of the Freedom of Magic movement were founded in those early years and to expose any of his history would likely bring down the group.

"I trust Cynder. I hope that you and the viewing public at home will also be able to do the same. Only two nights ago, he saved the life of a young boy who had been thrown into a freezing cold canal." I tried changing the subject, but Marybelle wouldn't be swayed.

"It's just been brought to my attention that as well as the proof of marriage I mentioned earlier, there is also a wedding photograph." On a screen behind her, a photograph of Cynder was displayed. He was looking very handsome in a suit. Next to him was Drusilla Bloom wearing what only could be described as a wedding dress.

The look of shock on my face as I took in the photo was not put on for the public. It was too late, they'd already seen it.

Anger and Passion Defeated

You trust me right?" Cynder had to run to keep up with me as I stormed down the corridor away from Marybelle and her crew. I wasn't sure if I was angry at Cynder or angry at the press, but I sure knew I was angry at someone. The whole interview had been a fiasco from the start. I'd gone into it believing that Drusilla was Cynder's sister or ex-foster sister or stepsister, but the proof she was his wife kept coming, and the more I tried to deny it, the more ridiculous and naive I looked. Cynder had done nothing to help matters. He's replied "no comment" to every question thrown at him, leaving me looking like a pathetic fool.

"I don't know what I feel right now. Just leave me alone!"

"I'm telling you the truth!" he shouted as I ran along the corridor, desperate to be away from him, from everyone.

"I've never lied to you, Charm," he said as I arrived at my bedroom door. He'd followed me the whole way.

"You didn't tell me that you were a freedom fighter. You never mentioned Drusilla until Leo found out about her. You may not have lied to me, but you sure kept some important facts to yourself."

"I'm sorry. Last year, I barely saw you. Every second I had with you was special, and I didn't want to waste it by talking about my past, and since I've been here, it's been nothing but meetings and interviews. We've not had a proper chance to talk alone. I'll tell you anything you want to know about my past if you give me the chance. What is it you want to know?"

"I want to know if I should really trust you. You are right, we've never really talked, not ever. Our whole relationship has been built on dancing and danger, but we barely know each other."

"I know enough to know that I love you, and that I have loved you from the moment you walked in on me doing the dishes last year."

"I'm sorry, Cynder. I'm not sure that's enough anymore."

I walked through the door of my bedroom, slamming it in his face and threw myself down face first on the bed.

I hated feeling sorry for myself, but no matter what I did, something always seemed to go wrong. I did trust Cynder, I'd trusted him all along, but the sheer amount of evidence Marybelle had produced was overwhelming. Every time I'd tried brushing it off, she'd come up with something else, and while I'd flapped about, trying to think up things to say, Cynder had kept quiet about the whole thing.

I wanted to be by myself to process everything, but even that was not to be. Only minutes later there was a knock at my door. I ignored it, hoping whoever it was would go away, especially if it was Cynder, but the door opened. I turned to find Luca standing at the end of my bed.

"What's the matter? Cynder said you were upset. Something about the interview. He didn't go into specifics, but he thought you might need someone to talk to."

"I'm not upset! I'm angry!" I replied, but as I said it, I noticed the tears rolling down my face. Luca was by my side in a flash, holding me. I let the tears of frustration fall, and I let Luca comfort me. I needed him so badly right now.

His arms engulfed me, taking away the pain I was feeling. He made no sound, but gently rocked me and stroked my hair until my tears subsided.

"What am I doing?" I asked, buried deep within his arms.

"Hmm?"

I looked up at his face. It showed nothing but love and concern for me. I'd asked him what I was doing, but the truth was I knew what I had been doing. I'd been messing with my own emotions and those of Cynder and Luca, and although I'd not physically cheated on Luca, emotionally I had. I'd told Marybelle right from the start that I was going to marry Luca, and yet, I'd let Cynder kiss me as recently as a couple of hours ago. I'd said stop and brushed it off as something innocent, but it wasn't innocent. Nothing about what I did with Cynder was innocent. It shouldn't matter to me whether he was married or single, except in terms of how people would view it, but it did matter, and I hated that. I needed to purge Cynder from my system. We all knew he was only here for the media and the public and yet this whole time, I'd been hoping for more. It was time to put that hope behind me and look to the man who was sitting in front of me. The man I'd promised my life to.

I leaned forward and kissed him slowly. He seemed surprised at first, and I couldn't blame him. I'd been pulling away from him for so long that he'd gotten used to it. As my lips parted his, he soon got over the shock and followed my lead, pulling closer to me, exploring me, his hands on my body, finding places I'd not let him touch before. To my surprise, I was enjoying it. Any fear or hesitation I'd felt in the past disappeared, leaving me with a wanton desire to discover him completely. I'd seen his body once before when I put him in his pajamas in Thalia, and then I'd been nervous, in a hurry to get it over with. Now there was an urgency, but at the same time, I was in no rush. The buttons on his shirt came open easily, letting me feel the warmth of his smooth chest as I ran my hand under the starched white material.

He groaned and kissed me harder, pushing me flat onto the bed. And then he was above me. His weight pinned me down, leaving me breathless. I'd waited so long for this, and he had too. Long enough.

His lips trailed down to my neck, giving me goosebumps and spreading heat throughout my body. Almost without thinking, I arched my hips up to meet his, and he groaned once again, urging me on. Pulling his shirt free from his trousers where he'd had it tucked in, I drew it down his arms and tossed it to the floor.

Our embrace became much more passionate as I marveled at the hardness of his muscular arms and the feel of his chest upon my own.

"Do you want this?" he whispered.

"Yes." I breathed back. I did want it, I needed it.

He began to undo the buttons on the front of my dress but stopped.

"I do want it. I'm ready!" I said urgently.

"I know, it's not that. Your buttons are stuck."

I looked down. They'd been fine when Xavi had dressed me earlier.

The dress itself was pretty basic with pretty gold buttons that buttoned down the whole length of it. I had a go with the top one, but it wouldn't open. The next two were the same.

"It's fine." I sat up, kissing Luca again. "I can pull the dress over my head."

He took my hand in his.

"I want this as much as you do. Hell, I want it more than you do, but maybe there is a reason those buttons don't open. You told me a while back that you wanted your first time to be special. It's not special if you are only doing it because you are upset."

"I'm not upset," I replied too quickly.

"Angry then. I don't want you to look back and remember it like this." He stood from the bed and retrieved his shirt. I watched as he pulled it back on and began to button it up.

"Please don't go!" I whispered, the tears threatening again. I was so ready for him.

"I'm not going anywhere." He lay back down on the bed and pulled me close. I rested my head on his bare chest where he'd not done his buttons up yet.

A thousand thoughts and emotions swirled around in my brain, but the tiredness I'd been fighting all day overcame me, and I fell asleep, safe in Luca's arms.

Later when I awoke, Luca went down to dinner, leaving me to freshen up. I ran to the bathroom and glanced at myself in the mirror. The mascara that had been carefully applied by one of Xavi's team was now smudged all around my eyes giving me the appearance of a panda. I washed my face clean of all my makeup and gave myself a long look in the mirror. At only nineteen years of age, I was a young queen, but the last year had taken its toll. The young, carefree girl I used to be was long gone. Instead, a weary woman stared back at me. I sighed. Looking down at my buttons, I tried the top one again. This time it opened easily as did the others. Fastening them back up I wondered why they hadn't earlier. It was almost like someone had fastened them shut with magic.

Chapter twenty-six – The garden party

The next week passed quickly. What with having to read more sensationalist crap every day from the newspapers, and having daily meetings with Leo and Dean about everything going on in the police force, I'd almost forgotten about my date with Luca. I'd barely seen him since our kissing session had come to an abrupt halt. He'd spent most of the week organizing the garden party with Cynder and Jenny. I was glad they were all so busy because it meant I hadn't had to see Cynder either. There was so much evidence that he was really married that appeared every day in the papers, that I'd given up and taken to not reading them at all. I had too many important things to deal with such as running a kingdom, to worry about my pathetic excuse for a love life.

The weather outside had warmed up considerably, and now spring was in full bloom. The showers that usually fell all April had kept at bay and on the morning of both the date and the garden party, the sun shone down, warming the palace gardens and bathing them in the unseasonable heat. It would make Xavi's job a little easier. She always hated it when I had to wear boots instead of pretty shoes.

The garden party was a ruse to get the Freedom of Magic into the grounds to have a meeting with them, but to make it work, an actual garden party had been planned for the early afternoon. After that, we would all retire inside and make plans for the future. Once that was over, I was free to go on my date with Luca. It exhausted me just thinking about it.

Jenny knocked on my bedroom door early and presented me with a silver tray with a fully cooked breakfast, a bowl of fruit, and a jug of coffee. There was also a small vase with a beautiful pink flower in it. It was so out of character that I almost thought I'd dreamed it until the smell of the bacon and coffee swirled around me.

"Has someone died?" I quipped, pouring myself a cup of the coffee and swirling a spoon of sugar into it.

"Only the pigs for the bacon and sausages," she replied back. "Luca asked me to bring you this. He wants you to have a day you'll remember forever. He asked me what way would you like to be woken the most and I told him you can't go wrong with bacon when it comes to you."

I grinned up at her. "You are not wrong," I replied, spearing a piece and taking a bite.

"I'll leave you alone, but he told me to tell you to go to Xavi and dress up for the occasion."

"I was planning to. Whatever I wear for the garden party will have to do for the date tonight. I'll not have time to change in between."

"I think Luca expects you to wear something extravagant. He's got something wonderful planned."

"He has?" My heart dropped. I'd told Luca to plan something special, but extravagant? I wasn't sure I was up for too much, especially as I had a busy day to get through first.

"Yes, he has!" Jenny clapped her hands together in glee.

"What exactly has he got planned?" I asked, suddenly feeling worried. Jenny rarely got this excited.

"I can't say!" She ran her hand across her mouth and pretend zipped it, before leaving my room with a big grin on her face.

Great! Just what I needed, something else to worry about.

Xavi was already waiting for me with her whole team when I arrived at the dressing room. Just as Jenny had been, she was filled with excitement about the coming day.

"I've got a garden party today," I began. "I need something light, just above the ankle maybe, with no heels." I didn't want to spend the afternoon on my tip toes for fear of sinking into the lawn.

"No, no, no."

"Excuse me?"

"You are going to be wearing something special today. I've already chosen it."

She clapped her hands and immediately two of the helpers brought out the longest dress I'd ever seen. Yards and yards of pink material floated behind it like a train. Another helper held out a pair of matching pink shoes.

"I can't wear that. It will get filthy out in the garden."

"Luca tells me that a marquee has been erected and flooring has been put down to cover the grass. You'll be fine, and what's more, You'll look stunning."

I sat in the chair waiting for Alezis to do my hair and feeling blindsided. Why was it that no occasion ever called for me to wear long pants and comfortable shoes? My mind flashed back to the few days I'd been on the run with Cynder where I'd been able to dress as I liked. Our date had been the same. I'd been allowed to be me. I threw the thought away. Thinking of Cynder hurt and I didn't want to feel anything but focused on the day ahead. What may look to the outside world as a day of fun and frivolity was actually a coordinated political event, and I, for one, couldn't wait to get the party part over and bring everyone inside for the meeting. Although Leo and Daniel had been keeping me up–to-date with everything that was going on at the police headquarters, it was fair to say that they were getting nowhere finding The Regent, despite hiring the best men and women to join the task force. I tried not to be disappointed, after all, they'd spent the first few days of the week doing interviews and hiring, but I'd hoped that with all the technology they had, they'd be able to come up with something in the past three days. A lead—anything.

Alezis combed my hair up, spending way too long making it into the most complicated updo I'd ever seen. It was going to be a nightmare to take down later that night. He must have used about a hundred pins to keep it in place, not to mention a whole can of hairspray. My make up was surprisingly light, just a touch of pink that matched the airy dress.

At midday exactly, I wandered downstairs to the main doors, holding on to the back of my dress for fear of tripping over it. It was quite the most cumbersome outfit and totally wrong for a meeting with a secret group of fighters. How I wished that I'd scheduled the garden party and the date with Luca on different days. Luca met me by the door, his eyes sparkling although not as much as his suit on which the silver buttons had been polished, so that they shone like stars. He was wearing the uniform of his country, a suit usually only worn on special occasions.

"You look stunning, my dear," he said, kissing my cheek.

"Don't you think this is a little too much for a garden party?" I asked, dropping the train at his feet.

"Nonsense. You'll be the belle of the ball!" He held his arm out, and I took it. I needed it to be able to walk steadily over the garden.

Xavi had been correct when she said that a marquee had been erected. I recognized it as the same one that had been put up on my wedding day to Xavier last year. A whole host of unpleasant memories flooded through me, but I swallowed them down. I was glad to see that the marquee was already full of guests.

"There's probably more Magi in this tent than in the rest of Silverwood put together," whispered Luca. I nudged him, not wanting anyone to overhear, but he was probably right. At the far end was a long table with food at one end and champagne glasses at the other. A number of the palace staff were busy putting them on trays and circulating through the crowd.

"Why are we serving alcohol? This is meant to be a serious meeting. I can't do that if everyone is drunk!"

"I thought it might loosen everyone up. It is a garden party. People expect a drink."

I sighed. I'd hoped for a quick sandwich and juice each before we could head indoors to deal with the reason these people were really here.

"Is that a band in the corner?" As I said it, the men and women picked up their instruments and began to play. People began to dance, others were drinking. Everyone was happy. It was a complete disaster. I should have paid more attention to what was being planned. Jenny flounced past in her best dress with a purple flower attached at the top.

"Isn't this magical?" she said, clearly the worse for wear after drinking too much.

"I'm going to call the meeting now before everyone gets too drunk. This is not what this garden party is supposed to be about."

"It's fine," repeated Luca. "Relax, here, have a glass of champagne." He took a couple of glasses from a passing waiter and handed one to me. "There is plenty of time for the meeting later. Everyone is having such a good time."

I looked around. Yes, they were having a good time, too much of one. Surprisingly, despite this being billed to the media as a Magi event, barely any of them were wearing purple. Unlike the magi I'd seen on the TV crossing back into the kingdom, who had almost exclusively worn purple, here, the men had elected to wear black, and the women wore ball gowns of every color. I could only assume that Luca and Jenny had added a dress code to the invitations.

I turned to ask Luca, but he was already gone—disappeared into the crowd to talk to someone. Being as I was the supposed host, I decided to follow suit and introduce myself to some people.

I found an elderly couple sitting at the edge of the marquee. As I approached, they both stood and bowed.

"Hello. It's nice to meet you. I'm so glad you could come today," I said with my widest smile. "I hope you don't mind me saying, but I imagined the Freedom of Magic members to be a little younger."

Ok, it was rude, but true none the less.

"What was that?" The old man cupped his ear. How he was a member of an active fighting group was beyond me.

"I was just saying it's nice to see you here," I repeated a little louder. Someone tugged at my arm, pulling me away before I had time to hear his reply.

I spun around, coming face to face with Cynder.

"What is this?" he asked angrily, before pulling me to a quiet end of the marquee.

"You know what this is. You helped organize it."

Cynder shook his head. "No. Luca told me that you didn't want me to help, so I left it up to him and Jenny. I've spent the week keeping out of your way. Leo and Daniel have been using me at the police headquarters."

"I know its way over the top, but we can still have the meeting later."

"How are we going to do that..."

"There you are. I thought I'd lost you." I turned to find Luca behind me. "I just went to speak to the band. They are playing our song next. Come dance with me."

Luca took my hand and led me away from a very angry-looking Cynder.

"Our song?" I asked as the band began to play.

"It's one we danced to at the ball. Please tell me you remember?"

I listened to the unfamiliar music and murmured uncommittedly. Most of the music sounded the same to me.

"Why did you not let Cynder help with this? He's annoyed that it's become a ball rather than a meeting. I can't say I blame him."

"Look, the guy is married. He's made the pair of us look fools. I think it's time we sent him home."

"We can't send him home. Not yet. I'm supposed to pick someone next month."

"So? You picked early last year. Just do the same again. Tomorrow when they do the interview about our date, you can tell them then. I doubt anyone would blame you after all the lies."

"We don't know for sure he's married. He says he isn't."

"All evidence to the contrary!" replied Luca.

I sighed. The newspapers had been full of the story for the past week, and it was showing no sign of going away. And yet, I wanted to believe Cynder. After all, why would he keep lying about it?

The song came to a close. As we ended the dance, Luca fell to the floor.

"Are you alright?" I asked in alarm. Out of his pocket, he pulled a small box. When he opened it, a huge diamond ring sparkled back at me.

"Charmaine, I know we are already engaged, but I never had the chance to propose properly. Now, here I am on bended knee in the presence of all these people, with the world watching. I love you. Will you marry me?"

A Proposal and a Loss

A roar went up among the people. I looked up to find the people had gathered around in a huge circle and dotted around the circle, were photographers. These weren't ordinary photographers, these were the media. I recognized some of them. Marybelle, stood out, microphone in hand pointing right at us.

Luca had set this all up. The room became deathly silent as the seconds ticked by. I could feel my cheeks coloring and my heart pounding as I realized there was no way out of this situation.

To say no now would be a disaster. Goodness only knew how many people were watching this live in their houses. I gazed around at the people again, frantic to find a way out, but apart from the television cameras all pointing at me, I could only see Jenny, waving at me with a huge grin on her face.

I looked back at Luca. I was already engaged to him. How hard would it be to say yes? And yet the word stuck in my throat. The competition between him and Cynder would be over for good.

Luca raised his eyebrows, waiting for my answer. I was out of time.

"Yes," I whispered. "Yes, I'll marry you."

A huge cheer went up, and Luca hugged me, twirling me around. As he slipped the heavy ring onto my finger, I caught a glimpse of Cynder leaving the marquee.

"I need the bathroom," I said quickly. Luca let me go, and I ran outside for some fresh air. I saw Cynder walking towards his guest house, so I picked up my dress and followed him.

"I didn't know he was going to do that," I said, as we both reached the house at the same time. "We can still salvage this. We can still hold the meeting. This doesn't have to change anything."

"This changes everything!" shouted Cynder, opening his door. Without invitation, I followed him through.

"You already knew I was engaged to him. I've never lied to you."

"And I've never lied to you, but you don't believe me, do you? You still think that Dru is my wife. What do I have to do to prove to you that she isn't?"

"I do believe you," I replied.

"It doesn't matter anyway," he said, pulling his bag out and throwing clothes into it. "The public will see the proposal and the competition will be done. I'll be out of your hair as soon as I've packed."

"You can't go. We need you for the meeting!" I said, clutching at straws. I couldn't bear to part with him on such bad terms.

"The meeting was never going to happen."

"What do you mean? Of course, it was. Let's go back and bring them all into the palace now."

"I tried to tell you earlier. Those people in there. I don't know who they are, but they aren't Magi, and they definitely aren't members of The Freedom of Magic." He zipped up his bag and darted past me angrily. The last I saw of him was him storming down the palace driveway. At the end, the guards opened the gates, and then he was gone.

"Are you ok?" asked Luca a little later. He'd found me on the opposite side of the house, sitting alone on a garden bench.

"Why did you do it?" I asked. "We were supposed to be meeting with the Freedom of Magic. Today was about coming up with a plan to fight the MDS."

"I'm sorry. I told you a little white lie, but you said last week that I should plan something spectacular for our date. It got me thinking. When I told Jenny my idea, she loved it. I couldn't tell Cynder of course, so I told him you didn't want him to help. To be honest, I didn't think you would want him to help after all the lies he told you. I thought you'd love it."

"It was beautiful," I replied, trying not to hurt his feelings. "But I felt blindsided. If only you'd told me what you were planning to do. I could have organized the meeting for another day."

"What man tells the girl he's going to propose to that he's going to propose to her in advance? It kinda spoils the surprise don't you think? If you are worried about the Freedom of Magic people, I'll ask Cynder to rearrange it."

"You can't. He's already left."

Luca was silent for a moment.

"That's good news though, right? The people were beginning to hate him anyway. It can be just you and me now, just as it should be. We get married in two months. Your poor mother has been planning it all by herself. Maybe it's about time, you let this whole Magi thing rest for a bit and spend some time looking at wedding dresses and the like? To be honest, you look exhausted. It's about time you took a break."

"But the Magi!"

"They are already here in Silverwood, thanks to you. They aren't going to go anywhere just because you are marrying me. Cynder has been outed as a liar. They'll understand why you couldn't marry him. The guy is already married! Leo and Dean are recruiting the Magi into the police force. When the Magi see that, they'll know it's safe to apply for other jobs and go to any university. You've done enough. It's time for you to focus on yourself."

I nodded wearily. So much of what he said made sense. I was exhausted and sick of my life revolving around the media. Maybe a couple of weeks off would do me good. Maybe I could even begin to get excited about my upcoming wedding. If I wasn't so preoccupied with the Magi, maybe I could persuade Mother to let me have the wedding I wanted rather than the all-singing-all-dancing extravaganza I knew her to be planning.

I took his hand and let him walk me back to the marquee, my heels digging into the soft ground as we walked, leaving a brown and green layer over the soft pink. As we both entered the marquee, everyone descended on us. People I didn't know hugged me and congratulated me. The women gushed over my new ring while the men patted Luca on the back and told him he'd made a great catch, as if I were no more than a salmon swimming upstream.

At some point, Marybelle, along with her camera crew bustled in.

She pointed her microphone right at me.

"Congratulations," she said, grinning widely. I noticed she'd had her teeth whitened and they now gleamed so brightly I was worried they'd glare on the camera.

"Thank you," I replied politely, feeling sick. I wasn't prepared for this interview one bit, but I could already guess how it was going to go.

"How are you feeling right now? It's a very exciting time."

Sick, nervous, sad, tired.

"I am excited. What girl wouldn't be when her prince proposes to her. Today has turned out to be a wonderful day. I'm very happy."

"It looks like the competition is over. Did the right man win?"

"Of course." I gripped Luca's hand for encouragement. "I said all along I was going to marry Prince Luca. We are both really happy."

"What about Cynder?" she asked, gazing around the marquee.

"I'm afraid he had to go, but I wish him well in his future endeavors. He has been nothing short of amazing in his time here at the palace, and I know that without him, there would be far fewer Magi here in Silverwood. I want the people watching this at home to know that I still support the Magi a hundred percent and me choosing to marry Luca has nothing to do with that. I said I would choose a man based on love, and I was true to that. The police force has implemented a new initiative focused on the recruitment of Magi, and as before, the universities are now open to everyone. I really hope that all you Magi out there stay to help us build a better future for Silverwood."

"Where is Cynder now?" Marybelle asked, clearly not interested in what I had to say about politics.

"I don't know. He decided that it was his time to leave. This week has been very hard on him. There have been a lot of rumors circulating which aren't true, and I, for one, believe him. I hope that now that this is all over, the media will leave him alone."

I tried to make it sound like a threat, but Marybelle wasn't biting.

"What now, for you and Prince Luca?"

"The prince and I have decided to take a small step back from our public life so we can concentrate on our upcoming wedding. As you can imagine, there is a lot to plan. We will still be fulfilling our royal duties but in a much less public way. The last few weeks have been fun, but appearing on TV all the time can be quite exhausting. In the fall, after our wedding, I hope to tour some of Silverwood's universities to see how the Magi are settling in."

It was not something I'd actually planned as it had just come to me in the spur of the moment, but it was a good idea.

Marybelle thanked me and nodded to her cameraman. The light on the camera turned off, and the interview was over.

I wanted to escape, to leave the marquee and spend the rest of the day alone in my room to process everything, but as with everything else in my life right now, I once again found myself in a situation I had little control over.

This was my engagement party, and although there was no chance I was going to enjoy it, I could at least try.

Leo and Elise were there along with my mother, Dean, and Daniel.

Elise was looking better than she had in a couple of weeks and now had that healthy pregnancy glow that people talk about. I watched as she and Leo danced to the music. They looked so good together. Leo only had eyes for her as he twirled her around the marquee, and she looked so happy. I wondered if I looked as happy as she did from an outside perspective. If I did, it was only good acting. I was trying to feel happy, but something big was lost to me. It wasn't just Cynder, although his leaving had left a gaping hole in my heart, especially under the circumstances. If only I could see him again to apologize, to make him realize that I did believe him and always had.

I knew he wouldn't go back to Thalia. The press would be all over him there, and that was if the king and queen gave him his job back. Luca had asked that they would all those weeks ago, but that was before the Drusilla scandal. I sipped at my champagne, hoping the alcohol would make me feel better, but it didn't. I was already numb.

The afternoon quickly turned into night, and eventually, the people began to leave. Apart from the few family members and Dean and Daniel, I didn't know any of them. I'd have asked Luca where they all came from, but I didn't have the energy. When it was finally late enough that I could make my excuses to leave, I told Luca I had a headache from all the champagne and headed to the marquee's exit.

I was just about to go outside when I felt a hand on my arm.

"Leo," I said when I saw who it was.

"Charmaine, I've been wanting to talk to you all day, but Elise said I should let you enjoy your big day first."

"What is it?"

"I want you to come into the police headquarters tomorrow. We have a lead on The Regent. We think we are getting close to capturing him."

The Regent

"How are things going?" I asked Dean who had come down to the headquarters lobby to meet me. Recruitment posters filled the entrance hall, and I was pleased to see a couple of people wearing purple taking down notes.

"It's actually going pretty well. We've had nearly fifty applications for this branch alone, but over the whole of Silverwood, we are looking at hundreds. When you first mentioned it, I wasn't sure if it would work, but it seems the Magi want some control in their own safety."

"That's great," I yawned.

"Busy day yesterday, huh? Daniel told me he was so surprised. Between you and me, he expected you to end up with Cynder."

"Yeah, well…" I trailed off. What else was there to say on the subject? "How are the current staff taking the influx of Magi?"

"There have been a number of people quitting and some low-level grumbles, but nothing we aren't handling. Leo is doing a great job."

"That's good to hear. I heard he had a lead on The Regent."

"I'll let you speak to him about it."

He led me to a small room with just a table and three chairs. One of which was occupied by Leo. Dean took the other one next to him, and I sat opposite.

"I feel like I'm being interrogated," I quipped.

"This is an interrogation room, but it's the only place I could think of that is private. I share an office upstairs, and Dean works in an office with the rest of the task force."

"Ok," I replied. "What is it you've found? Do you know who it is yet?"

"Not exactly, but we do know that it is someone high up—higher up than we thought. I think we underestimated the reach of the MDS. The Regent is someone at the very top."

"Top of what?" I asked, confused.

"Someone in a really powerful position."

"Could it be Pittser? He is a very well known celebrity since telling all those lies on TV."

"No. It's not him. He's a member of the MDS, but he's not the boss. We have intel that he was the one that shot at you in Thalia. But unfortunately, he's gone underground, and we can't find him. We don't even know if he's in Silverwood or Thalia, although we have men and women in the field looking for him."

"So what else do you know about The Regent?"

"We know it's a man and we know he has a lot of political clout. He needs it to keep his identity secret. His followers are exceptionally loyal, although many don't know who he actually is. He's clever because only a few select members of the MDS know who he really is. The rest only know him as The Regent. We also know he has a lot of money and isn't afraid to spend it."

"That doesn't really narrow it down that much. There are many people in powerful positions here in Silverwood; surgeons, lawyers, judges, even the police."

"That's why I've chosen to speak with you down here rather than in my office upstairs."

"You don't think it's Mr. Copper, surely?" He'd come across as such a nice guy, but I knew that he was the one who currently shared an office with Leo.

"Not as such, but I can't rule him out. He's in the perfect position. He has power and money and what better place to hide than in full view. Few people would suspect him."

"But you do?"

"No, but I'm not prepared to make mistakes, based on a gut feeling. He comes across as genuine, but The Regent didn't get to where he is by being anything but brilliant."

An idea suddenly occurred to me. "What about Grenfall. He was vehemently anti-Magi and an asshole to boot."

"I had the same thought," replied Leo. "but he was a bit too perfect as a suspect. We think our man is keeping his anti-Magi beliefs to himself to avoid suspicion. Grenfall couldn't keep his mouth shut about how much he despised the Magi."

"We have been tracking him, though," cut in Dean. "We've had a couple of our task force on him for days."

"And?" I asked. I could quite imagine Grenfall heading some secret group to bring down the Magi despite what Leo said. He seemed like the type and fit the profile perfectly. Plus, I didn't like the guy!

"Nothing. He's spent the last week drinking alone in a pub."

"That's sad."

"Yeah, but not suspicious. He's talked to no one except the barman, and then, only to order drinks."

"Any other leads?" I asked, feeling hopeless.

"A couple," answered Leo, "but nothing concrete. The task force members are working well together, and we are gathering information, but it's going to be a while before we know for sure."

"So why call me in here? You could have told me this at the party yesterday."

Leo sighed and rubbed his temples.

"Your love life is really none of my business, but I do feel pretty bad about finding that photo of Cynder. I think this whole marriage to Drusilla Bloom thing has spiraled out of control."

"It's ok. You were looking out for me. I understand that."

"It's not ok. If I'd not stirred the pot, none of this would have happened. I've kept some of the task force to one side to look into Cynder's past for you."

"And?"

"Are you sure you want to hear it?"

"Yes, of course, I'm sure. What is it?"

"His parents were killed in a fire when he was a child. Apparently, there had been a lot of threats towards them as they were Magi. The official line is that it was an accident, but..."

"There was a strong smell of petrol, and the doors to the restaurant had been blocked off," I interrupted him.

"How do you know?" asked Leo.

"He told me." I felt relieved that at least this was the truth.

"The trail goes a bit murky after this point, but he lived with a number of people. Some Magi, some not Magi. At one point in his mid-teens, he lived with the Blooms. I think the Countess Bloom thought she was doing him a huge favor, but by all accounts, he was nothing more than a slave for the two years he lived there. She made him refer to her as step-mother and her daughters as sisters throughout the time he was with them. She liked to show him off to her well-to-do friends, but when he wasn't out with her and her daughters, he lived in rags, sleeping among the fireplace ashes in the basement. When it stopped being cool or when she got bored with him, she threw him out in the streets. He lived

324

on park benches for the next six months before a Magi family took him in."

My heart went out to him. He'd told me much of this already, but he'd not told me he'd been forced to wear rags and sleep in ashes. How cold he must have been living on the streets."

"So he wasn't married to Drusilla Bloom?"

"No. All the proof the media found is fabricated. We've managed to get a lot of it and have our experts go over it. It's all fake, but it's good. Whoever made the wedding photos and the fake certificates knew what they were doing. It wouldn't have come cheap."

"So the countess or her daughters paid for someone to do this?"

Leo shook his head. "We don't think so. She might have the title and the nice house, but since her husband died twenty years ago, she and her daughters have managed to squander every penny they had. There is no way that any of them would have been able to afford good forgery."

"So who then? And why?"

"We think The Regent did it. He must have offered to do it for her. She accepted for the fame. Dragging her one-time foster son's name through the mud didn't matter to her if it meant one of her daughters became famous. That family would give anything for fame."

"Why would The Regent care?"

"He hates the Magi, remember? Having a mage in such a high position would be an abomination to him. Killing Cynder wasn't an option with all the security at the palace. After all, he'd already tried to have you murdered unsuccessfully. There was no way he'd be able to get past your guards. Instead, he did the next best thing. He painted him as a liar and a cheat. With Cynder leaving, he got exactly what he wanted."

I closed my eyes. Cynder leaving had so many repercussions on Silverwood as a whole, not to mention the effect it was having on me. I'd barely slept all night the night before. Every time I closed my eyes, I saw him out there with no place to go and no money. He'd been in that position before, and I knew he'd survive, but I wanted more for him. He deserved so much more than the hand he'd been dealt. When he first came to the palace, he'd been promised a handsome amount of money if he were to lose, but he'd left so abruptly that I'd not have the chance to give it to him. Now the MDS would be gloating at their win.

"Will this affect our plans for the Magi?"

Dean and Leo looked at each other. Neither spoke.

"What is it?"

"There's something else. Something you should know."

"What?" Why did I get the feeling that it wasn't going to be good news. Nothing ever was these days.

"The MDS are hatching another assassination plot. We don't know what it is, but we know it's going to be big."

"When?" I asked in alarm. Another assassination plot meant more security, more guards, and a more visible police force. I wasn't sure if I could handle another disaster like the one last year.

"We don't know the date, but we suspect it might be your wedding. It worked before, if only by accident. What better way to get their cause on the news than by doing something that will have all the media out in force, plus the sheer numbers of people."

"My wedding?" I gulped. I'd already had one ruined wedding. I couldn't bear another.

"We will get a lot more guards on duty on the week leading up to it, but your current guards should be aware. We'll do our best to keep everyone safe."

I could barely wrap my head around it all. Yesterday, I still had two men to choose from and a wedding to look forward to. Just twenty-four hours later, one of the men was gone, and someone wanted to kill me.

"I want you to leave," I said to Leo.

"I'm sorry? I know this must be distressing, but I can assure you, I'm doing everything I can."

"No, it's not you," I said, realizing how he could have misunderstood my intentions. "You are brilliant. It's just that Elise is pregnant. I don't want anything to happen to her. Can you take my mother too?"

"As much as I want Elise to be safe, I don't think taking her away from the palace is a good idea right now. She was fine for the party yesterday, but the pregnancy is hitting her hard. She can't travel. I'll make sure she is safe, as I will your mother and everyone else in the palace. If we all evacuate now, The Regent and the rest of the MDS will know. We are safer at the palace than anywhere right now. I've instructed quite a high number of the police to guard the palace leading up to the wedding."

I wasn't so sure, but I nodded my head. I had to trust him even though the thought of my sister's life being in danger terrified me much more than my own safety.

"What about the Freedom of Magic? Can they help us? They've been gathering information on the MDS for years."

"I'm sure they could be very useful; however, we have one problem with that. We don't know who they are and without Cynder to tell us, we have no way to contact them."

Wedding Plans

The next two months passed slowly and in a state of fear. I warned the royal guard to be extra cautious and, true to his word, Leo sent police to bulk up their numbers. I wasn't sure if the extra security made me feel safer or more nervous, but I couldn't get a moment alone at all. The palace was always filled, and I felt like I was constantly being watched. Guards stood in every corridor, and yet, every unexplained noise had my heart jumping. All packages and letters for us were diverted to a local sorting office where specialized bomb squads opened them and checked their contents. Despite the fact that I kept the media out of the palace, I had more eyes on me than ever. The only solitude I got was when I was in my room at night. I'd not heard from Cynder in over two months. Luca's parents confirmed that he hadn't returned to Thalia or, at least, not to his job at the royal castle, and the media hadn't caught up with him. It was probably for the best, but every night, I gazed out of my window looking for a light in his old apartment that never came.

Most of my days were filled with wedding plans. My mother, Xavi, Jenny, and occasionally Elise when she felt up to it, would sit with me in the dressing room going through swatches and photos of wedding gowns. The only good thing that happened over the two months leading up to the wedding was the fact I got to stop an order of the most flouncy horrible meringue gown I'd ever seen that my mother had picked out for me. Instead, I sketched out something, something plain that Xavi promised to have made for me. I was in no doubt she wouldn't be able to make it without adding her own touches, but anything was better than the meringue gown. Elise's bridesmaid dress was a much easier choice. She picked out a beautiful pale golden dress that could be let out to cover her burgeoning belly. Thus, the theme of the wedding became gold and white. It enabled my mother to pick matching flowers and centerpieces and the million other things that a royal wedding seemed to require. At least, they were all happy, and partly, so was I. It was nice to spend time with them. I'd been so busy in the previous months that I'd forgotten what it was like to be around family.

Luca took up a lot of my duties, leaving me to relax as much as possible, and, as such, I saw very little of him. The only people I saw to do with work on a frequent basis were Leo and, occasionally, Dean when he came up to the palace.

Little progress was made on the identity of The Regent, although they had narrowed it down to someone who had connections to the capital. I tried not to worry about it. After all, the palace security was at an all-time high. Even the demonstrations outside the palace seemed to have dwindled to a few hard-core people with banners.

All in all, in the week running up to the wedding, I was beginning to come out of my funk and actually look forward to the occasion. The cathedral was booked and decorated. The palace ballroom, swathed in bunches of gold and white material with flowers to match looked as beautiful as it had ever been, and I even had a dress I was halfway happy with.

On the morning of the wedding, I woke up to glorious sunshine filtering through the curtains. Opening them wide, I knew it was going to be a magical day. People had come out in droves to see us and were already jostling for a good view at the back gates. I knew that there would be ten times that number at the front gates.

Jenny kindly brought me a breakfast of fruit, and when I complained about the lack of bacon sandwiches, she winked and lifted the silver cover, revealing one.

"How are you feeling?" she asked as I grabbed for the sandwich.

"Good, I suppose."

"You suppose?" She arched her brow, sitting on my bed. She knew me too well.

"I know marrying Luca is the right thing to do. He's been so busy lately, I've barely seen him, and it's just that..."

"Yes?" she encouraged.

"I've not really missed him. Is that terrible."

"Oh, honey. You've had a lot on your plate. This last year has been pretty terrible. You've still seen him every day even if it's only been at dinner. Once you are married, things will change."

"Will they?" I wasn't so sure.

"You'll not have to worry about flowers and dresses for a start. I know how boring you've found all this wedding planning stuff. You and

Luca will be running the kingdom together. It will be wonderful."

"Hmmm," I sighed non-commitedly.

"Is this about Cynder?"

"No," I lied. I'd not seen him for months and had given up scouring the newspapers for information. Just as he had done last year, he'd completely disappeared. I'd thought about hiring private investigators to search for him, but it was kinder on all of us to just let him go.

"Good," Jenny said, seemingly satisfied with my answer. "I'll see you in the dressing room in half an hour."

When I finally got down there, Xavi had double the number of beauticians lined up to make me beautiful for my big day. My mother and Elise were already sitting at a couple of stations having their hair done.

"You all know the wedding isn't until two and it's only eight in the morning right?" I asked Xavi, who rolled her eyes.

"This is the biggest day of your life. Everyone in the land will be watching on TV unless they've come to the capital to catch a glimpse of you in the flesh."

"But six hours..."

"Should be enough to get everything done. Now go into the marble room to get a good scrub down."

Now it was my turn to roll my eyes. I did as she asked and entered the room where I'd be loofahed and scrubbed until my skin shined.

Five hours later and I was transformed. I had to admit that the crew had done an amazing job with me. I let the dressers carefully lower the dress over my head. It was perfect. Simple, flowing, and white. It was beautiful. A simple golden sash matching Elise's dress was wrapped around my middle, and a simple diamond tiara was placed upon my head. Of all the looks Xavi had dressed me in, this was my all-time favorite. I looked elegant but not over the top.

"You look stunning!" Elise came over to me and gazed at my reflection in the huge mirror. My mother took up my other side. We did look beautiful. My mother filled with grace and the pride of every mother on her daughter's wedding day, Elise with her swollen tummy that she managed to make look elegant, and me in the center looking every inch the bride.

"Time to go!" yelled Xavi.

I gave my mother and sister a shy smile and headed out the door.

There were so many people accompanying me to the palace's main door, that I could barely tell who was who. My mother and sister kept to my side the whole way, and Daniel, whom I'd asked to walk me down the aisle, was waiting for me at the door.

Behind us, were all the beauticians plus a great number of guards who would be keeping me safe all day.

Leo came bounding up just as the main doors opened. I noticed the worried look on his face straight away.

"What is it? Is it Luca?" Luca had chosen Leo to be his best man, so they should both already be at the cathedral waiting for my entrance.

"I need to talk to you," he whispered.

"You three go on ahead," I said to Daniel, Mother, and Elise. "I'll meet you in the carriage in a minute."

I noticed a worried look pass between them, but they did as I asked. I could already hear the crowds screaming and cheering at the gates at the end of the driveway.

"Luca is fine. He's already gone to the cathedral," assured Leo, keeping his voice low so only I could hear.

"So what is it?"

"We've had a tip-off that The Regent is in town. We think the MDS are planning something huge today, but we don't know what."

"We have so many guards, and the cathedral and palace have been checked thoroughly. Luca has been doing a great job of keeping everything safe."

"He has. I'm sure everything will be fine, I just want you to be alert. We know The Regent is after you. I want the window of your carriage closed at all times along with the curtains."

"But I'm expected to wave to the people. You've seen them. There must be ten thousand people out there."

"Any one of whom could kill you if they got a chance. I'm doing what I can. I know Luca has made sure you have plenty of guards here and with you, and I've got all the officers I can spare on duty too."

"With all the people looking out for me, I'm sure I'll be fine, but I'll keep the carriage window shut as you ask. Thank you for your help with everything. You've been amazing."

"Just looking out for my queen," he said, kissing my cheek.

"Shouldn't you be looking out for the Prince right now? You are his best man."

"Gotcha!"

He gave me a final peck and left me alone in the grand entrance hall.

Two guards stood by the door and quickly escorted me to the carriage.

I recognized it as the pumpkin carriage that Daniel had magicked up a few months previously. Dean sat proudly wearing a white suit in the driver's seat holding the reigns of six beautiful white horses.

I stepped up into the carriage and immediately we started to move. Taking Leo's advice, I closed the curtains. Even though I could no longer see the crowds, I could hear them. The cheering was almost deafening, making me smile.

Even though I'd been taking a break from public view for the past couple of months, I knew that Silverwood's universities and colleges were experiencing record numbers of Magi enrollments and the recruitment drive for the police had been hugely successful. The fear that the Magi would leave again after Cynder did, had not come to pass, and even more encouragingly, the Magi were still coming back into the kingdom. All in all, I had a lot to be grateful for.

Jenny had been right. Today was the beginning of a bright new future with Luca, and I could finally lay to rest everything that had happened in the past year. I ignored the pang that stabbed my heart at the thought of Cynder. He was gone for good.

The carriage came to a halt, and a guard opened the door for us. Daniel climbed out first to help my mother and Elise down the steps. Mother hurried into the cathedral to take her place, leaving just the three of us. Guards held up screens to allow us to get into the cathedral without being seen by the crowds. They might not have been able to see us, but they knew we were there. The screams and cheers were deafening as I climbed out of the carriage. After the wedding, the screens would be taken down, and Luca and I would walk back to the carriage in full view of everyone. For now, I was grateful for the privacy they afforded me. Elise fussed around me, pulling my dress straight and handing me my bouquet of white flowers tied in a gold ribbon. As I'd been very specific about not wanting a long train, she had nothing to hold behind me, so she went first, walking the huge aisle to the front. I heard the wedding march begin to play as she passed through the huge oak doors of the cathedral.

"Ready?" asked Daniel and he held out his arm to me.

"As I'll ever be."

I took a deep breath and together, we walked step by step towards my future husband.

The Wedding

I gave my broadest smile as I walked down the aisle. There were so many faces I recognized, including Luca's family. Because of Luca's dedication and hard work, Silverwood was now safe enough for Seraphia to attend the wedding, which pleased me no end. I'd not seen her, nor any of them since Cynder had taken me from their palace. If they held a grudge against me, they didn't show it. Luca's parents smiled with genuine happiness as I slowly walked past them.

At the front of the church stood Luca. I'd never seen him looking so utterly gorgeous. He was dressed smartly in his royal attire, but it was the look of joy on his face as he watched me walk up to him that topped any outfit.

Daniel kissed my cheek and passed my hand to Luca.

His hands were cold and clammy which I could understand. He looked as nervous as I felt. Getting married was nerve-wracking enough for anyone, but our wedding was being broadcast into the homes of everyone in Silverwood, not to mention the surrounding kingdoms. Outside the palace and the cathedral, huge screens had been erected so that those who had chosen to come out, could also watch. He must also know about the threat against us.

The priest began his speech, but I could barely hear it. I was too busy gazing up at the man who would stand by me for the rest of my life.

He smiled down as though everything was fine, but his pale face gave him away. I noticed a bead of sweat appear on his forehead. I hoped it was nerves and he was not coming down with something. I desperately wanted to ask him if he was alright, but I couldn't interrupt the priest when hundreds of thousands of people were watching.

As the priest welcomed the people to the cathedral and introduced the reason we were all here, I took the time to really look at the man I was going to marry, the man I was going to grow old with. He truly was beautiful, but I couldn't shake the feeling that something was wrong. On the surface, he seemed calm and collected, but I felt the slight tremor in his hand.

"Is there any reason that these two shouldn't be joined in matrimony today? Speak now or forever hold your peace."

The cathedral was deathly silent as everyone waited for someone to speak. Even the massive throng of people outside quietened down.

I looked out over the hundreds of people packed into the pews. My heart hammered, terrified that someone would say something to stop the wedding, and then it dawned on me that my fear was actually that someone wouldn't. I'd spent nearly a year to get used to the fact that I was going to be Luca's bride and now the time had come, Luca's nerves were beginning to rub off on me. Was I ready? I wasn't sure.

No one spoke, and so the priest continued.

"Luca James Alexander Phillip Tremaine do you take Charmaine Elizabeth Mary Annesley to be your lawfully wedded wife?"

As he looked at me, with fear rather than love in his eyes, I felt my stomach lurch. He'd dressed for the occasion, but now that I was looking at him, I saw he'd forgotten to shave, and his eyes were red as though he'd not slept well the night before. Could this just be nerves?

"I do."

"And do you Charmaine Elizabeth Mary Annesley take Luca James Alexander Phillip Tremaine to be your lawfully wedded husband?"

At this point at my wedding to Xavier, thousands of people had crashed through the palace gates, starting a riot that would kill both Xavier and my father. It made me feel sick when I realized I hoped the same thing would happen now. Anything to stop this. I loved Luca, at least I thought I did, but I didn't want to marry him. I'd had so many chances to make love with him in the past year, and yet, it had not happened between us. Wasn't that enough to tell me that this was all wrong? I'd given myself excuse after excuse, but if I really loved him, surely I wouldn't need to make excuses?

I waited as long as I could get away with until I couldn't wait any longer.

"I do."

Luca smiled and nodded his head. The sweat dripped down. He pulled a handkerchief from his pocket and dabbed himself with it, before pulling out a small box with my wedding ring in it. A plain gold band that symbolized our lasting union.

"With this ring..." he began the speech that millions had said before him. When it was my turn, Daniel passed me another box with another gold band. I repeated the words, trying to sound like I was being sincere.

The priest closed his book and smiled. "I now pronounce you man and wife."

A great cheer went up both from inside the cathedral and from all those people outside. I took Luca's hand, and we walked down the aisle as man and wife, smiling and waving at everyone as we passed. Leo raced ahead to make sure we were safe as we stood outside the large oak doors to give the media a chance to film us. We waved, and we smiled some more as the carriage pulled up in front of us. A similar carriage pulled up behind to take Mother, Leo, Elise, and Daniel to the palace. Behind that one stood another and another for all those guests heading back to the palace for our wedding reception. Luca and I were still waving as flowers and confetti were thrown at us. I saw Elise, Mother, and Daniel get into the carriage behind ours.

"It's time for us to go," I whispered at Luca. "Leo, we are fine. Go be with Elise."

Leo nodded and after a quick scan of the area, left us to get the carriage home. I stepped up into the carriage, but before Luca had time to follow, the carriage set off. It raced at such a pace that I lost my balance, falling into the pumpkin orange upholstery. I could hear the screams as we careened out of control through the crowd. Gone were the cheers to be replaced by the sound of terror. I pulled myself up as best I could and grabbed for the door. I could barely make out the frightened faces we passed as we were going so fast. The door slammed shut, trapping me in, so I opened the window.

The crowd parted with many people diving out of our way for fear of being run over. Pretty soon, the cathedral was just a speck in the distance behind us, and the crowds had thinned out into nothing. Behind me, I could see that our carriage wasn't the only one. Whoever had taken me had also taken Mother, Leo, Elise, and Daniel too. Their carriage was right behind mine.

"Stop!"

I shouted up to the driver, but it was no use. He was either ignoring me or couldn't hear me. I couldn't jump out as we were going at a breakneck speed, so I had to sit and wait for the journey to come to an end wherever that may be.

I tried to understand who would do this. The only people I could think of were the MDS. Leo had warned me that something like this was being planned, but why take the others too? Maybe they wanted to murder the whole royal family. Get rid of us all at the same time. It would tie up any loose ends. It angered me that The Regent, whoever he was, was probably safe back at the capital, pretending to show concern. He wouldn't be one of the drivers. No, he'd have someone else to do the dirty work, while he pretended to be outraged. When we were all dead, he'd show grief publicly but be plotting to take over behind the scenes. It was perfect. I just couldn't understand why there were no guards following us. There had been so many at the wedding and along the route back to the palace. Where were they all now?

I thought of Luca. My driver, whoever he was had royally messed up by setting off moments too soon. Luca was still back at the cathedral. The thought of it made me feel a little better. Luca had been the one who had worked with the guards these past few months. If anyone could sort this out, it was him.

I sat seething as the town turned into the countryside. Every so often, I'd put my head out of the window to see if the carriage behind was still following us. I could see the driver from here, but I didn't recognize him. It didn't matter who it was anyway. Some faceless MDS lackey who would, no doubt, have a weapon ready to murder us all as soon as they got to their destination.

We drove for hours, and pretty soon, I was hopelessly lost. The scenery changed from rolling hills and pretty fields to sparse moorland, purple with wild heather.

We were going to have to stop soon, I realized. I'd not seen any signs of civilization for at least an hour, and the bumpiness of the carriage told me that we were now on dirt tracks. The horses would be tired. I wondered just how long I had left to live.

Glancing around the carriage interior, I searched for something to hit my driver with when we finally stopped. Apart from my bouquet, I had nothing at hand.

"Fat lot of damage some white lilies are going to do," I mused aloud, feeling angry at my situation.

I wasn't even scared anymore. Anger flooded through me as I thought about Elise behind me, pregnant. This journey would be no good for her. Who would do this despicable thing to a pregnant woman? I might not have long to live, but I was sure going to give my kidnapper a piece of my mind when the carriage stopped.

I didn't have long to wait. I felt the carriage begin to slow down and finally stop beside an old farmhouse.

As soon as the door opened, I was ready. I pulled my arm back, and with as much force as I could muster, punched my kidnapper square in the nose. He fell back, hitting the ground hard. Maybe, just maybe, I'd be able to escape, but as I looked up, I could see more members of the MDS begin to pour out of the farmhouse. I jumped down, ready to kick the driver. I might not be able to escape, but I wasn't going down without a fight.

I looked down at his face. Blood poured from his nose where I'd punched him. He sat up and gave me a crooked grin.

"Hi, my Lucky Charm."

It was Cynder.

After

Behind me, I could hear a fight. I looked over to see Leo punching the driver of the second carriage while Elise, Mother, and Daniel looked on.

"What are you doing?" I hissed at Cynder.

My mind whirled with both emotion and shattered thoughts.

"He's The Regent!" shouted Leo, laying a final blow to his opponent and knocking him out completely.

It was no good, though. The people who had filed out of the farmhouse descended on him. There were too many of them, and despite us all putting up a fight, we were all led into the house. I was dismayed to see that Daniel joined them. He was in on this all along.

It was huge, with a large sitting room, big enough to cram us all in. On the outside, it looked deserted, but inside, it was decorated in a modern fashion.

Knowing that we were outnumbered, we all sat quietly on the sofa as the thirty or so members of the MDS stood around us.

"You lied about everything!" I screamed at Cynder. "There never was any Freedom of Magic was there? It was fabricated to throw us off the scent. How could you do this? Elise is pregnant!"

I put my arm around my sobbing sister. "I'm ok, I feel the baby kicking," she whispered between sobs.

"And you, Daniel," I yelled. "I trusted you. I trusted both of you!"

"It's not what you think," said Cynder.

"I don't care what it is. Luca will find me. He's been working with the palace guards, recruiting so many of them we almost have an army. They'll find us."

"They won't, but that's not the point," replied Cynder. "I'm not The Regent."

"I don't even care anymore if you are him or just one of his servants. More the fool, you!"

"Charm, listen to me. Please!"

"Don't you dare call me Charm. I'm not your Lucky Charm. I'm Queen Charmaine!"

"Will someone switch on the TV, please?"

"The TV?" I asked astonished. "You want us all to watch a movie. Great, let's have popcorn!" I was being sarcastic, but I couldn't help myself. I was unbelievably angry. If I wasn't surrounded by so many people, I would have punched Cynder again.

"I want you to know the truth."

The TV turned on. There I was coming out of the cathedral with Luca, smiling for the cameras. Below me, were the words 'recap of today's events.' Seconds later, I watched as I toppled over in the carriage when Cynder spurred the horses on. I saw the shocked look of Luca as he tried to chase us but was stopped by the second carriage cutting off his path. Behind him, I could make out Dean chasing behind him. Poor Dean. He was supposed to be my driver. I wondered if Cynder had hurt him to get his place on the carriage.

With folded arms, I glared at Cynder.

"Keep watching!" he said, without even looking my way.

The crowds descended into a panic as our carriages ploughed through them. It was a miracle no one was hurt. I gripped Elise's hand tightly, my eyes fixed on the screen.

Luca hailed another carriage and with a few of the guards, got in. He followed our carriages rather than heading to the palace on the official route. Somehow, the crowds had closed in, not letting him pass. At least, he'd tried to rescue me. Eventually, the carriage cut through the crowd. He was behind us. We'd gotten a bit of a head start, but he would catch up with us.

"He'll find us!" I said. "We only had a ten-minute head start."

"He wasn't following us," replied Cynder.

Back on the screen, Marybelle rushed to the camera and began to talk, recapping for everyone what the scene looked like from her point of view, A totally pointless endeavor, as we could all see the confusion around her. As she was talking, there was a huge bang followed by even more screams.

Marybelle faltered and then looked out to something behind the camera. Raising her hand, she gently pushed the camera so it showed the thing she had seen. In the distance, a plume of smoke filled the air. Even at the distance from the cathedral, I could see where it had come from. The palace had gone up in flames.

The picture cut to an anchorman. Behind him, was a live feed of the palace. It was completely consumed in flames.

"Those were the scenes four hours ago at the cathedral. Back at the palace, fire-fighters have been working tirelessly since then to get the blaze under control, but sources say the palace has been completely gutted by the flames. A number of explosions were heard which suggested more than one bomb, although the fire sergeant has yet to confirm this.

"A number of palace staff are still unaccounted for, and there is no word yet on the whereabouts of the queen and the rest of the royal family.

"Prince Luca is also missing. The acting chief of police has issued a statement that they knew something was going to happen, but even with the heightened security, they weren't prepared for the magnitude of today's events.

"A number of people are still fighting for their lives after being crushed in the crowds of people fleeing the scene. If you know someone who was there and are worried about them, we've set up this hotline for you to call..."

The sound on the TV was shut off although the picture remained.

"You blew up my palace?" I screamed. I didn't care that I was completely outnumbered. I stood up and punched Cynder's chest.

Someone pulled me back, pinning my arms behind me, so I spat in his face instead.

"Let her go!" said Cynder, wiping his face with his sleeve.

My arms fell to my sides.

"I'm not The Regent, and I never lied to you," he said.

"So then, who is?" I asked, not really caring anymore.

"It's your husband. Luca is The Regent."

I stared up at him, unable to process what he was telling me.

"I don't believe you."

"Believe him," said Daniel, coming up beside him and resting his hand on his shoulder.

"None of this was planned, us bringing you all here. We only found out this morning who The Regent was. At first, I didn't believe it myself, but as I thought about it, it made perfect sense. He has access to you and the palace. He was the one who provided all the security who, let's face it, were next to useless today."

"He's been helping me promote Magi rights for the past year!"

"And I'm a Mage," said Cynder "but you still accused me of being The Regent. Also, just for the record, we aren't the MDS. The MDS are all those people who have been recruited over the past few months as your palace guards. I even recognized some of them on the TV."

"You are the Freedom of Magic," I said quietly, trying to wrap my head around everything that was happening.

"Give the girl a cigar," shouted someone at the back, causing Cynder to glare at her."

"We knew someone had been providing fake documents to Drusilla Bloom. She's not rich enough or smart enough to figure out how to do it on her own. Thanks to you opening up the police force, we managed to get a couple of our own into the task force so we could keep tabs ourselves on The Regent. A lot of what we know is thanks to you, Leo."

I turned to look at him. It was then I noticed he had a black eye from the fight earlier.

Up until this morning, we knew exactly what you knew. That The Regent was planning something. A lot of the Freedom of Magic were already planning to be at the wedding to protect you in case anything should happen, but this morning we received a tip-off. We found out that Luca was The Regent. It was too late to contact you, Leo. You were too busy with the wedding. If we had have been able to get through to you, we might have been able to stop this before it started."

"I told Copper that I couldn't be reached today."

"And I didn't know Inspector Copper. For all we knew, he was one of them." I was frantic, knowing Luca was going to do something big. I got on my horse and rode as fast as I could to the capital, just in time to see you say your vows on the big screen. I gathered up the Freedom of Magic people and told them what to do, Then it was just a case of pulling the drivers from the front two carriages and driving off quickly before anyone could stop us. Once we had gone, our people closed around the other carriages so no one could follow. As I said, Luca wasn't intending to follow you. He was making his escape."

"I..." I had no words. It couldn't be true.

"He wants to rule the kingdom. He doesn't care in what capacity, whether as a prince or a president. With you out of the way, he's free to do that. He is not the fan of the Magi he pretends to be. If you look into his past, you'll see that he opposed Seraphia when she married his brother. It's only in the last year or so he's had this amazing turnaround."

"Since the ball?" I asked.

"Exactly!"

The room went quiet. I looked over at Leo. He nodded his head.

"I believe him. I also believe Daniel."

"I actually didn't know what was going on until I got here," said Daniel. "But I know these people, and I trust them with my life."

"If you don't believe us, you are free to go now," said Cynder looking directly at me. "We won't follow you. Your horses and carriages are still outside. I don't want you to go. I don't think any of you are safe in the capital at the moment. I suspect Luca will show up on TV at some point, blaming us or someone else. He'll become the kingdom's hero and all the while he is publicly grieving, he'll have his best men looking to kill you all. I can only keep you safe here, but I'm not going to keep any of you by force."

I waited to see if anyone would get up but no one moved. Cynder looked at me almost beseeching me to believe him, and I found that I did. There was more in the way he looked at me then, than there had been all the way through my wedding with Luca. No wonder Luca's hands had been cold and clammy. He knew that the palace was going to blow up. He knew I was going to be inside it when it did. I wondered what excuse he was going to give me for him to leave just before it happened.

I thought back through the past couple of months when he'd been absent all day. He'd told me he was recruiting palace guards, and I'd believed him. Instead, he was hatching a murder plot, no doubt inspired by Xavier and my own father. He must have thought it hilarious to wait for our wedding day, echoing the disaster that had happened last year. Perhaps he only chose today to be guaranteed that we would all be at the palace. It occurred to me that he wasn't just planning to kill my family, but his own too. If Cynder hadn't rescued me when he did, the palace would be filled with hundreds of people there for the wedding reception. Cynder had saved hundreds of lives, not just those of us here. I felt sick at the thought of it.

"Can you all leave us?" Cynder said to his people. "Our guests need a bed, and I suspect they will be hungry. We have a long day ahead of us tomorrow, and I'm sure they've had enough to deal with already today."

A couple of women took Mother, Elise, Leo, and Daniel through a door. The rest of the people left through other doors until it was just Cynder and me in the room.

"I was going to leave you to live in peace. I'm sorry this has happened to you." He moved forward and got to his knees in front of me so that we were now almost eye level as I sat on the sofa.

"You saved our lives," I said. "I don't know how to begin to thank you."

He took my hand and sat next to me on the sofa. Our eyes both went to the picture on the screen which showed the charred remains of the palace.

"You can thank me by fighting them. You are the best queen Silverwood has ever had. The Magi need you. Everyone needs you. Please don't give up."

I wasn't about to give up. My fighting spirit was angry. I was going to bring Luca down and turn this around no matter what it took.

"Anything else?" I asked, gripping his hand tightly, knowing that this time I wasn't going to let go.

"You might want to think about getting a divorce."

From the depths of my despair, a laugh bubbled to the surface. I would win. With Cynder by my side, I knew that this was just the beginning.

Available now

Charmed

Back to the Capital

Luca looked every inch the man in despair as I watched him on the TV. His beauty was not diminished at all by the tear tracks down his face. If anything, the sorrow made him all the more beautiful. It was a shame it was all fake. Fake tears, fake sorrow, masking a monster. And yet, I couldn't turn the TV off. It was one in the morning, and I'd watched this particular interview three times already in the past twelve hours. The first two times I'd been surrounded by my family and the members of the Freedom of Magic group as we huddled around the sofa, trying to take in everything that had happened.

The palace was gone. Barely anything survived the catastrophic fire that had torn through it. The cause had finally been confirmed as a number of bombs placed at strategic points throughout the building for maximum impact. So much for extra security! Of course, when the person in charge of the extra security was the one who planted the bombs, there was little anyone could do.

"Come to bed," I heard Cynder's voice behind me, but I didn't turn around. I should have been sleeping as the others were, but I couldn't. I wasn't sure if I'd ever be able to sleep again.

I felt his hand on my shoulder.

I turned to him and stifled a yawn. "I'm sorry. Did I wake you?"

He slipped in next to me on the sofa. Just having him close brought me comfort.

"No," he whispered. "I couldn't sleep either. I've brought you some hot milk."

I took the milk gratefully and gave him a sad smile.

"I should have known," I mumbled. Just acknowledging my part in this made me feel sick to my stomach.

Cynder put his arm around me. "You've had it so tough this past year. A lot of people have not been who you thought they were. First your father, now your fiancé. There is no way you could have known. Please don't put the blame on yourself."

"I was with him every day," I argued, "every single day for a year. Only an idiot would not have suspected something."

Cynder stroked my cheek, causing me to take my eyes from the TV and look at him directly. "The only idiot I can see is him. He threw away everything and for what?"

"He didn't throw away everything, though, did he? He's quite the hero now. The whole of Silverwood feels sorry for him, and he's been tipped to become the new king. King! Not President, but actual royalty. He's the happiest person on the planet right now. He's gotten everything he ever wanted."

Cynder made a sound that could have been a *huh*. "I wasn't talking about that. I was talking about you. He lost you. No title, no matter how powerful or glamorous could compare to being by your side. He is the fool here."

"Hmm," I made a noncommittal noise. The only people that had lost were my family and I. And we *had* lost. We'd lost it all. Everything we had was burned to cinders—our clothes, our belongings, our home. That paled into insignificance as I contemplated the loss of life. The majority of our staff were at the wedding when the bombs went off, but of those left behind to get the palace ready for the wedding reception, most had perished. A total of ninety-seven people had died yesterday. Ninety-seven families had lost a loved one all thanks to the greed of one man.

"Look at it this way," assured Cynder. "He can't really become king because you are still alive. As soon as you show your face, he'll be done for."

"And he knows that! You said yourself; he'll have all the MDS looking for us. Nowhere is safe. We can't even go to the press ourselves because we don't know if they are members of the Magi Death Squad. You were right when you said there was nothing we could do."

"I never said that at all," he replied, referring to the meeting we'd had earlier in the day. "I said that we need to sit tight for a few days until we come up with a plan. You know we are going to fight this, right?"

I nodded slowly, not sure what I knew anymore. We both silently sipped our milk, watching Luca shedding his crocodile tears on the TV.

"How unlucky can one person get. I've been engaged twice, and both times, my fiancée has tried to murder me on my wedding day." I began to giggle. There was nothing funny about the situation, but my nerves were so tightly stretched that giggling was a nervous reaction.

"It's not a coincidence. Either Luca pulled this stunt as some weird homage to Xavier, or the thing with your wedding last year had something to do with Luca in the first place. It won't happen the next time," he whispered, pulling me closer to him.

His arms tightened around me, shielding me from the world like a warm cocoon. He picked up the remote and turned off the TV.

It hadn't occurred to me that Luca had anything to do with the atrocities of last year. I'd thought of them as two completely separate incidents, but it made sense that Luca was somehow involved. I just didn't know how. I fell asleep on the sofa with Cynder stroking my head.

I woke up the next morning to a whole group of people making breakfast in the open plan kitchen. They were all tiptoeing around and whispering so as not to wake us, but there were so many of them, it was impossible to sleep through.

I yawned and sat up straight, waking Cynder with the motion.

"Good morning, Your Majesty," said one of the women.

I recognized that voice. Looking up, I saw I was right.

"Agatha?"

My old maid broke into a grin, one I couldn't help but match as I saw her.

"Is it really you? I've missed you so much. I thought you were staying with your aunt and uncle?" I leapt up and hugged her tightly.

"I was, but when I heard of the Freedom of Magic, I decided to join. I couldn't find a job. No one would hire me because of who I was, so this seemed like the best option. I wouldn't have had the courage to do it if it weren't for you."

"What do you mean?" I asked, taking a step back.

"Well, it was that last talk we had together. It made me see just how much of a slave I was."

I remembered the talk well. I'd asked her if it bothered her that she was a mage who was only allowed to use her wand to fold my clothes. At the time, she'd said it didn't bother her and that she liked her job. I was glad to see she had changed her mind. She was worth so much more than being a maid.

"I'm glad to hear it," I replied, and I genuinely was.

"I should go and help make breakfast," she said, moving towards the kitchen.

"No." I stopped her. "Let me do it. You've spent way too long looking after me. Take a seat, and let me look after you for a change."

Her eyes widened as she gave me a shy grin.

I made my way into the mess of people in the kitchen. There was someone cooking eggs and bacon, another person laying out bowls for cereal, a couple were counting mugs for coffee.

I grabbed a bit of everything and threw it on a plate which I gave to Agatha. She accepted it gratefully.

I headed back into the kitchen, keen to make myself useful and distance myself from my title. "Can I help?" I offered.

A collective round of no's followed by a chorus of "Just sit down, we'll serve you" went up. It had been this way my entire life. Would no one ever let me do anything for myself?

"You saved my life yesterday, and you are keeping me here with great danger to yourselves. Here, I'm not the queen. I'm just a person like the rest of you, and I want to help."

"Maybe they just think you can't cook!" whispered Cynder playfully in my ear. I grinned and gave him a swipe which he dodged.

"You can make toast for everyone," said the woman who'd been frying the eggs. She broke off to pass me a loaf of bread and a knife. With curly grey hair topping off a ruddy face, she was the quintessential grandmother type. Her half-moon glasses were steamed up, so she peered over the top of them.

"Thank you," I replied, taking the bread from her and fetching the butter.

"We usually fend for ourselves around here," she said, going back to the bacon and eggs, "but what with everything going on, we thought it would be nice to welcome you with a proper breakfast. There are thirty of us altogether, and we can't fit around the kitchen table, so we'll have to take it in turns to eat."

"Alannah," said Cynder sidling up to her and stealing a piece of bacon right from the pan, "you know you'll not stop cooking until we are all fed. You can't help yourself."

"Looks like you've no problem with helping yourself," she said, hitting him playfully with the wooden spoon she was holding.

I sliced, toasted, and buttered mountains of toast. Every time I put a slice down, someone would come and take it. After I'd gotten through three loaves, I finally took a couple of slices for myself and added an egg and bacon to my plate. Alannah was right; there was no space around the table, so I sat next to Cynder on the sofa. Someone had turned on the TV again. I watched silently, eating my toast as my so-called husband continued the charade.

This interview was one I'd not seen before. He'd probably filmed it this morning. He was wearing a smart suit with a purple flower in the lapel. Oh, how I hated him for that!

The fake tears were still streaming down his face as he spoke. He really was quite the actor.

I chewed on a slice of toast as I listened to him.

"We had our whole lives in front of us," he cried. "I'd been looking forward to our wedding for months, and I still can't understand why anyone would do this. Why would someone kidnap my beloved?"

"The public is in mourning today alongside you," said a voice just off camera. I recognized it immediately as the voice of Frederick Pittser. So it didn't take long for him to crawl out of the woodwork. Without Leo at the police station and with Luca in charge, Pittser had nothing to fear anymore although I noticed he didn't show his face.

"Yes," replied Luca solemnly, "and I want to thank everyone for the overwhelming support they've shown at this terrible time. I will continue to support the public back in the way Her Majesty would have wanted."

I resisted the urge to throw my plate at the television.

"There is a slight possibility that the queen is still alive," Pittser reminded him.

Luca looked up mournfully. "I hope so, but the truth of the matter is, whoever blew up the palace obviously wanted her dead. Why would they take her otherwise? I'm sorry to say that although I'd give anything to see her one last time, I fear she is already gone."

"Oh, you'll see me again alright!" I shouted at the TV. Cynder gripped my hand, quietening me.

"If she is alive," continued Pittser "and somehow watching this, what would you say to her?"

Luca turned to the camera. His eyes pierced mine as though he could really see me through the lens.

"I'll find you, Charmaine. I'll not rest until I do!"

To any one of the hundreds of thousands of people watching, it would look like a broken

369

man doing anything he could to find his beloved, but I saw it for what it was—a threat. He was coming for me, and he would find me. Well, not if I found him first!

I was still seething with anger when Leo and Mother appeared. She still looked as graceful as ever, even after everything she had been through. Someone passed them both a plate of food. Mother took her's to the kitchen table, where there was now space, but Leo sat on the arm of the sofa next to me.

"How's Elise?" I asked, noticing she wasn't with him.

"She's feeling rough. The journey yesterday did her no good. She's too sick to eat."

"I've got a remedy for that!" said Alannah. She bustled into the kitchen and began taking things from the cupboards and pouring them all into a large bowl.

"One glass of this, and she'll be right as rain in no time!"

"Is it a Mage potion?" asked Leo suspiciously, looking at the weird concoction she was making.

"No, it's my mother's recipe and her mother's before her."

"What's happening today? Anything I should know about?" Leo nodded towards the now blank screen of the TV.

"We are going to have a proper meeting when everyone is up," said Cynder matter-of-factly. "All you've missed is thinly veiled threats from Luca. Pittser's suddenly come out of hiding too."

Leo nodded his head. "I've been thinking. Maybe I should go back. Chief Inspector Copper won't know what's going on. He needs my help, and he needs to know the truth."

Cynder shook his head. "No one is going back yet until we've come up with a plan. It's too risky. They know you are with Charm, and they suspect that Charm is with us. You go back there, and you won't be able to come back here."

"Actually, I am going back!" We all turned to see who had spoken. Daniel stood there looking distraught. "Dean is still there. Luca knows I'm with you. Who do you think he'll be going after first? I've been thinking about it all night. Dean will be a target. Luca will think I was in on this, and if I'm in on it, he'll think Dean is too."

"You don't know that he's been captured," Cynder replied cautiously.

"And I don't know that he hasn't. Luca or his men will have Dean and will be holding him

371

prisoner until we give Charmaine up. Why wouldn't they? I'm going back to the capital to find him."